FLYIN' KAI:
A Pelican's Tale

Share in the excitement of Kai's speed diving, surfing, and endless encounters as he searches for more meaning in life. Feeling restricted by parents, school and friends, Kai flies from his Anacapa Island home to the mainland in search of a legendary magical mountain. Teaming with a blue-footed booby from México, the two experience and observe the damage that mankind is inflicting upon nature and wildlife.

Flyin' Kai: A Pelican's Tale is a great read for all ages and strikes hard at the hearts of young adults, the environmentally sensitive and older baby boomers.

A contemporary "Smokey the Bear," famous for his iconic "ONLY YOU CAN PREVENT FOREST FIRES," Kai is a deeply beloved and substantial character that implores "ONLY YOU CAN SAVE THE SEAS."

Dorrance Publishing Co
585 Alpha Drive
Pittsburgh, PA 15238
Visit our website at *www.dorrancebookstore.com*

ISBN: 978-1-6393-7116-7
eISBN: 978-1-6393-7928-6

Flyin' Kai:
A Pelican's Tale

by

DUNCAN P. FORGEY

DORRANCE
PUBLISHING CO
EST. 1920
PITTSBURGH, PENNSYLVANIA 15238

ACKNOWLEDGEMENTS

My many thanks to these special individuals for sharing in my journey.

My Mother Travis
My Wife Madelynn
Leslie Andrews Howell
Anne Pearce Kramer

Plus, the boatload of incredible friends, students, and colleagues I've known along the way.

Animal Portraitures by B. Duncan Forgey

Dedicated to Earth's environment
and all of its inhabitants.

---

*Civilization is so thin that it is only
a skin on a wonderful animal.*

– George Edwin Burnell

ONE

Before mankind came to our region, oceans were so full of fish that when agitated, the moisture they created turned to rain and thunderstorms. Vast forests of seaweed extended far from shore and were so thick that families of otters played tag upon their backs. Giant flocks of seagulls blotted out sunlight for half a day as they migrated to and from the sea. Tuna were the size of whales, and whales were so big, their wakes caused waves to break on the shoreline. Porpoise pods overtook entire sea passages, and bales of turtles formed offshore islands.

– Pelican Lore

In the beginning, Earth experienced a difficult birth. Fathered by an endless universe and born to a reluctant solar system, it lay stillborn and lifeless for millions of years. Immersed in chaos, fire, and trembling from its core, great rivers of lava slithered across its surface like burning snakes. From a succession of volcanoes, massive clouds of poison gas embraced the youthful planet like a protective blanket.

The Mother of Nature engaged in a cataclysmic struggle between life and death. She pitted forces of the Earth against forces of the Heavens. It was a war to the bitter end. Lightning and fire dominated, leaving burnt soil. The surface of Earth was made of vibrant primary colors, yearning for the softening effects of pastels that life would bring. Creation was not yet able to emerge, leaving flora and fauna in perpetual hiding.

Life began with the first drop of rain falling from orange-red skies. Sensing the power of water, the clouds became dark. They carried soothing liquid to the farthest reaches of Earth. Storm after storm released decillions of raindrops, cooling one sector at a time. Lakes, rivers, puddles, and ponds were created. Ice was stored to the far north and south of the emerging planet. Vast oceans arose to levels never before seen, turning huge volcanic mountains into islands. A planet of seas was created, bringing forth fish, animals, insects, and birds. Life was born, and it flourished.

As time progressed, the Mother of Nature experienced dangerous trends that kept the environment in a constant state of flux. Again and again, Earth's core spilled forth lava and toxins, threatening all life and leaving a palpable fear in its wake. As eons passed, life soldiered on.

Pelicans were especially hard hit by the tumultuous activities of Earth. Sensing that something was needed to save their species, the pelicans of Anacapa Island, in an act of desperation, united to face this threat. Never before had a species joined together and pledged

9

communal protection. Because of this act, all life on Earth became forever bound by a common thread.

As the Anacapa pelicans discussed, meditated, and prayed for answers, waters rose, and pollution devastated the skies. The colony asked for knowledge that would stave off their extinction. After five full moons passed, they received their answer. It came in a rare and unsettling way. A supersized moon rose in the eastern sky, casting a mustard-red tint. The moon was so intense that the stars were erased, leaving long, eerie shadows on Earth. The pelicans of Anacapa were truly unsettled by these strange happenings. Meanwhile, a dense cloud bank rolled silently atop the still black sea. As if under divine direction, the pall crept straight toward the pelican colony and stopped, fully-crested, at the entrance to their cove. Loud claps of thunder announced its arrival. A symphony of hues, as brilliant as if extracted from the truest of rainbows, threw scattered spears of moonshine at the birds as lightning strikes reflected back from the cloud's umbrella. From deep within the epicenter, the darkness split revealing a great pelican.

She was not just any pelican, but one dressed in feathers of vivid yellow, bright rose-red, earthy brown, and virgin white. Her size and weight were more than five times that of the biggest bird in the colony. She was a brown pelican like the others, but one with a deep and spiritual aura surrounding her. She was truly a magnificent bird.

"I am Sorté," she announced in a melodic and soothing tone, wings lifted high in the air. "I am the mother of all pelicans and have heard your concerns. I will instruct you how to remedy your fears. If you listen, pelicans of Anacapa can survive these and all future challenges. But...if you do not listen, your colony will disappear forever."

The pelican pod stood in silence, mesmerized by this spirit bird.

"You are, indeed, faced with serious challenges," the enormous bird continued. "There are evils all about, and the Mother of Nature is angry. She will punish all those not following her wishes. As a colony, you must remain strong. I, Sorté, will be part of your lives forever. Our partnership gives you a path to everlasting existence."

Sorté floated effortlessly in the sky, appearing weightless despite her large size. She softly proclaimed, "I have burned the *LAWS OF NATURE* into the rocks on the west end of the island. Learn and put to memory each of these laws. Then, teach them. In two generations, they will erode back into the rising sea and be forever gone. However, they must not be lost. It is the sole responsibility of each generation to pass this wisdom and knowledge on to the next. These covenants must live on in order for you to survive."

Sorté's voice was like a song, relaxing the birds.

"Pelicans in the future must live with caution. There will come a day when you will encounter a new species. This species will bring forth hardship and danger to Earth. If you understand, teach, and live by the *LAWS OF NATURE*, you can survive.

"This new breed will arrive in floating vessels. They will kill indiscriminately, bring forth diseases, and enter into intense wars. Driven by greed and accumulation, they will inflict great harm on the environment. Considering themselves the most powerful species on Earth, they will take from nature, not partner with it. These 'human animals' will be blind to the needs of others and bring death and unhappiness to your way of life. When this occurs, do not forget the writings on the rocks. Everything on Earth is interconnected, and the oceans act as the vital link for all of survival. These newcomers will not take time to understand this, and unknowingly, they will kill the oceans with avarice and shortsightedness unless they are stopped."

Sorté hesitated before continuing her oration.

"Fellow pelicans, remember, the oceans are responsible for everything that lives, from the deepest sea canyons to the tallest of mountain peaks."

With that, Sorté swung her gold-flaked wing toward the crowd dousing them with energy. A deep feeling of brotherhood spread among the pelicans.

"Do not let mankind win, or pelicans will be lost forever. Keep our relationship alive and always honor the Mother of Nature. Whenever you experience tough times, I will help. You will survive trials by keeping hope, strength, courage, and direction."

This visit by such a magnificent pelican was unlike anything the flock had ever experienced. She was able to change the color of the moon, make clouds appear, float without flying, and speak of the future as if she had already been there. She was truly a gift from the Creator. Members of Anacapa's colony became believers that day. They were convinced that Sorté was half-bird and half-god. She would surely keep them safe.

Effortlessly moving her wings, Sorté rose, creating a beautifully scented breeze. The mesmerized pelicans smelled orchids as she floated backward into the cloud. Its walls closed slowly like a celestial clamshell. Then, all darkened, dissolved, and disappeared. The moon lost its unusual size and oddly colored brilliance. The pelican colony of Anacapa was awakened and warned about a changing world. Future birds of Anacapa would be told about that day through pelican lore and would never forget.

One hundred full moons after Sorté visited the island, a new species arrived in large wooden vessels with wings of cloth. Just as Sorté prophesized, the ways of nature would never be the same. Cloaked in dirty clothing and carrying sticks of fire and noise, these intruders wreaked havoc upon the pelicans' world. For no apparent purpose, they attacked nature with vengeance. It became clear that they outsmarted others by strength and deception, often using death as an answer for solving problems.

Within four generations after their arrival, the pelicans of Anacapa felt a deep and negative impact upon their way of life. They watched as these interlopers robbed the surrounding waters of fish, whales, otters, and anything else they could catch. The natural world became dramatically different. Sadly, these creatures never left. Instead, like insects, they bred exponentially, spreading across the world like waters from a tsunami. The pelicans of Anacapa called them "people," and they have never forgotten the parting words of Sorté, their spirit bird:

"The world will be at grave risk, as long as mankind rules the seas."

LAWS OF NATURE

Oceans are many different rivers encircling the Earth.
All life is born of the seas.
Every droplet of water has an individual soul,
providing the gift of life.
The Creator's love lives within every creature on Earth.
Each generation must teach the next to respect nature.
Life on Earth is purposeful.
No species has the right to overshadow another.
Nature is meant to self-destruct so that it may
bring forth a renaissance of new life.
Elements needed to create life are within all creatures.
No two lives are the same, each showing uniqueness
among all of Earth's occupants.
Great climatic change defines generations
and cleanses the Earth.

TWO

Plunge boldly into the thick of life, and seize it where you will,
it is always interesting.

– Johann Wolfgang von Goethe

Acting more like a hummingbird than a pelican, Kai ascends quickly until he becomes part of the sky. Free from school, an excitement vibrates throughout his feathered body as he quickly moves toward his favorite dive spot. Speed diving is his addiction. Despite the dangers involved, he believes that testing his boundaries will allow him to push himself beyond normal limits. With each dive, he plunges deeper into maturity. Beneath him lays a spectacular volcanic rise circling a crystal blue bay—a view out of an ancient dream. Because it is situated at a bend on the island, this location creates the secrecy and solitude Kai craves. He has named this coveted cove Nirvana.

Nirvana watches over and protects him like a silent partner. The cove's spiritual wisdom is wind-whispered into his ears, even though Kai thinks they are his own thoughts. Today is a classic diving day when the cove offers a minimum of westerly winds and a calm sea. These conditions are perfect for speed diving. It is his personal invitation to a grand ball, with Nirvana as his date. Kai accepts without hesitation. Nirvana, like a magician, allows Kai to spend as much time as needed to practice his craft. He continues until the air under his feathers cools his overheated body, indicating that soon the day will be coming to an end.

When Kai's practice is complete, Nirvana whispers, "There is time for one more dive."

The young pelican looks down at the large cove shaped like a half-moon and declares that this dive will be the one to break all his previous speed records. He will become famous today.

Most pelicans have never heard about what Kai is attempting, let alone tried it themselves. Previous dives have taught him all the skills necessary to be successful: when to tuck his wings, when to pull out, and how to keep his concentration. At these high speeds, anything can go wrong. Despite all of his experience, he will need Nirvana's wisdom, as well as a bit of luck.

Kai reaches his desired altitude of two hundred and fifty feet and transitions into a high-level float. Lying on his back like a resting sea otter, the damp stratus clouds feel like soft pillows underneath his feathered form. He stretches out his body and asks Sorté, the ancient spirit bird, for protection and success.

"Sorté, watch over me, and fly with me to sea level," he states in the form of a prayer.

Rotating his wings unnaturally, he is able to maintain an upside-down position long enough to lower his breathing and drop his heart rate. After visualizing the dive all day, Kai is sure that it will be the most extreme yet. Both Sorté and Nirvana join him as he readies.

Kai has endlessly reviewed all of his previous dives leading up to this moment. He reflects on his first feeding dives, where he was the fastest and most aggressive of all the young fledglings. His entire life, his father has unsuccessfully tried to slow him down. All Kai could hear was his mind and body telling him to go faster. It didn't take long before his dives had little to do with gathering food, and became more about the thrills. Never doubting his ability to catch fish, it was speed and danger that lured him to his beloved Nirvana. This is where he pushes to the edge of control and balance, allowing himself to knock on the doors of death.

Kai instinctively knows the necessary steps for a successful speed dive. All his moves must be sequential and executed properly, or he will spiral out of control. Today, he set a goal to break his previous record of ninety miles per hour. Because he will be traveling at a speed for which his body is not designed, he must expect the unexpected.

His inner voice announces, *It is time. Sorté, we are ready.*

Flipping over, belly to the brine, he faces the vivid blue blanket of sea. He is way above the point where he started his last dive. Suddenly, Dread appears.

"Look how far away the ocean is," Dread says tauntingly.

"Dread be gone," Kai responds out loud, giving voice to his guides,

Nirvana and Sorté. Nirvana has taught him to replace fear with affirmations emphasizing success.

"Positive thoughts yield victory," she whispers to him.

Kai starts a numberless countdown and thanks Sorté for a perfect day, ideal conditions, and his own personal health.

"Sorté, wrap your protective wings around me, and I will make you proud. Give me the strength to finish this record-breaking dive, and I will repay you with love and loyalty," he says aloud. He takes a deep breath of Anacapa's pure air and exhales slowly. Even though conditions are mild, it is likely that there will be changes in wind speed or direction as he drops toward the ocean's glassy tableau.

Mentally and physically settled, he begins his dive.

His first circle is quite slow with an extremely wide arc. This is when Kai visualizes the line he will be taking. He decides to track his path using a large rock just south of the cove and a fishing boat sitting to the west. Triangulating these with the cove's entrance, he creates a flight plan in his head. Dropping several feet for the next loop, his weight and momentum cause his speed to increase. As he completes the second circle, his body feels the mounting energy, which is an indicator of what is to come. Accelerating again, he engages in a series of decreasing, descending circles, dropping in altitude. By his fifth tightening loop, Kai's speed has increased to the point where he must squint his eyes in response to the mounting wind pressure. He has achieved a descending speed equivalent to a windy winter afternoon of forty-five miles per hour. Even though he feels the stress caused by the wind's increasing resistance, he remains calm. He has been here before and knows exactly what to do.

His dive resembles a whirlpool of water accelerating and disappearing into a drain. The air's resistance soon feels like he is swimming upstream through water; his face stinging as the wind hits him. Traveling at storm speeds of seventy-five miles per hour, his muscles begin to ache as he fights his way through the battering currents of air. He plunges downward, using the fishing boat as his target. Kai tightens his circles and streamlines his awkward torso. He digs his head into the impeding wind. Nearing a new record, his confidence surges as he prepares for the additional challenges yet to come.

The boat grows quickly in size, and Kai knows instinctively that he has entered into life-threatening danger. As the ocean surface rises, there is less room for error. Hitting the water at this speed would be like slamming into a granite boulder. His vision blurs from tears, and his muscles cramp. He makes a final move to mold his oblong body into a bullet-like posture.

"You must be careful, smart, and very, very lucky!" Dread says.

Like a surfer wiping out on a twenty-five foot wave, his body feels as if it may break apart. Kai mentally taps into the powers of Sorté to keep himself steady. A gritty smile appears on his large, awkward bill. Because of the cyclone-like winds, the gular on his throat is flapping wildly, and both his eyes are drawn down to tiny slits. Kai pulls his wings in tighter and tighter. Using only his tail feathers for steering, he's now a spinning, high-speed dart.

One hundred and ten miles per hour. Dread worries this is a suicide dive.

"Out, damn Dread," he tells himself, as Nirvana nudges him along.

Pain is wracking his body! This speed is like flying inside a hurricane. His circles have disappeared; he is now a kamikaze pilot with the roar of a jet in his ears. Kai struggles to maintain control within the ferocious wind. In an instant, he sees the name of the boat. It is the *Emma B,* a trawler, illegally poaching in the protected waters of the *Channel Islands National Marine Sanctuary.*

Kai lets out a loud scream, barely audible due to the winds blasting past his ears.

"I've done it!"

"It is too early to celebrate," Nirvana whispers.

The pelican's crooked smile has turned into a grimace. His focused mind keeps his concentration acute, helping him to overcome the pounding of his heart deep within his chest. His breathing is hampered by the wind's force, causing him to gulp for air.

"Pull out! Pull out!" The voices of both Sorté and Nirvana are shouting. It is like a chorus of gods. "A few more seconds, and it will be too late."

The adolescent Kai loves the sensation of speed and is intoxicated by what he is experiencing. But he knows what he must do, or he will end up plummeting to the sea surface. If he loses concentration, he will not be the fastest pelican ever—he will be a dead one. He pushes on his wings and intense pain rockets through him. His primary feathers cannot catch the wind because his wings are glued to his body. The pressure is far greater than in any of his previous dives. He has entered totally new territory. Panic tries to seep in.

"Out, Panic!" he counters. "Concentrate, I must concentrate!"

But his wings do not move, even though he is using every ounce of strength that he can muster. Finally, with a monstrous screech and a burst of exasperation, his wings begin to move just before he is due to crash near the port side of the *Emma B*. With help from his celestial guides, his scapulars catch a lip of wind. The blast of air tears his wings open, threatening to catapult them too high, too fast, breaking his fragile bones and making him drop to the ocean like a cannon ball. But with Herculean strength, his muscular wings remain firm, allowing him to level off.

Flying parallel to the surface at a high rate of speed, he misses hitting the sea caps by only a length of a swordfish. Hurling across the ocean, he is shaken but alive. Elation explodes through his mind as he enjoys this dragster-like glide.

Level and stable, he zooms past the stern of the poacher's boat at seventy miles per hour. Numerous men are on deck, engrossed in a trance of killing fish. The ecstatic fishermen do not notice the bird because they are concerned only with what is in the water. A large school of yellowtail surrounds the *Emma B*, and the activity on board is chaotic. The men are shin deep in protesting fish, with more spilling over the gunnels. Countless fish flail in puddles of blood, scales, and seawater on the wooden deck. They gasp for oxygen unavailable to them in the thin surrounding air. The terror in their eyes reveals the intensity of the shock they are experiencing after being plucked from the security of their homes. Their lives will be gone soon. The yellowtail are the latest victims of man.

High above in the crow's nest, a lookout scans the horizon for the Coast Guard whose boats patrol these sanctuary islands for illegal fishing. But the *Emma B*'s spotter has been watching this crazy pelican instead of the surrounding ocean. Not sure what he has just witnessed, he knows he has never seen any bird act like this before.

At a declining rate of speed, Kai's anxiety is replaced by a calmness born from pride. He can now enjoy his fifty miles per hour cruising speed. He tucks his wings to maintain this fast glide as long as possible. As he approaches a group of pelicans, he senses a problem. If he cannot react quickly enough, there is the very real possibility of a collision. The other pelicans are moving slowly away from him, flying serenely home from a feed. Kai is going too fast to avoid the line of birds that lies out in front of him. They are totally unaware of this comet speeding toward them.

At the last second, Kai recognizes the group as that of Feathertop's family. Feathertop is his best friend on Anacapa, and she is flying four off the front. Looking over her shoulder, she sees him and smiles, momentarily distracting Kai. Desperately, he opens his right wing to slow down, and it jerks him hard to the right, barely missing Feathertop's grandmother at the rear of the line. The old pelican panics as she falls four feet onto the ocean surface in an embarrassing splat. Even though the grandmother and Kai have always had a great deal of respect for each other, she lets out a stream of unkind words as she falls. The others double back to help the older bird.

Deep in Kai's chest is that uncomfortable feeling that comes with shame.

"That was really bad," exclaims Dread. "You are in deep trouble!"

Realizing that he has royally screwed up, Kai looks over his shoulder and sees the many faces of displeasure among the family of pelicans. Feathertop and the others assist the assaulted grandmother as she scrambles back into the air. Kai's velocity propels him, and he unwisely chooses to continue home.

Kai's father, gliding high above, is camouflaged among the shadows of the dark cliffs. He watches his son with a combination of trepidation and pride. Kai does not know he is there but instinctively feels his father's presence. Kai loves his father and remembers his many lectures and lessons about life.

"The Creator made pelicans to be calm," his father has repeated to him over and over. "Cease this dangerous diving," he has warned Kai. "It will end badly."

But, Kai's inner voice boasts, *I am the fastest pelican alive. I have flown at speeds never to be matched. You will be proud of me, Father. I am one of a kind!*

However, the shame of knocking Feathertop's grandmother out of the air has clouded his accomplishment, casting an ominous shadow over his record-breaking day.

THREE

The Mediaeval Bestiary tells that the pelican is very fond of its brood, but when young ones begin to grow they rebel against the male bird and provoke his anger.

– The Reverend E. Chobham Brewer LL.D.

Even the underlying guilt Kai feels after knocking down Feathertop's grandmother does not diminish his inner pride regarding today's dive. He knows that he has done something special in the pelican world. He has achieved his greatest accomplishment. On his way home, he executes a series of large celebratory rolls.

"Take that, you eagles and hawks!" he yells to the wind. "I am the top pelican and the fastest ever!"

Kai is not finished. He has a plan for a grand finale. With confidence verging on cockiness, he rises rapidly upon the invisible hand of an updraft and then transitions into an extra-large barrel roll, all the while shrieking a sharp victory cry. He savors his accomplishment much like a movie star receiving his first *Oscar*. On the backside of the large arc, he picks up speed. Heading down the opposite side of the vertical circle, he breaks out in the direction of the family cave.

Watch this! his inner voice boasts. Deep down he wishes his father would envy him just a little.

His timing is perfect, but unfortunately, his overheated body and exhausted mind cause him to misjudge the landing. He is traveling way too fast. Coming in hot, the ledge approaches too soon. He slams his tired wings up and out to create as much drag as possible. He lands just left of the mouth of the cave and hits hard. His webbed feet, ill-equipped to grab the loose dirt, cause him to flip over, bouncing head over feathered rear-end in three dizzying tumbles. He stops beneath a dusty mushroom-shaped cloud.

Covered with dirt, Kai utters a long, low moan, sounding like a demented ghost, "Ooooohhhh."

Every muscle in his body aches. He is afraid to move, not knowing if he has broken any bones. After lying perfectly still for a few moments, he slowly moves his right leg, then his left leg, then one wing at a time. Finally, he unravels his neck. Miraculously, nothing feels damaged despite the pain and discomfort haunting every cell and fiber of his body. Assured that all is well, he continues to untangle himself. It is time to mend his body as well as his bruised pride.

Kai opens his eyes to a shadowy figure outlined by the late afternoon sky. He knows that silhouette well and what comes with it. It is his father, wings at his waist, standing silent in his authority. Kai senses the intensity of his father's stare—it feels as if his grandfather and great-grandfather are also there, burning through those eyes. From his father's expression, it is obvious, once again, that parental concern has turned into disappointment. Once again, Kai is in trouble.

If only Pops knew about my dive, he would be proud, Kai speculates. *But more than likely, he only saw the crash landing. This could turn out badly.*

He prepares for the worst, feeling like a small fledgling about to be punished instead of the young pelican that just flew faster than anyone thought could be possible.

Looking down at his disheveled son, his father hopes he can find the right words. He sees his younger self in his son, which makes him want to smile, but he knows he must keep a stern exterior. He needs to teach his son responsibility.

"I watched you today," he says leaning over Kai. "I went to Eagle Point, so I could see what you were up to. I saw the entire dive. It scared me. In just a matter of seconds, you could have died."

Happy to hear his father saw him break the record, he responds "But Pops, I didn't crash! I went faster than ever!"

"I have never seen such a stupid stunt!" his father bellows.

"Don't call me stupid!" the son responds, reacting to this hurtful word.

"Pelicans are not designed to dive from great heights at that speed. The Creator made pelicans to be calm," the father repeats for the umpteenth time. "What you did was risk your life and the happiness of this family, and for WHAT? A fast dive for no fish. That is stupid if you ask me!"

Kai heaves a great sigh and tries to calm down, but his feathers are static with anger and will not settle back onto his chest. He is fighting frustration rising from deep within his heart. Even knowing his father may be partially right, he believes he is right, too. This is the classic father-son conundrum.

His father plants his weight evenly on both feet and squats down.

"Son, each creature has been designed for a purpose. Every bird has a specialty. Hawks, eagles, and falcons are built for speed and maneuverability...*not* pelicans!"

Here comes the lecture, Kai thinks as he rolls over, stretches his aching wings, and then slowly sits up. He can now see clearly into his father's eyes. They are dark, like the ocean before a storm. Kai knows his dad is set in his ways and cannot understand why his son does what he does. *Times are different and I am not like the other pelicans,* his inner voice says. *Why can't Pops see that?*

"Raptor birds are top guns of the bird world." His father continues, "They are designed for the kind of stunt you pulled off today. But you are not such a bird! You are destined to ride the seas like generations of pelicans before you." His father is almost beak-to-beak with his son, their ancestral energies mingling and at odds. "You must remember the words passed down from Sorté about the pelicans' role in the world."

"Yes, Pops, but Sorté HAS approved what I do, and she flies within me."

"That is ridiculous. Sorté wants us to take care of ourselves, not kill ourselves for no good reason." As the father speaks, he suspects that he may have already lost his son's attention, so he mentions Feathertop's name. Kai really likes Feathertop and is still trying to deal with the guilt about her grandmother. Her name reels the young pelican back to hear his father's words.

"Feathertop would make a fine mate, and both our families would be happy with the union."

Union! Kai thinks. *Father is once again telling me to pick a mate and commit to raising a family. That will never happen,* his inner voice declares. All Kai thinks about is speed, adventure, and travel. He is not ready for the responsibilities of being a mate and father. He is not ready to settle down.

"You must make it right with Feathertop's clan," his father says sternly. "Kai, you know I am right."

Feelings of guilt and remorse overwhelm him and rise in his throat like vomit. Kai knows he must atone for his transgressions even though he cannot agree that what he did was wrong.

Feathertop will understand, his inner voice declares. *Feathertop is always there for me through all my challenges. She has told me so many times that she will support me.*

Knowing his family is inside the cave, he glances past his father and wishes he was there, too. He looks up at the blue sky and the surrounding cliffs filled with birds. Trying to deflect his father's angry glare, his thoughts wander. Kai is very smart but easily distracted. The savants in school try to teach him how to focus on what is being said, but his mind is so active, he often travels to places far beyond Anacapa.

Kai's attention slowly returns as he hears his father recounting the story about DDT.

"When pelicans and other birds were decimated by man-made poisons, it became imperative that pelicans stick together," the father says, referring to weakened eggs and young fledglings who were killed in the past. "Mankind has huge plants where they make many poisons for purposes that are uniquely their own. However, these companies kill off nature with their complex chemicals. A huge population of pelicans, many of whom were from Anacapa, died from the toxins sent down rivers to the ocean. It was a time of great tragedy for our colony. Sorté warned about this, saying it was essential for our survival that we never let our guard down. You must realize the importance of what I am saying!" Kai's father then hesitates, waiting for a response from his son.

Kai realizes this history is important but doesn't know why his father keeps bringing it up over and over again. It was a sad time, but today, Kai wants to celebrate his accomplishment, not hear about all these deaths so many years ago. In his heart, he loves and respects his father, and he hears the sorrow whenever he talks about this chemical holocaust.

It must have been awful, Kai thinks to himself.

"Son, listen to me! At any moment your life here on Earth may come to an end. Unnecessary risks like speed diving only increase your chances of dying young. As you grow older, you will learn to lessen your risky behaviors. Sorté told us that we must use wisdom and dignity to help save the oceans. That is our main priority. Your diving is selfish and does not help us in this cause."

Noting his father's urgency, Kai believes that some of what he says may be true. But once again, he simply cannot agree.

I have plenty of time to do what I want before I conform to the ways of others, he thinks, believing he has his whole life ahead of him to settle down and be responsible. *Besides, life on Anacapa shows no signs of all this danger and impending doom Pops always talks about.*

"What do you plan on eating?" his father demands, changing the subject. "You did not fish this afternoon. Keep this up, and you will become a burden to others. You are hungry, yet you have no food."

"I will fish now," Kai blurts out without thinking.

"It is too late. The fish have gone deeper in the water," his father reminds him. "It will be dark soon. Fishing is over for the day. Young pelican, you have wasted half a day and not lived up to your responsibilities to the family or the colony."

Kai wants to jump up and yell to the sky, *Wasted a day? How can I waste a day when I broke a record for speed? This is a day like no other.* But he knows better. He once again swallows his frustration.

"You must NOT think only of yourself!" his father drives home, his voice reaching a crescendo.

Just then, Kai's mother unexpectedly emerges from the cave. She is carrying fish in her pouch like she used to when Kai was young.

"Kai, you must be hungry," she says in a soft and loving tone. Her smile makes her youngster feel safe and secure. Father, unappreciative of this untimely interruption, glowers at his mate and retreats back into the cave. He has lost the momentum, thanks to the mother.

Mom sits down next to her son. Her face is soft, but there is an intensity in her usually kind eyes. She understands her son's thoughts, but she, too, is worried. As he eats, neither of them says anything. Very little needs to be said. Both know the father is correct, but they also know it really doesn't matter. This young adolescent will soon make his exit from Anacapa.

This one is different, she thinks. *Kai is not ready to settle down. He has the heart of an explorer and the strength of a leader. Someday, he will be a valuable asset for the colony, if only he gets past the challenges in his young life.*

Her thoughts scare her. Her son is infatuated with the land on the other side of the water known as the Endless City. She does not want to lose her son to the dangers in the world of mankind, but she understands there is a journey ahead for him.

"Mom, tell me about the Magical Mountain again," Kai asks with a mouthful of fish.

"Son, it has been generations since Anacapa birds have visited the great mountain. No one knows what it is like today, but in the past, it was a special place. It was home to the Creator. The mountain healed the sick and was full of good spirits. Legends tell us that all who visited the Magical Mountain lived long and productive lives. It was a place of great good for all the birds and animals of Earth."

Echoing the father's concerns, she has impatience in her voice.

"Son, you have been told over and over that the Magical Mountain is no more. It lost its magic when mankind changed it and began a different way of life. Your great-grandfather was one of the last to journey there. Until his passing, he told stories of man's rapid expansion, noxious dirty air, and polluted waters. When he and the others returned from the mainland, they were sick from toxins and tainted food. No birds from Anacapa have returned since. The savants have made visits to the Endless City taboo."

Kai gobbles down the last two fish while his mother continues, "Since I was a fledgling, all I have ever been told is to avoid the Endless City because, like a rattlesnake, it is full of poison. Son, listen to the wishes of your ancestors and great-grandfather, whose spirits tell you to stay home. You should start a family of your own and experience the joys of Anacapa."

As Mom wraps her wings around her son, she feels a tension running throughout his body. She knows this resistance to her words is the force driving Kai's life. He is determined to find out about the mountain and the city one way or another. She closes her eyes and prays:

My great Sorté, please watch over my son. When he chooses to leave, keep him safe in his endeavors. Oh, great Creator, bring him home alive and healthy.

They lay wrapped together until mother and son fall into a deep sleep. Lying beneath the stars of the universe, the mother's mind slips into dreamland.

Kai is flying alone over a confused and hostile ocean spotted with debris. It is as if a great storm has lifted mankind's trash and placed it into every part of the sea. He is thirsty and exhausted after a long flight. Sharp winds have battered him for many hours. Looking for somewhere to rest, the sea spreads out like a watery desert. Finally, he sees an odd, low-lying isle on the horizon, moving like a branch in the wind. As he gets closer, it glistens in the reappearing sunlight and shapeshifts as swells pass through it. Unlike normal islands, Kai cannot see waves breaking along its rim. He decides that it may be an atoll due to its small size and lack of height. Void of normal colors, it shows no rocks, no trees, no sand, and no dirt. He glides above the mysterious isle. It is unrecognizable and sits in the middle of the ocean where there has never been an island before.

Spotting small clusters of birds near the center, he decides to land. Coming in cautiously, Kai sets down near a congregation of frigate birds and terns. These are fellow sea birds and great travelers, so he feels safe amongst them. As his feet hit the surface, he immediately slips and slides until he falls into a bunch of what appear to be empty bottles.

The unnatural feel of the island is exaggerated when Kai examines it closely. It is built not by nature but with oddly shaped objects of varying sizes. They feel slick and oily. The island lacks solidity because nothing is grown together. Instead, the flotsam is like a giant jigsaw puzzle, pushed together by the strength of the sea's currents. Kai shuffles to get atop the bottles but loses traction several times and falls backwards. Not only is the surface slippery, but it is also unsteady, rising and falling as swells move through it.

Looking closely at the other birds, they appear sad. The two frigate birds are emaciated and coughing so hard that their red pouches inflate unintentionally. Others are bent over and huddled uncharacteristically for proud birds of the sea. None of them acknowledge Kai.

As Kai looks around, Dread says, "Something is terribly wrong."

Kai wonders what the unfamiliar odor is. It is not the smell of flowers but instead a chemical stench leaking from inside the island itself. The smell of old medicines, chemicals, and rotting food make this a most undesirable place. He walks over the objects, most of which are a dull white or clear plastic. Many items have large decals of man-made colors that identify each piece. Human writings printed on the objects boast of the source of the trash.

Why would humans admit to trashing the Earth...Kai ponders.

Because there are no beaches, no reefs, no plants and no trees, Kai cannot imagine how this island came to be.

"Where am I?" he asks, hoping to learn what direction he can fly to get away from this ghoulish place. "Why does such a weird island exist?" he says, groping for answers from no one in particular.

The biggest of the frigate birds looks at Kai from behind clouded eyes.

"You have landed on Plastic Island Number Twelve," he answers, followed by a cough emanating from deep within his chest. He must wait for his pouch to deflate before he talks again. "It is one of many floating islands that have invaded our oceans. All of this material has escaped from man's lands and rides the currents until they meet up and form islands. There is an avalanche of plastic traveling like a tsunami all around the oceans," declares the frigate, sounding as if he is discussing the end of the world.

The entire time Kai listens, he needs to shuffle his feet for stability. Like standing on quicksand, he sinks deeper into the island with every movement. He notices too late that other birds are perched on boxes or large bouquets of nets and rope in search of stability. Kai, however, is standing on straws, bottles, paper, and plastic wraps, plus thousands of other miniscule objects too small to identify. The plastics are interlinked into a complex bundle that will not break up even though it is not firm enough to stand on. Like a giant octopus, the plastic island wraps its tentacles around Kai, now struggling to maintain his balance.

"I have inadvertently eaten too much of this plastic by fishing too close to land," the frigate continues. "My stomach is blocked and does not work. Like the others, I am waiting here to die. Hopefully, our remains will tell mankind that we cannot live with this waste."

All inhabitants of Plastic Island Number Twelve have one characteristic in common—they appear to have accepted their fate, like prisoners in a death camp.

Kai's feet have disappeared into the junk, and he is now up to his stomach in garbage. Freaking out, he desperately tries to fly away. This only entangles him more. Like a scuba diver swimming in thick seaweed, the more he struggles, the tighter his bonds become. In a short time, his wings are weighted down by the impenetrable plastic.

It is too late. He is hopelessly ensnarled, like a fly in a spider's web. As he relaxes, the aggressive hands of trash drag him deeper. He screams for help, but the other birds ignore him.

"Mother, help me!" is the last thing he says before disappearing into the belly of the beast.

Kai's mother awakens from her dream with a start. Her heart is beating rapidly, and her breath comes in short, labored puffs. This visionary nightmare reveals not only the contamination that mankind has created, but to her, it is a reminder that her son is truly contemplating a trip to one of the sources of this trash.

It cannot be safe, she thinks, as her mind fills with a whole new level of anxiety.

His mother gazes at Kai sleeping comfortably, and she cries in silence. Pelican lore has warned about the dangers of the human assault on the environment. This abuse of the Earth has only gotten worse over time. But her intuition tells her that she won't be able to stop her son. He will follow the path of his ancestors before him and seek a mountain that may not even exist.

Unable to sleep, she lays awake, covering her boy with her wings in a futile effort to protect him from the unknown.

He sleeps soundly, like a newborn who only knows his mother's love.

FOUR

*Looking northward, he saw a tiny bird flying towards him
from far across the water,
flying low over the waves and struggling to stay in the air.
Fluttering over the surf, it fell hard to the sand.
And, when our chief's spirit picked it up and stroked its feathers,
it turned its eye toward him and said,
"The path of my flight is your bearing. Sail!"*

(Polynesian tale of an exiled South Pacific chief whose dream
led him to follow shorebirds to the unexplored northern sea
and the discovery of Hawai'i.)

– Herb Kawainui Kāne

Kai awakens to the austere voice of his father giving him instructions for the day. He treats the young pelican like a child and chides him for yesterday's actions.

"Son, you WILL behave today," he orders. "You WILL fish with the family, and right after that, you WILL go to school. After school, you WILL NOT fly or dive outside of the cove. There is no room for negotiations. I want to see the son I know is within you; not this rebellious one sitting in front of me."

Looking to his mother for support, he sees she has already retreated back into the cave to help the other youngsters get ready for the day. It is Kai and his dad, alone on the bluff.

"But that is not fair," Kai objects.

His words are barely out of his mouth when his father talks over him.

"You are restricted to the cove. Do you hear me, young man? Keep talking, and it will get worse," his father says, upping the ante. In his parental logic, the punishment should fit the crime. In this case, too much freedom necessitates restrictions.

Kai knows from experience that further discussion is not an option. So, he acknowledges his father with a sound somewhere between a grunt and an okay. This further irritates his dad, who makes an abrupt turn and marches back to the cave to rally the rest of the family.

Alone on the ledge, Kai feels the toll of yesterday's dive. His body aches in the chill of the new morn. He can hardly lift his wings. This makes him slightly grateful for his father's restriction because it will give his body time to rest.

In the east, the mainland wakes up to the emerging day. An explosion of orange, gray, and purple merge to color the billowed clouds. Sunlight is at war with the dark sky and the mossy green surface of the Pacific Ocean. The beauty of the sunrise is not lost on young Kai. He whispers an affirmation of gratitude to the forthcoming sun.

"Our Creator has gifted us with yet another beautiful day on Anacapa. Please help me make the most of it."

Kai stretches his body and starts his daily exercises as the rest of the colony comes alive. He focuses on the mainland while doing his workout. On the horizon, there is the familiar grayish tone surrounding a thin, brown line. This recurring stripe looks as if it has been shaded by a mythical giant using a number two pencil. The dust-colored band shows itself every day and disappears only with rain and darkness. Kai knows instinctively that it is not of natural origins. Throughout his childhood, Kai has inquired about the brown line. No matter whom he asked, he always got the same explanation:

"It is a line of human life. It comes from all of mankind's machines, contraptions, and fires. It is an expression of the human need for heating, cooling, travel, and manufacturing. The greed of mankind and his huge corporations routinely change the environment to fit humans and their way of life. Unlike nature, which adapts to its surroundings, mankind alters all that surrounds him."

In the course of his short life, this coffee-colored line has peaked the young pelican's curiosity of the mainland more than anything else. It is hard for him to fathom how much activity it takes to yield such an immense layer of airborne debris each and every day. His fixation on the humans' lifestyle draws him to the mainland like a marlin is pulled toward warmer waters. For other young pelicans, fishing, school, and home are all they need for a satisfactory life and a quiet mind. Kai, on the other hand, is different. He craves more mental stimulation than he thinks Anacapa can offer. Questions about life on the mainland consume his thoughts.

Flipping over on his stomach, Kai starts a series of exercises in order to strengthen his shoulders and wings. He devoutly adheres to a program of calisthenics and meditation, which makes him stronger than other pelicans. This intensive training enables him to work through fatigue and pain and is key to his high-speed diving.

His mom, dad, and three siblings exit the cave and gather around him. Standing side by side, they appear as if readying for a family photo. To his left is his younger brother, Churchill. He is the tallest and skinniest of the clan. Churchill's lanky frame makes his faintly colored feathers appear too large for his body. Headstrong like his brother Kai, Churchill looks up to his older brother's accomplishments, which makes his father uneasy.

Next to Churchill is Maria Tallchief. She is the middle fledgling and only daughter. Her sun-bleached feathers and vivacious attitude make her quite unique. "MT," as she is called, is very popular and always full of energy. Like her namesake, she is a fabulous dancer, possesses an infectious laugh, and spreads social unity with her charm. But she also has a temper. If challenged about something she deems important, she is quick to respond.

Rikki is the youngest and is unusually small for his age. He was born a "preemie." His mother became sick after coming in contact with a fuel spill near the mainland. His egg was birthed with a crack. Rikki does everything right; he is a pleaser. Excelling in school, Rikki never gets into trouble. Because of weaker bones and other physical challenges, there are days others need to fish for him. His family is devoted, knowing that Rikki's life will always be tough.

The surrounding cove and cliffs are wild with activity. Every cave, nest, bush, and tree is alive with birds. They are talking, cawing, kipping, squealing, whistling, and singing their welcome to yet another day. There are petrels, auklets, cormorants, murres, and gulls, plus hundreds of pelicans, all preparing for the ritual of the morning fish.

Pelicans are the most organized of all the sea birds. While other species fly in bunches and flocks, pelican clans assemble in the air by forming trains. They consist of a "V" or straight-line formation led by a family elder, with the remainder of the pelicans following behind. By pumping their wings consecutively, it looks as though the lead bird is pulling while the caboose birds are pushing. Hence, the name train. Pelicans fly wing to wing like a group of synchronized swimmers. While in motion, their formations create harmony and beauty up and down coastlines around the world. Unlike migratory birds who are in constant motion, pelicans are excellent gliders and give the impression of a group of Sunday motorcycle riders cruising on a quiet country road.

The start of each day begins like a marathon with thousands of birds diving off the cliffs. It resembles a meteor shower on a moonless night. Kai's father sounds like a sergeant addressing his troops.

"Stick together and be safe," he commands. "Now go!"

The family obediently dives off the cliff. As he drops, Kai lets out a scream, freediving until caught by an updraft. As the family train forms, cousins, aunties, uncles, and close friends travel together. Kai's father drops into the lead, with his eldest son at the number four position. Feathertop snuggles up next to Kai. Figuring his dad has orchestrated Feathertop's visit because of yesterday's events, Kai smiles. He welcomes any opportunity to spend a day with her, regardless of the circumstances.

Kai stares at her bright colors, unique feathered head, and soothing smile. His inner voice declares loudly, *She is indeed quite pretty.* His happy eyes relay that message to her silently. Feathertop is equally delighted to be with Kai's family for the day. The feeling of comfort is mutual.

As the train starts to move, the two simultaneously look at each other as they synchronize off the father's stroke.

Feathertop calls out, "Hey Kai. Feeling okay today?"

"Oh, hey there Feather," he responds quickly. "You look great! Oh yeah, I'm good," and for that moment, the discomfort in his body fades. "Is your grandmother okay? I feel terrible about yesterday."

"Yeah, she's fine. Grammy Grace was startled, but she was not hurt. Grammy, living up to her name, is always graceful. She forgives you and knows it was not intentional. Your problem is with my dad. He is upset that you did not come back to help or apologize. You definitely need to talk to him."

"Told you so," Guilt whispers.

"Yep, that is a good idea," Kai responds without really thinking. He immediately changes the subject. "After fishing, let's go to

Pinniped Point. I want to show you Nirvana. It is my favorite place on the island and is really pretty in the late morning. It is where I was diving yesterday."

"We have school after fishing. Did you forget?"

"Oh shoot. Yeah, I did," he says, conveniently forgetting the terms of his grounding as well. The excitement of being with Feathertop has trumped all else. "Well then, how about after class?"

"Great," she answers, their wings flapping in perfect harmony.

Being with Feathertop always has a calming effect on Kai. He has totally forgotten his problems at home, his tired muscles, and sore body.

Morning trains are normally not a place for a lot of conversation, so the two follow the stroke patterns of the other pelicans while silently enjoying each other's company. A short time later, they arrive above the fishing grounds. The water is churning with anchovies. The train breaks up with individual birds trimming their wings, tucking their heads, and dive bombing into frothing water.

"Let's go for it!" Kai challenges Feather.

Never one to shy away from a dare, Feathertop responds with an enthusiastic, "You're on."

With that, they jackknife in sync and torpedo themselves into the water, scooping up fish at will. Kai is very hungry after missing yesterday's afternoon feed. When Feathertop surfaces, she has a wriggling anchovy sticking out the side of her beak. Wet and disheveled, she is still alluring.

The feeding continues until everyone is full. Throughout the morning, they break into groups and socialize while digesting their meals. Feathertop's wings touch Kai as she paddles around. Neither one pulls away. Both have the same deep feelings of affection for one another. They are too young to understand their emotions, but their hearts are full of optimism and innocence. Both are sure they have a future together.

The train re-forms for the trip home. Kai's dad takes the lead, carrying extra fish for Rikki, who remained at home once again. The return trip is filled with laughter and stories. Hitchhikers are allowed as part of homebound trains, and the previously assigned spots are jumbled up. It is a long-standing tradition that returning trains are a mixture of birds from different families, which encourages socialization amongst them. Pelicans believe that by knowing and liking each other, it diffuses conflicts and stress, making for a happier colony.

Glancing back, Kai's dad hopes that being with Feathertop may help squelch his son's fire for adventure and danger. What he sees is promising. Both youngsters seem relaxed and comfortable with each other. However, his concern is not completely gone. This represents only a speck in time in the life of two teenagers. At this age, personal satisfaction comes and goes quickly. He hopes that their feelings will deepen and stop his son's dangerous behaviors.

As the train reaches the entrance to the cove, the adults continue up to the cliffs, and the youngsters break off for school.

FIVE

Educating the mind without educating the heart is no education at all.

– Aristotle

Today's lesson is held in the miniature amphitheater. Its main feature is a large middle stone that has been flattened by millions of years of erosion. Outlined by a ring of large San Onofre breccia boulders, the smooth surface provides an ideal stage for colony activities such as school, meetings, and celebrations. The ten students arrive, frenzied from the morning feed. They tell exaggerated tales about how many fish they caught, the size of the shark they saw, and the type of boat that sped by. Sitting in a semi-circle awaiting their savant, several students exchange teenage gossip about others in the colony. Kai does not participate in these shallow conversations. Besides, he has Feathertop to hold his attention.

One student, Hector, is a bit overweight, insecure, and always looking for praise and reinforcement. He deliberately sits in the front row closest to the savant. This is so the teacher sees him and can easily acknowledge his efforts. Kai does not like it when Hector asks questions, causing the students to stay longer. It is Kai's belief that assigned class times should be adhered to. All the savants love students who participate in discussions, so Hector is one of their favorites.

Immediately behind Hector are identical twins, Monica and Leia. They are two rascally female birds who look so much alike they are often mistaken for each other. Only a very small black mark on Leia's left leg sets them apart. They are known to pull off pranks. Using their looks to confuse others, they switch places during exams to help the other sister pass a subject that is difficult. Both are light-hearted and full of fun.

Sitting patiently in the center of the class are four youngsters, all from the same family. Two are natural and two adopted. Their father and mother are very influential in the colony and live outside of the cove in an area where the more prominent pelicans nest. For this reason, these four must be well behaved so as to not bring shame upon their father, who is one of the colony's elders. The rest of the group includes Kai's brother, Churchill, and several other birds who attend school as required. These pelicans are satisfied at being unexceptional.

Feathertop and Kai always sit together. They have been doing so since they first started school as young fledglings. Kai finds there is something grounding about being close to her. She is a good student, and Kai learns from her every day. He tries to pay attention to the various subjects, partially for knowledge and understanding, but more importantly, to please Feathertop. Even so, Kai often daydreams about fantastic feats outside of school. He insists they sit farthest from the stage, so they are not under the watchful eye of the savant. Today, he has put an empty row in front of them in an attempt to move even further back. Kai thinks he is hiding in the back of the class, but he attracts the teacher's attention more often than not. Feathertop thinks this is dumb, but as she understands Kai better than most, she goes along with it. Feathertop knows that Kai's mind seldom rests and she finds this appealing. He is more complex than other youngsters in the colony. Even though Kai is not the best student, Feathertop, like many others, thinks he is a potential leader with a great future.

Today's savant is Master Benjamin. He slip-slides in from the left side of the stage. The kids have nicknamed him "Master B." He is the oldest of the savants and is the most knowledgeable in pelican lore. There is an air of wisdom around Master B that is enhanced by his older appearance, peppered beak, and grayed feathers. He brings history alive with his lessons. When he lectures, it is as if he is living in the historical moment, not just talking about the past. The backdrop of the dry hillside behind him neatly matches the gray-brown color of the old pelican's neck feathers. Due to current drought conditions, the normal mat of healthy plants blanketing the hillsides is all but gone, leaving only patches of green dotting the dry, brown landscape.

The professor swaggers confidently to center stage, turns his back to the students, and waits for silence from the buzzing teens. Hector immediately shushes the class.

Hurry, so we can go, Kai's inner voice pleads in silence. Anxious to have Feathertop to himself, he makes a vow to sit quietly until class is over. Then, they can fly to Nirvana.

Master B begins by ceremonially fluffing his feathers signaling the importance of the lesson to come. Kai winces and rolls his eyes. Master B talks longer than other savants because of his slow mannerisms and vast knowledge of all things pelican. The class settles in.

"Today, we are going to hear about some very important pelicans who were great leaders and heroes in history," Master B begins. His voice is calm and melodic like an owl's call. His intro grabs the attention of everyone in the room; even Kai's. "It is vital to understand how these famous pelicans have paved the way for all of us. We will see how mankind has interacted with the natural world over the past centuries. And, we will talk about great pelicans throughout history that have tried to befriend and help humans."

Master B looks over his classroom. His gaze drifts to Kai, who is already beginning to lose interest. As the lesson starts, Master B directs his words specifically to Kai.

If pelican leaders in the past were great heroes, then why is everyone trying to stop me from becoming great? Kai's inner voice challenges. *All I am ever told is to be normal like everyone else. I do not want to be like Hector. I want to be like myself,* he argues silently.

The contradiction is so obvious to him that he cannot understand why others do not see it. He wobbles to get more comfortable. Feathertop, sensing this internal dialogue, brushes up against him with her wing to quiet his thoughts. When he looks up, she gives him a soothing smile, and he relaxes.

Kai understands this lesson is meant to give young pelicans pride in their ancestors, but he knows all too well that, if given a chance, Master B will challenge Kai's personal goal of exploring the world of mankind in search of the Magical Mountain.

Master B, and even Feathertop, will attempt to get me to abandon future adventures. They all want me to live a more sedentary life, he tells himself.

Master B starts by talking about the ancient story of the human's Trojan War.

"There was a great white pelican named Setivius who flew through flaming arrows to warn the king of Troy about a giant wooden horse that Greek soldiers would deliver to the city. It would be disguised as a gift announcing an end to the fighting. Setivius told the Trojans of Greek soldiers hiding inside the belly of the horse. They were prepared to open the city's gates, allowing the rest of the invading Greek army into the city. This led to a disaster. The wooden horse was merely a decoy to lure the Trojans into weakness," Master B says. He is at home on stage and loves "storytelling," as he calls history.

"Nobody listened to the noble pelican Setivius. The Trojans were too busy celebrating their perceived victory. Drunk with food and wine, they rejoiced late into the evening. It was their time to thank the gods for helping them defeat the Greeks. The vanity of human gods has been the root of wars throughout human history, resulting in incomprehensible death tolls. This is in opposition to the Mother of Nature because she believes that all creatures are born from the same God. Besides, why believe a talking pelican whose advice would end this great celebration?"

Master B went on, "They rebuffed the pelican's advice, and the result was indeed catastrophic. The battle was lost, and the war quickly ended. The great city of Troy fell. Years later, when Homer, the greatest writer of the period, wrote about the story of Troy, he included Setivius. But as time went by, the pelican was edited out by subsequent historians. They decided that a talking pelican was too unbelievable, thus saving face for the important people in Troy's history. This is just one example of how mankind ignores natural history in favor of human history. Humans describe natural events like earthquakes and volcanoes as 'disasters,' unlike war, which has become a human obsession and the greatest way to show their power and strength. Wars are glorified and repeated many times in each generation as mankind searches for a winner. But there is rarely a winner when it comes to war. Like the many Trojans, Setivius' place in history died an inglorious death."

Kai is starting to get really annoyed.

"The pelican should have been a hero that day. But instead, the soldiers in a wooden horse were victors because the pelican was ignored," he whispers loudly to Feathertop. "Besides, this happened so many years ago, what does this have to do with my life today?"

Master B, now warmed up, executes a dance-like spin at the conclusion of this episode, energizing the class.

"The lesson to be learned here is about deception. Be wary of someone bearing gifts, especially if they were once enemies. Always verify what is about to happen, and if anything seems too good to be true, be cautious." Master B's wisdom is timely and true. He stares down at his students and notices Kai looking out to sea.

"All great pelicans have risked their lives to do what they believe is right. Do not forget that," Master B says loudly, still trying to recapture Kai's wandering mind.

Kai's eyes meet his teacher's in a tug-of-war of generations. His inner voice yells, *Precisely! That is what I am doing, and nobody acknowledges me for it.*

The hypocrisy is not lost on Kai. He believes something is wrong with older pelicans and their line of thinking. He hears his father's voice ringing in his head, *Learn as much as you can in class and stay out of trouble,* clearly endorsing what is taught in school. But in classes like this, they teach about great pelicans who risked everything to do the right thing, regardless of what others thought. Kai wants to experience life the way great pelicans in history did. *These famous pelicans did not learn from a teacher. They learned by living, doing, and risking,* his inner voice states so loudly, it echoes inside his head.

Feathertop shifts in her seat again, so their bodies brush. She can sense his tension and see his taut muscles. There is energy shooting through his body, which both impresses and concerns her.

There is so much boxed up inside him, she thinks.

Master B jumps into the air like a circus ringmaster, lands, and continues the lesson.

"Next, there is the story of Nimus, an Australian pelican who flew four thousand miles to warn the human explorer Magellan of dangers he would face in the Philippines. The pelican foresaw Magellan's death at the hands of other humans and tried to steer him away from Mactan Island. Magellan's angry crew was devastated by his death. Because Nimus was a talking pelican, they considered her a 'sea witch,' which was a common belief among sailors of that era. Nimus was killed by the crew out of ignorance and fear. Magellan, killed by a poison arrow, was unable to complete his around the world voyage.

"The lesson here is one of trust versus greed. Had Magellan believed and trusted Nimus, he would have lived. But the explorer's greed inspired him to go on. He was determined to claim more lands for his king in spite of the warning. This is one of many examples of people dying because of an addiction for fame and riches."

Kai doesn't know anything of the greed or material possessions that drove Magellan, but he wonders about a world that places them higher than trust.

I think living a good life and caring for others is more important than gold or money, his inner voice concludes. *From this story, Magellan sounds a lot like the new species that Sorté had warned about in her prophecy.*

Master B winds up telling this tale by doing a short tap routine on the smooth surface of the rock. For a bird his age, the savant's agility is quite impressive. The students like it when he dances, and Master B enjoys the students because they keep him feeling young.

Another story, Kai moans internally. *It's painful to sit through another story when I could be out creating my own stories. Every story I have to sit through takes me further from my future,* his inner voice states logically.

"I would have done things differently," Kai says to Feathertop, loud enough that it is overheard by everyone, including Master B. The savant scowls as Kai shifts in his seat, wishing he could fly away. He does not realize how his voice carries and is torn between the feelings that he treasures and the rules that are placed upon him in school.

"Hang in there," Feathertop whispers. "Master B is watching. You are a bit too antsy. He is our savant and should be treated with respect." Back on center stage, Master B says, "Class, what can we learn from these examples?" Hector, waving his wing excitedly, cannot wait to answer. "Hector, what do you think?"

Hector, straightens up, happy to be acknowledged.

"The message is that pelicans, as stated by our beloved Sorté, are supposed to help others. It is our nature. Unfortunately, most of the time humans think they do not need our help. They seem to think that we are of no value to them."

"That is correct!" the savant enthusiastically responds. "Always remember that we are good for others, so do not let them sway you. Let me tell you about an instance when a pelican did the right thing and was accepted by humans resulting in people's lives being saved."

Master B clears his throat and readies for yet another pelican tale.

"It is not unusual for powerful and deadly storms to troll the ocean off British Columbia. Several years ago, there was an out of season storm travelling south from the Bering Sea. Ominous clouds, heavy with rain, wind, and lightning came quickly toward Canada. It was late spring and the tempest was totally unexpected. Many mariners were caught unprepared for such a destructive storm. This is the story of one boat that floundered and was ready to sink.

"Over a calm sea and hours before the storm's arrival, Tecumseh, a five year-old brown pelican, wandered out to explore the open ocean. This was not his natural behavior, but youthful enthusiasm drove him off on an adventure, not suspecting there would be any problems. Just short of reaching his destination, he saw the coal-black storm front moving rapidly in his direction. He turned and flew toward home as fast as he could, but the storm eventually overtook him. The swirling winds kept increasing in intensity for hours as he fought his way home.

"Afraid he was going to get pounded by the freezing winds, he took refuge on a sixty-five foot luxury boat that lay dead in the water, completely surrounded by menacing waves and battering winds. The boat's name was *Blondie,* and onboard was a Seattle couple and their two teenage children. They were doing a routine delivery to Anchorage. Not expecting such a devastating storm because of the time of year, they went to sea unprepared for the high winds and huge waves. *Blondie* was a boat built for recreation, not designed for heavy seas.

"By the time Tecumseh landed on its stern, both engines were dead, and the boat was taking on water. All four crewmembers were manually trying to keep it afloat. Power had failed, and they had to do everything by hand, desperately fighting back fear and panic. The mother shared her deep concerns and let the bird know what needed to be done. If help was not found soon, the boat would sink and her family would perish. Tecumseh knew he had to help. He allowed her to duct tape a SOS message to his leg with a set of bearings denoting their location. The communication was awkward, but both the human and the bird were children of the same God at that moment.

"Tecumseh flew off and spent the next several hours battling icy winds. The frigid gusts felt like razor blades lashing him as he trudged toward the mainland. Eventually, finding a Coast Guard cutter, he landed on its bridge.

"Tecumseh was able to get the attention of the captain who saw the message taped to his leg. The captain ordered his ship to follow the coordinates written down by the mother. Without understanding or questioning the situation, the Coast Guard cutter arrived where

Blondie was supposed to be. After a short search, they found the boat and were able to rescue the family just before *Blondie* was swallowed up by the raging ocean.

"There was an emotional reunion between the family and the pelican. To this day, the captain of the rescue boat cannot explain the actions of the brown pelican, but he now is a believer in the close relationship between man and nature. He leads efforts among other humans to protect the environment and its residents. The captain placed the pelican in his official report, which led to a picture of Tecumseh being hung in the Coast Guard Academy to this day."

Master B finishes the story by executing a pirouette turn with the agility of a classical dancer, his wings tight against his body while spinning on one leg. He breaks into a musical chant about loving to teach and then slowly moves off stage, dismissing the class.

Within seconds of his disappearance, Kai declares, "Hurry up! Let's get going," nudging Feathertop in the side. She smiles and follows. Rising to the sky in unison, they turn toward Kai's beloved Nirvana. But Feathertop soon falls behind, as the overly excited Kai flies too fast. She strokes to keep up. Looking at him from behind, it is apparent that Kai is truly a strong bird and happens to have very cute tail feathers. Feeling secure with him in the lead, they sail over Main Peak, drop down to Arch Rock and then head east. "Kai, why do you call this place Nirvana?" she asks when she finally catches up to him.

"It means a place that is free from personal suffering...a place of humility and salvation," he responds automatically with a tone and attitude she has never heard before.

"My, oh my, that is quite impressive," she says.

"Not really. I learned this from savant Susanna in one of her classes on pelican culture. The name seemed to match the beauty of this place."

"We took that class together, and I do not remember her talking about Nirvana."

"She didn't. I stayed afterwards for a one-on-one discussion about cultures from around the world. She believes in working toward Nirvana in her own life."

Feathertop is filled with pride by her friend's philosophical thoughts.

"I like the idea of a world free from suffering," she responds. "Could there be such a place?"

"I am taking you there." Kai looks back and hollers, "Feather, here we go!" as they aim high into the sky.

Not used to heights, Feathertop struggles with internal fears. At two hundred and fifty feet, Kai floats softly in the air, awaiting her arrival. Looking down, he sees her struggling as though she is climbing a very tall but invisible ladder. When she arrives, her face is strained and apprehensive.

"Look around, Feather, isn't this gorgeous? This is where I start my dives." He points with his wing and announces proudly, "That is Nirvana!"

Feathertop, never having been so high, is completely unnerved. She is so shaken that she cannot fully enjoy the beautiful vista that lies beneath them.

"Kai, are you insane? Look how high we are! You are surely going to get hurt, or even killed, diving from this altitude. I don't like this," she says with deep concern. "I want down!"

"It's okay, Feather, just trust me. I will show you the way," he says, trying to calm her fears. "I promise that you won't get hurt. Just follow me. All you have to do is concentrate on the beauty around you."

Kai starts a slow descent just as if he were starting a dive. He is careful to go very slow, ten miles per hour, the entire way down. *Not too fast,* his inner voice commands. At exactly the same time, Feathertop instructs him to do the same. Kai is a natural teacher and wants her to enjoy the experience. Using the larger circles of his dives, he flies in slow motion. Their descent is like a beautiful, spiraling dance. On the way, Kai tries to make it fun. Feathertop maintains her composure all the way to the ocean surface, giving Kai the impression that she may have enjoyed it.

"What do you think?" he asks optimistically.

"Kai, now I know what the others are talking about. You are putting yourself in great peril every time you do one of these crazy stunts. It scares me," she says in a tone of voice that surprises him.

"I am not crazy," he spurts out, reacting yet again to the one word that upsets him.

Feathertop senses his deep disappointment, but she is confused and scared. She wants to support her friend, but she cannot understand his macho desire to do such dangerous stunts.

In order to protect him from himself, he will need to change, she concludes. Feathertop issues an unexpected ultimatum, "Goodbye Kai, I am going home! I simply cannot support you in this. You must give up your speed diving!"

He watches in stunned silence as she turns and flies off.

"If Feathertop does not understand, then there is no one in Sorté who backs me. I am alone," he says out loud. He does not go after her. Understanding how fear can change people, he watches as she glides beyond the cliffs and disappears. Kai, saddened by her curt response and quick exit, cannot see that she is sobbing.

He banks left and flies to a massive black stone burped up eons ago from deep within the Earth's crust. Kai often comes here to gaze at the vastness of the ocean and view some of the world's most beautiful sunsets. Nirvana wind-whispers in his ear, "Stay true to who you are, and all will turn out in your favor. Do not forget your goals, but keep your love true to only one at a time." His relationship with his beloved Nirvana is truly a beautiful thing.

Feathertop does not understand what happiness entails, so she will simply have to wait, he and his inner voice agree.

In a moment of clarity, he stands tall and shouts out to the vast ocean.

"Tomorrow, I will start my search for the Magical Mountain. Tomorrow, I will go to the mainland!"

Kai knows his life is about to change dramatically because for the first time he is ready to leave everything behind; his schooling, his family, and his cherished Feathertop.

SIX

One way to get the most out of life is to look upon it as an adventure!

– William Feather

Kai awakens before sunrise. His mind immediately prepares for departure. To the east are brilliant yellow beams bursting forth like beacons. The sun will soon follow, beckoning life to share in a new day. By the time the firmament lightens to a baby blue, a new brown line has already started to form, revealing that humans have, once again, begun their complex way of living.

If mankind knows how ruinous this pollution can be, why does he continue to manufacture all this trash? What is the purpose? he asks himself, hoping to learn the answer very soon. *What activity could possibly cause so much waste, day in and day out?*

"DO NOT GO! Man has devastated the environment with man-made chemicals," Dread says, using the voice of Kai's beloved Auntie Aphrodite.

Kai's deceased Auntie Aphrodite was an outspoken and opinionated savant. She was an advocate for a clean environment. More than anyone on Anacapa, she spread warnings about the decaying oceans. She spent hours discussing life with Kai. Despite his young age, Auntie Aphrodite always treated him like an equal. He maintains a deep respect for her and her ideas. But because of his deeply entrenched idealism, he is having a difficult time believing that humans can be as uncaring as Auntie said. The only humans he has closely encountered are the brown-suited rangers that protect the *Channel Islands National Marine Sanctuary*. These round-hatted workers are always helpful and watch out for the animals and birds of the islands. However, he knows Auntie Aphrodite was a rock of reality. He can only assume she knew about a different side of human behavior.

"DO NOT GO!" Dread screams along with Auntie.

Kai suppresses Dread's fatalistic thoughts.

All will be good. Sorté will watch over me, his inner voice counters. *Dread, be gone!*

"Guns, chemicals and giant jellyfish-shaped bombs can kill entire ecosystems in an instant," Kai remembers Auntie Aphrodite saying, as an image of her shimmers in front of him like a phantom. She stands with the coastline behind her, corralled by the brown line. Kai's inner voice stays strong, despite the attempted beatdown by Dread.

I am ready to go, no matter what! All is well at home. I am not needed. This should not take too long. Besides, Dad always takes care of everything, Kai's inner voice declares in a strong closing argument. Ignoring his pounding telltale heart, he intends to sneak away and fulfill a lifelong dream.

"Out, Dread, out," he repeats for the final time. "Hello, mainland, here I come!"

Following in the footsteps of other great pelicans, he runs to the cliff's edge and drops into the moist air. Gliding low to maintain secrecy, he rounds the rock reef that protects Fishbowl Cove and finalizes his covert exit. His mother, hidden by the early morning darkness, watches from the blufftop. She is crying as he disappears from sight. This is the day she has feared for a long time.

Once over the open ocean, the sight of the mainland draws Kai like a fish to chum.

This is the beginning of a great adventure, he thinks, smiling to the eastern sky. The daring pelican celebrates that he is free from the constraints of parents, school, and colony rules. Heading east, he aims directly at the rising sun. It seems logical that such a powerful place as the Magical Mountain would be located near the rising sun. So, east it is.

Rising and falling with air currents, he follows the trail of the sun's glitter across the swells. This newfound freedom is exhilarating.

"Let the adventure begin!" he screams with the zest of a buccaneer boarding a treasure ship. What he is doing may be wrong in the eyes of some, but he knows it feels really good as adrenaline streams through his blood. The excited pelican establishes a progressive rhythm resembling one used centuries ago by ancient South Sea Islanders in tree trunk canoes. He measures his breath to save energy for the long trip ahead. Once in sync with the energy of the sea, he slips into a trance. His inner voice reminds him, *This is not a race.*

Ocean swells driven by a storm somewhere to the south increase in size and frequency. His creative mind senses an opportunity to turn the monotony of long distance flying into fun. Gliding low to the water, he rises to the summit of a swell then skims down the other side into the trough. The supply of swells is endless on the ribbed nature of the ocean. He quickly loves this new game and names it "swell surfing." It has some of the same movements as the porpoise and human surfers he has seen on Santa Rosa Island and the beaches north of Santa Barbara. But these are ocean swells and will never break. He makes a vow that when he reaches shore, he will ride real waves that break upon the beaches. In the meantime, he continues to practice and play.

By pulling his inside wing tight against his body, he is able to angle across the swell, getting him within inches of the water. Using his tail feathers like fins on a surfboard, he goes right or left, up or down. He concentrates on finding the right spot to take off, then calculates how to speed up and slow down utilizing different wing positions. His speed increases the closer he gets to the swell's inner energy. The key to success is starting out with a perfect glide. Swell after swell after swell, Kai surfs the open ocean.

"Someday..." he repeats to the world, "...I will surf real waves, at real beaches, where humans surf."

Thoughts of family temporarily interrupt his delightful play. Kai feels like a soldier going off to a foreign war. He remembers the good times of the past, looking forward to better times upon his return. But during this absence, Kai must keep alive images of his life on Anacapa and his love of those he leaves behind. Despite missing family and Feathertop, he must do what he has set out to do. He concentrates on pushing all thoughts of home out of his mind. Kai is on his way to find the Magical Mountain and must focus on this alone.

By midday, the golden pathway is eradicated by the sun sitting high overhead, and nature's colors are bleached due to the brightness of the sun. He keeps his head down, concentrating on the spectrum of vivid blues and greens beneath him. It is beautiful and hypnotic. Altering his course to the southeast, he flies parallel to the gun-metal blue mainland stretching out as far as he can see.

Kai crests the biggest swell yet, drops down tight, and cuts to the right. He picks up speed, his eye only inches from the swell wall. His breast feathers are ruffled from the breeze ricocheting off the water.

Suddenly, from out of the blue, a pointy black object pierces the wave and slices through the swell. It comes straight at him. He collides with a large fin and is knocked into the water. The fin instantly disappears like a periscope. Recovering, Kai scrambles back into the air, just as a huge black shadow rolls beneath him. It is a very large shark, propelling herself with a scythe-shaped fin moving back and forth with the grace of a hula dancer.

"Shark!" he shouts to no one, startled by the intensity of his own voice.

Kai watches as the monstrous fish thrashes in the water. Sharks do not like their space invaded, and this is exactly what Kai has done. Bending his wings, Kai rises straight up putting as much distance between him and the shark as possible. He looks down upon a big thresher shark, easily the length of two or three sea lions. Pelicans are taught to respect sharks. Savants, however, warn that sharks are not to be trusted. But like all of the Creator's critters, sharks have an important role in the sea. They act as equalizers. Sharks swam with dinosaurs millions of years ago, and little has changed. They cruise the oceans, simply searching for meals and mates. Two small remora fish ride the shark's gigantic back. Their job is to clean the shark as she swims. This relationship exemplifies the complexity of nature. One species becomes protected by and dependent upon another. Looking down at this scene, Kai feels a kindred spirit with the shark, despite an underlying fear. Ancient peoples worshipped and feared these behemoths, but today people kill sharks for fun, food, and supposed magical properties in their dried fins. Sharks are losing their battle with mankind and may someday disappear.

Kai's attention is diverted to a disturbance further west. He banks and flies quickly toward a chaotic group of gulls working the waters. Gulls annoy Kai because of their incessant bickering, but on the other hand, this behavior is a great indicator that food is nearby. Gulls are the ocean's dinner bell. They are not shy about announcing when fish are in the water, especially during a feeding frenzy. Hunger is gnawing at Kai, so he hurries to join them.

When he arrives, he sees a large school of anchovies spiraling clockwise beneath him. Watching as their bellies sparkle in the sunlight, he goes into a vertical stall, flips over, tucks his wings, and dives headfirst into a huge bullseye of tiny fish. Just before impact, he notices large bonito and barracuda feeding on the smaller fish. He reminds himself to stay close to the surface to avoid being attacked by one of these very aggressive fish. Eyes shut, he drives his bill into the water, opens his beak, and readies to gather a meal. Fish are flapping around him as his inner voice exclaims, *"Food, wonderful food. Life is good!"*

Abruptly, a powerful blow clobbers him on the left side of his head. It feels as though he has dived headfirst into a large rock. *But there are no boulders in the open ocean!* yells his inner voice just before he goes unconscious. Lying rag-dolled in the turbulent water, he is surrounded by a feeding frenzy, putting him at great risk. Regaining his senses slowly, he finds himself underwater and fearful of drowning.

Dread yells, "Find the surface. You are going to die!"

The sea, awash with fish, blood, and chaos, has become a potential tomb. Whether he drowns or is attacked by one of the larger fish, he is in extreme danger. It is then that he sees light penetrating from above.

Where there is light, there is air. Where there is air, there is a chance to fly away, his frightened thoughts tell him. Frantically, he kicks for the surface.

On Anacapa, Kai's distant mother shakes from a cold shot of adrenaline. She senses her wayward son is in trouble. It is a mother's sixth sense. Remembering her nightmare, she is concerned for her child's safety and offers a quick prayer to Sorté.

Kai sees the same thresher shark. She is using her tail like a giant whip, which allows her to immobilize the bigger fish and scoop them

up. Kai knows immediately, it must have been the shark's powerful tail that hit him. Like Kai, the shark also noticed the feeding frenzy and rushed over, where they arrived simultaneously. The thresher writhes about, chomping indiscriminately at floating and panicked fish. Large bonito are decapitated in seconds by her powerful jaws and razor-sharp teeth. Half-bodies float in the scarlet stew, as she kills and eats without restraint.

Danger surrounds the pelican. Stunned and scared, Kai makes for a quick retreat. Beneath him, the shark makes a sharp U-turn and charges a group of bonito. They race toward the surface with the shark in pursuit, putting Kai directly in the line of attack. Swirling her huge tail, she is traveling much faster than the pelican.

"I must get out of here!" Kai screams in concert with Dread. Once bursting through the surface, they both chant, "Fly! Fly! Fly!"

He runs across the water, pumping his wings with every bit of energy he can muster. Two terrified bonito blast out of the water, their eyes bulging with panic. Kai elevates and banks hard right, barely missing the bonito as they breach. The shark snaps her huge jaws around both fish, and, in a matter of seconds, they are gone. Kai is within a foot of the beast and looks directly into the monster's cold right eye. All he sees is thousands upon thousands of years of darkness. The shark falls back into the sea with a giant splash and disappears beneath the surface. The killing field quiets almost immediately except for the squawking of retreating gulls.

The muddy red water is disturbing to the naïve pelican, so he flies quickly. Looking over his shoulder, he sees a series of ocean swells cleansing the carnage and sweeping the ocean surface clean. Pumping hard, Kai distances himself from the slaughter and turns east toward the mainland and a large mountain with double peaks.

Maybe that is where I am heading, maybe that is the Magical Mountain. Keep flying!

Beneath him, he comes upon a number of boats travelling in a straight line. Fascinated by humans and their yachts, he drops down to observe. There is one luxurious boat, several older ones, and two smaller sailboats cruising the soft swells of the Pacific. Two of them are driven quietly by the wind, but the rest are being pushed along by loud black smoke. Regardless of the type of boat, the human occupants seem mellow and are enjoying the warm sun and rolling sea. As Kai passes, two children jump up and frantically wave at him. He dips his right wing in return.

He is now close enough to see the skyline. The brown line is gone, replaced by a purple-gray haze. Kai is convinced that this is more of man's floating trash. He increases the rhythm of his strokes, knowing he will soon arrive at his destination.

Back on Anacapa, his mother hugs little Rikki tightly. She yearns for Kai to be home.

SEVEN

I always pass on good advice. It is the only thing to do with it.
It is never of any use to oneself.

– Oscar Wilde

Kai is close enough to see the sweeping outline of the Endless City. It spreads beyond the coastal bluffs and long sandy beaches. There are checkered structures of varying sizes growing out of the ground, stretching north and south with great density. Kai's entire line of vision is dominated by man's metropolis. The scene is as daunting as it is impressive. Man's domain is far greater than Kai expected. He slows his stroke, so he can take in as much of it as possible.

A humming sound lies over the city like a wet blanket, blending diverse sounds into a consistent drone. As Kai closes in, he hears an intense racket bouncing across the water. It comes from a red, light-house-shaped buoy whose bell rings with each passing swell. This man-made contraption is strategically placed near the entrance to a very active harbor, funneling incoming boats into the long arms of two rock jetties.

Clang...Clang...Clang... announces the buoy to incoming vessels; not as a welcome, but rather a warning: "Danger is approaching...take heed!"

Other sounds distinguish themselves as part of the humdrum noise coming from mankind's lifestyle. It seems that everyone is in a hurry to get somewhere. The ocean is loaded with people and their boats. Further inland, a cacophony of sirens, automobile horns, and a chorus of sailboat riggings can be heard. For a bird accustomed to the silence and serenity of Anacapa, these sounds are harsh and grating, but Kai accepts them as his welcome to the mainland.

Kai breathes in large doses of oxygen to calm his nerves and notices a distinctive taste and odor in the air. His nostrils, throat, and lungs object to the abrasive chemical tang. He approaches the buoy, raises his head and wings, thus creating a stall. Hanging just above, he studies the rocking motion and makes a perfect soft landing on the top.

The pelican has landed! his inner voice bellows, coinciding with Kai's huge and prideful smile.

Gently swaying atop this perch, Kai studies the incredibly complex scene. It takes a few moments to comprehend. There, in front of him, is the Endless City in all its splendor. It is an elaborate assortment of man's accomplishments, machinery, and lifestyles. He is so confused by the sight that it makes him light-headed. He never realized how much activity mankind can pack into one locale at the same time. There are innumerable homes and tall buildings. There is very little greenery despite everything being made from earth and trees. The larger structures sit high in the air with bold letters spelling out their names. People and their devices are everywhere. Cars, bicycles, boats, and planes buzz about like bees working an active hive.

"This is perfect," he says, smiling with satisfaction. "I have finally reached my destination. My lifelong obsession of seeing the Endless City has come to pass." Closing his eyes, he takes time to relax and thank Sorté for a safe journey.

Suddenly, these pleasant thoughts are interrupted by a bellowing and angry voice coming from below.

"How stupid can you be?" someone shouts with hostility.

Looking down, he sees four sea lions lying on the base of the buoy. Their bodies are intertwined like seaweed after a squall. Two females lay still and a third is squirming and groaning in obvious pain. A very large bull yells at the young female to be quiet.

"It really hurts," the youngest cries out. "Can't you do something?"

Her left front fin is wedged beneath one of the metal flanges attached to the tower. She lets out a horrendous squeal as the other females bump her, attempting to get comfortable.

"Don't touch me again, you idiots," she screams at her companions. "You have no idea how much pain I'm in. Do not make matters worse," she begs.

"Pull hard and break it loose," the bull lion commands impatiently. "I do not have time for this nonsense. Either get it loose, or be quiet. I need my rest."

"It hurts really bad," the young sea lion pleads. "What am I supposed to do?"

"That is your problem, not mine. That is the price you pay for your stupidity," the bull replies, his voice dripping with condemnation. "It is time to take my nap. Leave me alone!"

"Please! Help me!" she says, her big brown eyes now full of tears. "You are our leader, and you must do something."

"You are not a child. It's not my responsibility to take care of you. Now be quiet, I want to sleep."

Watching the scene unfold from above, it is obvious to Kai that the stuck sea lion is scared and desperate for help. He feels sorry for her, knowing her pain is real. He cannot believe the others are refusing to help. The bull is definitely in charge. The other two females totally ignore the snared sea lion. Each time the dominating bull speaks, they exchange snickers and whispers full of unkind remarks about the younger sea lion.

If the bull is any indicator of what is going to happen, the trapped sea lion has no hope. The bull and his groupies are useless, Kai surmises. *I will help, because that is what pelicans do,* his inner voice reminds him.

Without hesitation and loud enough for all to hear, Kai leans over and states calmly, "First, you must push your flipper in to release the pressure, then lift and pull it out gently. Do not yank on it, or you'll injure it more."

All four heads jerk skyward, looking to identify the interloper.

"And what makes this any of your business?" asks the bull, feeling his position of authority has been challenged by some impertinent pelican.

"I'm making it my business," answers Kai from his roost. "I've been taught that if I can help another soul, then I must. It is the way of pelicans."

"Why should we care what a pelican thinks?" the bull snorts with laughter. The other two females mirror him with chuckles as the younger sea lion looks down at her injured fin. She ponders the pelican's advice.

"You need not care. However, good advice is good advice, no matter the source," says Kai wisely, not realizing that these are the words of his father. Unfortunately, the meaning is lost on these self-absorbed sea lions.

As the bull is readying a retort, the youngest sea lion lets out an exuberant, "Hooray, Hooray! I'm free. Free at last!"

Her joyful celebration can be heard over the clanging of the buoy. The other sea lions grumble loudly with disapproval.

"Thank you, thank you!" she shouts, a huge smile breaking out on her face. "You are one very smart pelican. I will never forget your kindness. I could have lost my fin, or even died, trapped here without food. Thank you," she says gratefully. "I don't recognize you. You're not from around here?" she inquires, stretching her sore fin.

"I have traveled from the north, all the way from Anacapa Island."

Total silence follows as the four sea lions stare in awe at Kai. These sea lions, who have never traveled more than several miles from their place of birth, have always thought Anacapa was a mythical place. They rationalize that this pelican must have magical powers, and that is why he was able to rescue the young sea lion.

The injured sea lion dives deep into the water, swims rapidly in circles testing her fin, then pops back up near the buoy.

"All is fine," she says, bobbing in the water. "Mr. Pelican, you came along just in the nick of time!"

"Please, my name is Kai."

The bull is very uncomfortable with all of this drivel. Here is a friendly and knowledgeable stranger making him look bad. The fact that he may come from a make-believe place does not matter. The bull's narrow line of thinking has been punctured, and he does not know how to respond. He looks at the other sea lions, failing to grasp what has just happened and then rolls over to take his nap.

"Is there anything I can do for you?" the young sea lion asks Kai.

"Yes, I have not eaten since yesterday and am very hungry. Plus, I have no place to stay. Can you recommend a good spot?"

The sea lion is quick to respond.

"You see that promontory?" she says, pointing with her injured fin. "That is Inspiration Point. It's a short flight to the south and is home to a small school of fish. It will be perfect for you. Do you like anchovies?"

"I love anchovies, thank you."

"Sleeping is a bit more challenging," she continues. "Bedding is on a first come, first served basis. There are lots of birds here, and all need a place to sleep. I recommend going inside the harbor, where it is protected. Go down between the two jetties, and it will open up into a large bay. Then, start looking," she suggests. "You'll find something."

"Thank you very much. Just one more thing, have any of you heard of the Magical Mountain?" he asks loud enough for all of them to hear.

No one acknowledges the question nor responds to it. The bull simply glares at Kai, obviously still unhappy with his intervention.

If they do not know that the Channel Islands are real, then they likely would not be familiar with the Magical Mountain, his inner voice rationalizes.

Bidding them goodbye, Kai drops from his perch, glides to Inspiration Point and dives into a school of anchovies. These fish, like the air, don't taste as good as at home. Each one is a bit sour and has a medicinal aftertaste.

"Beggars cannot be choosers," he concludes as he satisfies his hunger. After his meal, Kai is exhilarated. He is smack dab on the doorstep of mankind and declares to the Endless City, "This is exactly where I want to be. Here I come!"

Starting a slow-motion pump, he flies up the two jetties to the mouth of the harbor, winging his way deeper into man's domain.

"Let me find somewhere to sleep. I am exhausted. This day has been very exciting with the Endless City, swell-surfing, the shark, and the sea lions. I cannot wait to see what comes next."

EIGHT

*It is a curious situation that the sea, from which life first arose,
should now be threatened by the activities of one form of that life.*

*But the sea, though changed in a sinister way,
will continue to exist; the threat is rather to life itself.*

– Rachel Carson

The bay's calm inner waters are surrounded by a peninsula, sandstone bluffs, and several islands. There are thousands of boats, from luxury yachts to rowboats, moored or stored among a maze of docks, piers, and anchorages. Masses of homes and buildings smother nature's inherent beauty. An endless river of cars, buses, and bicycles shuttle people about. Even the largest of bird colonies cannot compare to this monstrous settlement. It is an outlandish world, even more intimidating than Kai imagined. His ever-active mind soaks up the sights and sounds like a sea sponge taking in salt water.

Originally created by the Mother of Nature, the bay has been transformed by man in order to maximize human benefits. Houses go on forever; some line up along the waterfront, while others cluster together like oysters in a bed. They are so close to each other that it is hard for him to determine when one home stops and another begins. This helps Kai understand why so many on Anacapa use the word "pandemonium" to describe the mainland.

*There are simply too many people...*he agrees.

As darkness crawls across the bay like an opportunistic fog, Kai's exhausted body screams for rest. Scanning the water below, all he sees are the artificial results of man's dominance over nature. From boats to docks to rooftops, it seems there are many places to settle in for the night. Everywhere, there are birds circling the bay and diving to claim spots.

"Hurry, Kai, they will all be gone soon," Dread warns.

So many different species of birds are competing for beds, they look like confetti sprinkling over the darkening harbor. At last, he spies an unoccupied mooring on the eastern edge of the bay. It is bigger than most, as it serves to anchor a large wooden sailboat. The vessel is already occupied by a number of brown pelicans. This will surely provide a comfy home for the evening. Kai is excited to make some new pelican friends.

Dropping down, he hovers above the round object. Knowing it will be unstable, Kai uses the patience he learned practicing for speed diving. He lowers himself cautiously. The second his feet touch the cold metal ball, his butt goes one way and his head the other. He over-corrects and topples into the water. After three attempts, he finally settles gently upon the curved back of the slick ball. Looking like a bad dancer, he executes a series of awkward adjustments, resulting in a rocking-chair-rhythm. Finally, a bit embarrassed, he gets all his parts in the right place and sits peacefully upon the sphere. The soft roll of the water, the bounce of the ball and the hum of background noise are like a cradlesong for his tired mind.

It is here I will spend the night, his inner voice celebrates. *Sleep is going to be extra special on this first night in the Endless City.*

Looking up at the old wooden boat, he sees its name, *Golden Opportunity.*

How symbolic for the beginning of my adventure, he thinks. *This is indeed my golden opportunity.*

The elderly ketch is a proud boat from a past era when life was simpler. The *Golden Opportunity* is made entirely out of wood and shows signs of neglect. She has chipped paint, some rusted metal, and strands of long, green algae clinging to her hull. Dressed in a torn and ragged canvas cover, her teak decks are bleached and parched by the sun. There is bird excrement forming a patchwork glue over the deck's surface.

"Hello friends!" Kai calls out, introducing himself to the nearby pelicans. All but one are sitting midships and are involved in a heated discussion. Kai cannot make out the words, but for whatever reason, they are very emotional. Too engrossed in their argument to acknowledge him, Kai feels ignored and hurt by this snub. These are fellow pelicans and should help one of their own. He looks down at his distorted reflection in the water, seeing a stranger in a strange land. He looks to the one lone pelican close by. This bird appears older than the others and lies quietly near the stern of the boat. His head rests on an orange life preserver, his wings and body spread out between the boat's rear hatch and the wheel. It appears he may be sleeping.

Kai calls out again, "Hello."

The old bird lifts his head slowly and focuses his eyes. Looking for the source, he calls out into the dusk, "Hello, is someone there?"

"Yes!" Kai answers excitedly. "I am over here on the mooring."

The older pelican turns and looks right at Kai, who is waving his wings to get his attention.

"My name is Kai," he says as he tries to stand up, his feet desperately searching for the proper balance point. The old pelican still does not respond, indicating he may be hard of hearing. "I have flown a long way," Kai continues, "all the way from the Channel Islands. An island called Anacapa. Have you heard of it?"

Still no response. Worried that the old bird is deaf and maybe blind, Kai hollers, "Can I stay here tonight? I need a place to sleep!"

The old grey bird cocks his head and looks directly at Kai. He stares into his eyes in silence. Outlined against the darkening sky, the old pelican is surrounded by newly-lit twinkling lights, reminding Kai of the ancestral spirits in the legend of Sorté. But this is part of a ritual mankind goes through each night. Humans, for reasons unknown, display millions of lights to illuminate their nighttime world instead of enjoying the dark veil of a star-studded sky.

Finally, the old bird speaks.

"I take it you are not from around here," he says slowly in a raspy voice. Each word is pronounced as if he thinks of it as he speaks. "You seem unfamiliar with the ways of the city." His gravelly tone is soothing to Kai, for this is the first pelican he has spoken to since he left home.

"Yes sir, I am from the north," Kai answers politely. "Please help me understand the ways of the Endless City. I have never been here. I do not want to miss out on anything."

"Son, there are many birds and people here." Kai feels the warmth of the word "son." He misses his father, despite his recent condemnation. "You must learn to adapt to the ways of the city, or you will find yourself in deep trouble," the old bird says seriously, his face worn and tired, his eyes sad and clouded with cataracts.

"We do not have caves or precipices like you are used to. That is because mankind has built homes where our ancestors used to live. Humans like being near the ocean and do not care that we were here first. In fact, many people seem bothered by our presence." The old bird's energy is picking up as he shifts from side to side as if riding the swells of an active sea.

"If we get too friendly, humans try to scare us away with fences, sharp projectiles, aggressive dogs, or plastic owls. It is amazing how stupid humans think we are. Take plastic owls, for example. There have been no owls in this bay for generations. Mankind drove them out with all their buildings." There is an underlying anger growing in his voice. "We are not afraid of plastic owls. We know they are not real. They never make a sound or move. They cannot hurt us. So, we avoid houses with plastic owls, not because we are scared, but because these homes are owned by people unfriendly to nature. They hold a disregard for animals and birds, and might as well hang a giant sign that reads, *NATURE NOT WELCOME. WE HATE BIRDS*. This is not a way to make friends, now is it?"

Kai cannot understand why there are no owls. Owls are important in the north because they are the guardians of the night and are known for their wisdom. Nighttime would not be the same without their restful calls. He starts to ask the old pelican this question, but the continuous monologue doesn't stop. He reminds Kai of some of the older birds back home.

"The caves that are left are unsafe and smell like urine and stale beer."

Kai does not understand the reference to urine or stale beer but assumes it is unpleasant. Just yards away, two more pelicans secure buoys for the night.

"Over the past five generations, we have learned to adapt in order to live with our human neighbors. First, our numbers were depleted by DDT. Today, we have new threats as DDT has been replaced by other pesticides designed to kill weeds and insects. In addition, there's West Nile Virus, Newcastle Disease, COVID-19, and whatever unknown viruses may show up as the balance of nature is disrupted. Humans continue to dump their toxic waste into our waters that eventually reach the sea, where these poisons get into our food and water. This is the result of humans yearning to be healthy, happy, and live forever. But what about the rest of us?

"Because of this, it is impossible for the natural world to live in harmony with people. We, like a wartime enemy without reinforcements, are at their mercy. A vast majority of humans remain unaware of our plight and see us only as pests or cute ocean birds."

The old bird drops his head and mumbles a silent prayer for all the pelican fledglings lost to poisons over the many decades. Millions of fledglings have been stripped of a future on Earth. Kai acknowledges by joining in a moment of silence, as if in communion with the elder pelican.

This conversation sounds similar to those Kai had with his father, his Auntie Aphrodite, and the savants. He is now hearing it repeated, almost word for word, from a mainland bird. For the young traveler, these words take on a whole new importance.

"Urban birds have lost their freedom," the pelican continues. "We must be careful, or we will go the way of the dodo, the passenger pigeon, and the great auk...extraordinary birds of previous eras. Do you know what happened to them?" he probes.

"No sir, I do not," Kai answers respectfully.

"The dodos were killed off in sixty years, and the passenger pigeons went from over five million to zero because they were cheap food for the humans. The great auk has a similar story. Man's cruelty knows no end."

The old bird raises his wings as if he is addressing a large crowd.

"Gone...no más...disappeared FOREVER!" He looks to his audience of one and repeats, "Gone, as in extinct, and never to return. These birds were not able to adapt, so they are no longer on the planet. Man shot them, ate them, or dressed in their feathers."

Kai raises his wing to catch the old bird's attention.

"Why didn't the birds leave? Why did they let this happen to them?"

The old pelican ignores him, because he knows that animals and birds cannot control man's cruelty alone. They need help from the Mother of Nature to curtail man's aggression. But even with disasters and pestilence, man always crawls back. Humans believe that the Earth is theirs to dominate. The old bird gets lost in his own thoughts and rambles on like he is speaking to an audience big enough to fill a stadium. His rantings are quickly turning to rage. Kai tries, but cannot stop him.

"This will be the fate of all the pelicans, if we are not careful. Pelicans are in jeopardy, despite our strength and wisdom. Pelicans are sensitive and caring, but this will not protect them. Fortunately, we are not sought for our feathers or our meat. But we are still at great risk. We, too, could become extinct in the blink of an eye, so we must stay strong! As a pelican, you must use your brain carefully. Live with caution, trust only those who are trustworthy. Be skeptical of anything that does not seem right, or you, too, will pay the ultimate consequence."

"Are you a teacher?" Kai asks.

"Oh no," the old bird laughs. "We have not had teachers for many generations. Daily life is our school. Mainland pelicans live one day at a time, futilely trying to keep up with the rapid changes inflicted upon us by mankind."

This resonates with Kai. Daily life is his school, too. He sees himself as a student of the world, and that is exactly what brought him to the Endless City and this mooring in the middle of mankind's chaos.

The bay acts as a perfect canvas. The multitude of surrounding lights are reflected in its calm waters. Thousands upon thousands of lights dance and shake hypnotically upon the surface of the bay. It is as if humans create a land of enchantment in this once all-natural environment. They have replaced the celestial sky with abstract lighting, mirrored in velvet black waters.

It is bewitching, Kai thinks. *If humans create such magic here in the city,* he rationalizes, *and nature is greater than man, then why can't there be a Magical Mountain? Maybe, just maybe, humans and nature live in harmony at the great mountain.* His mind is full of visions of this powerful place. It only seems logical that nature and mankind could combine forces to work as one.

Without any warning, Kai is slammed out of his thoughts by a hard body blow to his backside. He is thrown into the water and skids across the surface on his behind. The impact is so strong, it knocks the air from his lungs and sends a blast of pain shooting up his spine. Time freezes as he lay face down in the water. Slowly regaining his senses, he flips over and gasps for oxygen.

"What was that—another shark?" Dread hollers.

As Kai turns, a sense of danger and foreboding falls over him. The old pelican is still rambling on, as if nothing happened. But anger quickly bubbles up inside Kai when he focuses on the culprit responsible for the hit. Bouncing on the buoy, like a kid on a trampoline, is another brown pelican. He is about Kai's age, and because of his familiarity with the buoy, he moves on it like a gymnast. Maintaining balance easily, he leaps up and down with his wings lifted on the exact spot that Kai had chosen to spend the night. This brash youngster taunts Kai with a challenging glare.

"What the...!" Kai screams at the bouncing newcomer who has colorings of a teenager with a slicked-back crest and starched facial feathers. The other pelican does not answer and stares at

Kai with the arrogance of a prizefighter declared the winner of a long bout.

"Hey dude," the pelican finally answers, "what are you doing on MY can?"

A drenched Kai tries to speak but gets interrupted, making him think that mainland pelicans don't know when to stop talking.

"You have no right to be here, this is my spot and ONLY mine. Each buoy is designated to one pelican, and this one is MINE. This mooring goes back five generations in my family, and I am the sixth," he says, his eyes clouded with self-importance. "It has been ours since it was first placed here. No stupid tourist is going to come along and sleep here on my watch. Does this look like a hotel to you?"

There is that word again.

"Stupid!" Kai's anger is almost to the boiling point. His first re-action is to fight back. His inner voice is yelling, *Pound the punk!* He has never felt such rage or seen any pelican behave in such a selfish and rude manner. Not knowing anything about a hotel, he digs deep to calm himself down and avoid an altercation with this rude bird. In an attempt to diffuse the situation, Kai swallows these strong feelings, takes a deep breath and says, "I am sorry you are upset. I was unaware this mooring was taken. All you had to do was explain it to me and ask me to move. Your actions are out of line. We don't need all this hostility."

The pelican continues flapping his wings and bouncing on the ball.

"Why should I do that? You are where you are not supposed to be. I told you my way. This is how big city birds settle things in the harbor. You need to know what the rules are. If you break a rule, you have to pay!"

"I am not afraid of you," responds Kai, his face contorted, readying for battle.

They stare and size each other up for what seems like an eternity.

"Maybe you could suggest somewhere I might sleep. I have traveled a long way and am very tired. I do not want to fight."

In a voice louder than a walrus wail, the bratty bird answers, "What do you think this is, 'The Marriot of Moorings'? Do I look like a travel agent? Have you ever heard the old saying, 'No Vacancy'? It is not my responsibility to find you a place. Go find your own."

This sounds like a bunch of gibberish to Kai. Marriot of Moorings, travel agents, and vacancy mean absolutely nothing to him. But the young bird's tone of voice is only making Kai madder.

"Go home, if you want a bed to sleep in. Maybe your mommy can tuck you in," the imp says, his words dripping in sarcasm.

Just as Kai is ready to jump into a fight, the older pelican interrupts, "Kai, you must learn to be selfish. Then, and only then, can you be useful to your clan and live a long and prosperous life among humans. Go find another place to sleep. Fighting with this one is not necessary," he adds, nodding his head in the direction of the bully. "There are plenty more places to go."

This advice does not help Kai deal with the annoying bird. The old bird is saying the exact opposite of what is taught back home. The well-being of the family, the clan, and the colony are of vital importance and come first on Anacapa. These mainlanders seem to place themselves above all else, thinking their opinions are more valuable. This is Kai's first lesson about the Endless City, and it comes hard. It contradicts what is believed back home. Because he is so tired and without a bed, he realizes that changing the situation is hopeless. He turns his back to both pelicans.

The older bird is still rambling on about the future.

"One day there will only be sharks left in the seas. All other sea creatures will be gone due to man's influences..."

The youngster continues to bounce and makes an in-your-face gesture at Kai, showing there is neither compromise nor civility in this neighborhood. Kai looks over his shoulder at his two urban cousins with a mixture of disappointment and compassion. He realizes that neither of these fellows can be trusted, and this is painful to the naïve bird. These two will never know the rewards of living in a tightly knit community or having a loving family.

Is this the result of what humans have done to them? his inner voice asks. *Or, are these birds simply born different than the pelicans back at home?*

Kai runs across the water stroking his wings, rises, and flies away into the night sky. He feels a roughness to this new world that sits like a bone lodged in his throat.

In a short while, Kai locates a private dock not far from the *Golden Opportunity.* It is empty except for a small fiberglass sabot sitting upside down and two large boats side tied to the dock. It is quite a distance from the nearest house, giving it a feeling of seclusion. Landing with ease, he settles down between the skiff and a plank walkway leading to a sidewalk. Comforted by the fact that he is virtually out of sight, Kai places his head on his back, and within minutes, he is experiencing a deep and much-needed sleep.

NINE

The harder the conflict...the more glorious the triumph.

– Thomas Paine

At dawn, Kai awakens from distant dreams soon forgotten. The hum of car engines and an early morning fishing boat grinding its way out of the harbor are the first sounds he hears. A screech of tires and the howl of a distant siren breaks through the calm. The first of many large jet planes powers overhead, leaving a trail of noise and black dust in its wake. Somewhere in the semi-darkness, a loud exchange between two sea lions breaks out.

Hopping atop the dingy, Kai rubs his eyes and stretches. Within seconds, he hears yet another unfamiliar sound. This one alerts him to a possible new danger. The noise sends Kai an odd, yet frightening feeling that he is being watched. He quickly exercises his wings, readying for a quick getaway, as the racket grows more intense. The commotion is emanating from a blue and white house standing at the head of the dock. It is an annoying combination of yaps, howls, and growls, coming from a narrow side yard enclosed by a three foot picket fence. Behind the fence is a large, white dog with randomly spaced black spots. The animal gyrates, acting extremely agitated. With only a measly fence holding him back, the canine searches for an escape. He must deal with the trespasser on his family's dock. That trespasser is Kai.

The Dalmatian is frantic, jumping up and down, with eyes locked on Kai. Kai returns the stare, displaying neither fear nor intimidation. He is confident that with the fence and the considerable distance separating the two, he need not worry. But these are the exact factors that increase the dog's determination. He wants this bird gone, or dead. Willing his strength into a huge leap, the Dalmatian clears the fence and runs toward the dock. He is consumed by centuries of bird-dogging instincts and locks onto his target. Racing full tilt across the sidewalk, he skids left onto the dock. Kai feels the compressions of the dog's footfalls as he gallops down the planked structure, sounding like castanets as his claws hit the wooden runway. Kai has never encountered such hysteria in any animal.

Due to the dog's speed and agility, Kai is now vulnerable. He jumps off the dingy, desperately flapping his wings as he runs across the dock. The dog is coming like a bat out of hell and is now only several bounds away. Due to his stiffness and exhaustion from yesterday's long flight, Kai struggles to coordinate his big feet and wings. He is not sure he will escape this barking banshee.

Meanwhile, the dog thankfully makes a misstep on the dew-covered ramp and rolls head over teakettle, barking and growling the entire time. His spots spin like lottery balls as he slams hard onto the float. Only three body lengths from Kai, he flips back on all fours and leaps in mid-air. He exposes bare teeth and lets out a menacing growl, announcing to the world that he wants to tear this bird apart, one feather at a time.

Stroking harder, Kai runs, wanting nothing more than to lift vertically like a hummingbird.

"Pump, pump, pump," he yells to himself as he hears the snarling and snapping dog close behind. Without looking back, Kai gains air, leaving the dock just as the dog desperately lunges for his torso. He hears the dog's jaws slam shut with the sound of a bear trap. Three of Kai's tail feathers protrude from his lips.

"Feathers! Nothing else!" the dog howls in disappointment. He watches as the pelican drops off the dock like an airplane from an aircraft carrier. Kai flies quickly to the sanctuary of the bay.

"I am alive! I am safe!" he celebrates.

On the edge of the dock, the dog barks incessantly. He coughs out one of the feathers, jumps and runs in tight circles out of pure frustration at his missed opportunity. His obnoxious voice bounces across the glassy water reaching the entire harbor.

Here I am, the best diving pelican on the coast, and some stupid dog almost takes me down, Kai thinks. The old pelican last night said, *"Think of yourself first,"* causing new emotions to rise in the young bird.

"Yes, yes, I must think of myself," he declares defiantly, looking over his shoulder at the crazed canine.

Seeing his feathers floating in the stagnant air makes him snap as his anger grows exponentially. He is now on the verge of rage. His tail feathers are extremely important to his flying and diving. In a single day, he has experienced a bratty pelican, ill-mannered sea lions, and now this incomprehensibly rude dog.

"All I wanted was a simple night's sleep and to be left alone. I am not going to let him off that easy. He will pay for this brazen and un-provoked attack," Kai declares defiantly, feeling a totally new emo-tion—revenge! He banks hard left, pumps his wings, and heads straight back toward the dock. His eyes have turned cold black, like the shark's.

"Let the battle begin!"

Putting the dog in *his* crosshairs, Kai attacks. Astounded by this reversal of roles, the Dalmatian becomes even more crazed. His inner wolf has been aroused. He shrieks and howls in decibels twice as loud as before. People are drawn from their houses, adding to the confusion.

The dog's pajama-clad owner exits his house, hollering fruitless commands as he runs down the dock to control his delinquent ped-igreed pet. Kai closes in, his gaze transfixed on the agitated animal. His mind is clear and focused. Kai's face shows the intensity of his record-breaking dive. He is fearless. He is in charge.

The dog gets confused. Hearing his owner, now only a short dis-tance away, the dog stares at the pelican closing in on him. Spinning like a whirling dervish, the dog ignores his owner's commands. He must take care of this insubordinate bird first, and then he will deal with his owner. But in these last seconds, it comes clear that all three—bird, dog and owner—will arrive at the edge of the dock at the same time. With Kai a short distance away, the dog crouches, growls, bares his teeth, and readies to pounce.

"The time has come!" Kai hollers. "Sweet revenge!"

Kai suddenly throws his wings forward and breaks into a stall. He hangs still in the morning air for a fraction of a second, his wings spread wide in a cruciform. The Dalmatian, surprised and angered by the aggressiveness of this strange bird, is like an excited child going after a piñata. He leaps.

"It is time for victory," declares the canine.

Simultaneously, Kai pumps his strong wings twice and goes vertical while at the same time the dog's owner trips on a dock line and flies through the air. The human lets out a loud groan as he lands hard on the dock and hits a metal cleat. As the dog soars over the water, he realizes his predicament. Kai, staring into the spotted animal's eyes, burns a message deep into his canine psyche: "Dogs cannot fly! Dogs cannot fly!" The dog panics, and with an exploding splash, is submersed in the brisk water. Kai breaks into hysterical laughter. Submerged in the cold water, the canine pokes his head up and sees the pelican laughing and treading air. Worse yet, he hears the cruel expletives of his prostrate owner.

The Dalmatian paddles himself to the beach, walks ashore, and shakes water loose from his coat. This once furious killer has been transformed into a hapless buffoon. This is not a pleasant outcome for the proud carriage dog whose ancestors accompanied ancient kings of Europe and hardy firefighters. He will have to live with the knowledge that he was publicly humiliated by a bird in front of everyone, including his girlfriend, a cute black poodle who lives next door.

The pelican floats calmly in the air and watches as the embarrassed animal is dragged back to his house by his limping owner, berating the dog for his stupidity. This further bruises the Dalmatian's already damaged ego.

Satisfied with a job well done, Kai releases out of his stall, turns west, and pumps his wings. Having overcome yet another challenge, the proud adolescent is off to explore more of the Endless City. The second day of his adventure has officially begun.

TEN

Ua Mau ke Ea o ka ʻĀina i ka Pono
(The life of the land is perpetuated in righteousness)

– Hawaiian saying and Hawaiʻi state motto

A lazy marine layer hangs over the harbor like wet cotton. It quickly becomes evident that humans get an early start. People and vehicles scurry about everywhere. Kai will soon learn that this early morning hustle is but a mere teardrop in a waterfall when compared to the midday and evening activities. When humans are fully engaged, the Endless City backs up like an overused sink. The flurry of human activity is exhilarating to this Anacapa tourist who is used to quiet and serenity. He executes a series of barrel rolls in celebration of his first full day on the mainland.

Flying east to west, he follows a long and densely populated peninsula rimmed with expansive beaches. Early beachgoers are out surfing, running, or walking. Spanning the entire length of the beachfront are houses and businesses, positioned side by side like neatly stacked shoe boxes. The only break in the conforming line of structures is a beachfront schoolyard. Its playground is teeming with children running and playing on the sand. This reminds Kai of his oceanfront school on Anacapa and brings forth the image of Feathertop's charming smile. For a moment, his heart aches just a little.

This nostalgic feeling is interrupted by gleeful sounds emanating from the schoolyard. It is the infectious laughter of happy kids. Their raucous shouting brings a smile to the pelican's face. Wanting to share in their joy, he swoops down to see what they are doing. Gliding mere feet above the brightly dressed students, he watches them frolic. Because he is still a child at heart, Kai can easily relate to their playfulness.

The young are much more carefree than the old, he ponders. *Even here, the youngsters display spontaneity that will most likely fade with age. Why is it that getting old means that opinions and habits become more entrenched? Oldsters, like yesterday's pelican, become set in their ways while children are open and receptive.*

Kai observes the children playing four square, tag-you're-it, and climbing monkey bars. Wanting to join in the fun, he creates another new game. After rising high in the air, he reverses direction and dives rapidly. Paralleling the blacktop just above their heads, he makes a high-pitched whistle, copycatting the eagles of Anacapa. Few kids notice at first, but as he repeats it, more huddle together to watch him. They shout encouragement, waving and screaming, "Pelly, Pelly," each time he dives. The dive-bombing bird plays to the loud cheers and screeches of admiring school children.

Suddenly, their exuberance is halted by an abrasive electronic buzzer. Immediately, these once carefree kids become subdued. Like herded cattle, they move toward the buildings, ending their real-life experiences until school is out.

Kai banks north, flying low and close to the breaking waves. He feels his relationship with the ocean growing with each new wave. Born far out to sea and traveling long distances, one by one, the swells transform into a wall of water and disappear upon the sand. The energy they carried for thousands of miles is gone in seconds.

"If I am to learn how to surf, I must start right now," he tells himself. "These waves are not that big, about the size of a tule bush back home. They are perfect. Each wave will be my teacher."

Kai quickly learns that to be a successful beach surfer, he must have a really tight glide allowing him to stay ahead of the curling tube. Moving closer and closer, he utilizes the small updraft on the face of each wave. After a couple of errors and near wipeouts, he tells himself, "The most important factor is when and where to take off. Right place—right time."

He quickly discovers that every wave is different, and a surfer must approach each one individually. As he hugs the wave's face, he moves nearer to the inner energy of the ocean. By listening to the snap of the wave's lip, he can calculate the level of energy it holds.

Offshore, a train of pelicans glides up the coast, reminding him of his family and Anacapa. Yesterday's bratty pelican is flying near the end of the formation, indicating a lack of importance within the clan. The bird looks childish next to the older birds in front of him. Kai offers up a loud and enthusiastic, "Hello," which is ignored by every pelican in the train.

He comes to an old wooden pier located at a large bend in the beach. The pier's boardwalk extends into the Pacific and is crowded with people walking and fishing. Waves are breaking on both sides of the pier, attracting a bunch of black-suited surfers. Kai flies in circles, searching for a good spot to observe these seal-like humans on surfboards. He lands just outside the impact zone to watch them scurry about, scouting for waves. On the horizon, humps of water alert them to incoming sets. Once the waves hit shallow water, they show themselves. Like mosquitoes on a pond, surfers scatter about to get to the right place at the right time. Kai notices that there are both female and male surfers and surfboards vary in length. The riders appear to be all different sizes and ages.

It is easy for Kai to distinguish the experienced surfers from the inexperienced ones. The best surfers catch the most waves, go faster, and stay on their boards longer. Some make sweeping turns and fly into the air at the end of a wave. Each participant tries to show off his or her level of skill and courage on each wave. In contrast, the poorer surfers are barely able to paddle. Lack of balance makes them flounder easily. They look like someone riding a bucking bronco for the first time. Their rides oftentimes end in a disaster. All in all, everyone seems to be having fun.

Kai flies low among the surfers, attempting to create a bond. After two hours, he becomes part of the pack and has developed his own style of riding waves. Eventually, he tires and realizes how hungry he is, having not eaten since yesterday.

"*Stop playing around; it is time for breakfast,*" he scolds himself, sounding remarkably like his father.

Rising out of the surf, he joins a group of gulls working the water offshore. With thoughts of the thresher shark still fresh, he dives carefully into the water. He sucks up a large gulp of water containing two fresh anchovies. Excited, he eats fish until he is satisfied. Flying ashore to digest and primp, he passes a couple of his surfing buddies. Dipping his right wing twice, the astonished surfers smile and flash him a two-fingered shaka in return.

Eventually settling on a seawall separating the sand from a blacktop parking lot full of cars, he lets out a huge sigh and enjoys a moment of reflection. His journey to the mainland is all good so far, and being a bit vain, he grooms himself for the first time since leaving Anacapa. He is starting to relax.

In front of him, a large semi-circle of birds suddenly breaks into a noisy commotion. On his left, a human father and his young son throw food at the birds. The birds jump about, yelling in loud boisterous squawks, as some square off against each other competing for the human food. The humans find this highly entertaining.

Kai has never seen this kind of fighting from such a diverse group of birds. There are a dozen gulls and an equal number of pigeons all squabbling for the leftovers. As the humans grow bored, they throw their remaining food, causing the skirmish to escalate into chaos. Birds challenge one another for a discarded bag of chips, donut parts, and skinny potatoes. They attack and retreat, trying to gain the advantage. Once the food is gone, an empty bag gets pushed by the wind to the parking lot, where it stacks up with other trash.

Another adult human with a small child approaches the wall. The little girl is fascinated by Kai. Her father grabs her arm and tells her to throw bits of food. This reignites the fracas and immediately sends the flock back into a frenzy. The little girl laughs hysterically.

Most notable among the birds is a large male California gull. He stands defiantly in the middle of the battlefield and takes whatever he wants. Kai is impressed by his size, aggressiveness, and his clever strategies. He is larger than the other gulls, has distinctive gray markings on his head, and a bright yellow beak that is accentuated by a spider-shaped black spot. He is as handsome as he is scary and uses his wings to keep balance because he only has one leg. His screeches are the loudest and most threatening of the group.

Intimidated by the one-legged gull, others challenge him from a safe distance and retreat when he charges. The smaller birds use diversion as a strategy to outwit the big gull. One pigeon flies above his head, getting his attention, while a second then sneaks behind and steals food. This bait and switch technique has taken months to perfect. Even a number of sparrows compete with the bigger birds by using decoys.

The one-legged gull screams, "I am Colossus, and I will not let you have MY food. Do not eat any of it, or I will make you pay!" He then charges several pigeons, who hurriedly scatter in different directions.

Colossus stands his ground and suddenly bolts forward as a smaller Bonaparte's gull tries to sneak up on him. While he chases the gull, two cagey pigeons use the Bonaparte's gull as a distraction, grab a bit of food, and scamper off half flying, half running. Colossus whips around and chases them in anger. The entire scene is bedlam, and the noise is frenzied. Humans laugh and continue to throw food, having created a form of live entertainment by watching the birds battle.

There do not seem to be any rules. Fascinated by the orchestrated moves of the various combatants, Kai realizes that this is a common occurrence. When humans stop throwing food, the fights end as quickly as they began. The birds settle down to await their next opportunity. Over the course of the day, this happens over and over again. One hundred yards to the south, another small child starts throwing parts of her donut. Every opportunistic bird near the beach races toward them. Tired from the fray and satisfied with his take, Colossus hops to the seawall, landing only a few feet from where Kai is resting.

"You are quite the fighter," Kai says, hoping to open a dialogue. "Congratulations! You got so many of the scraps. Very impressive."

Colossus cocks his head side to side, examining this inquisitive pelican.

"What the heck is a pelican doing on the sea wall?" he inquires in a derisive tone. "Pelicans are supposed to stay down on the beach near the fishermen or at the water's edge. Why are you here?"

"I have traveled very far and am preening myself. I noticed that your food games are rowdy and fun to watch when you play with the others."

"Play?" the gull scoffs. "This is not play. This is strictly business! This is bird versus bird. There is no love lost in these circles. It is survival of the fittest. Every bird for himself is the credo we live by." As the gull turns to look at Kai, the sun accentuates his spider spot.

"Where are you from? It is obvious you are not from around here," Colossus states with authority.

"The Channel Islands," the pelican answers obediently. "Anacapa."

"Well, I don't know about life out in the channel, but in the city, you must work for every morsel of food you get. It is a matter of life and death. There are too many birds and not enough fish. Humans are very wasteful, so many of us fight for their edible trash. People rarely eat everything, so there are always leftovers. Then we get our shot at it. Potatoes, donuts, bread, meats, nuts, and just about anything else they eat. That is what is happening down there right now," Colossus says pointing to the squawking birds two blocks south.

"I am Colossus," he continues proudly puffing out his breast feathers.

"I am a scavenger and a very good one! Survival is simply a function of supply and demand. If there is too much people-food, then their leftovers end up on the beach, in the streets, or in trashcans. I have become adept at dumpster diving, or as you just saw, trash talking and beach fighting. My favorite food is the donut. Donuts are soft, sweet, and filling. Humans eat them in the morning and throw leftovers to us. Most of them come from that little shop by the pier," he points to a sign that reads *Seaside Donuts*.

"We have learned to eat like humans and by midday the menu changes," Colossus says bouncing on his one leg, eyes intense and intimidating. "Later in the day, humans eat more potatoes and sandwiches. Lunch comes from over there," indicating *Da Kine Burger* and *Oceanfront Deli*.

"Human food gives me sustenance, as you can see by my robust belly. I never go hungry. There is plenty to go around. But I must fight those crafty pigeons. They rush in and eat as fast as possible. They are sneaky little hustlers and often work in pairs, one to distract and one to steal. I use my size and voice to scare them. It gets very nasty," he declares with pride.

"Then there are other gulls," Colossus continues with contempt in his voice. "They will try to force me out of the circle and chase me away. That is when sparks really fly. I have worked all my life to perfect my skills and persona. My reputation is that of a bad-ass. I never lose a fight."

"Now, what about you?" the gull asks. "What brings an ocean bird to the shores of the Endless City?"

"I came to explore and learn about humans. I want to experience great adventures that will make my life more interesting. Plus, I am looking for the Magical Mountain," Kai adds, hoping for a reaction from the gull.

"I don't know what will make your life more interesting in this mad house," the seagull exclaims. "We are overpopulated, we have dirty air and spoiled water, and most of the inhabitants have unpleasant attitudes. Is this the 'interesting' part of life that you are seeking?"

The pelican ponders this for a second.

"I have noticed that most of those I've met are not very friendly and some are downright rude. The interrelationship between humans and other species is startling. On Anacapa, there are so few humans that everything is in a state of natural balance. Life barely presents a challenge. Days come and days go with very little excitement. It is all preordained by the Mother of Nature and her natural ecosystems. Kind of humdrum, really. I have not found that kind of balance here."

"Boy, you are one naïve bird!" the gull interjects with a caustic laugh. "It is not that all is well in the world of mankind or nature. It is simply what you are used to. Everything that looks natural here is out of control. There are constant challenges, nothing stays the same and we live one day at a time. Nature is in danger and food chains are broken and disappearing. Species are vanishing rapidly, so they are forced to become scavengers and share the human lifestyle. When donuts replace fish for nourishment, something is definitely out of kilter. But there is always excitement and high-energy." The gull's eyes sparkle as he talks, but his tone is matter of fact.

"If species do not adapt to humans, they disappear. Look at the grizzly bear. These powerful and beautiful bears used to live in all the surrounding mountains. They have been extinct for generations due to man's cruelty. Ironically, it is the grizzly bear that is on the California state flag. It is as if the humans are celebrating their victory over the grizzly. This is a warning to the rest of nature that extinction can happen to any one of us.

"After eons of time, some species of whales, salmon, otters, and insects have disappeared from our coast. Abalone, marlin, sharks, and lobster are losing their battles for survival. Look at your own brown pelicans and the DDT madness. You, my friend, are lucky to be alive. And your city cousins are still dying of poisons. Today, pelicans are dying of viruses and man's cruelty. A pelican friend of mine was captured and had his beak cut off. Can you imagine that? We are at the mercy of mankind." The gull's voice rises like steam from a kettle, as his internalized rage begins to boil over.

"Look at my leg!" he yells. "Gone! Gone because of some inconsiderate human. Now, you listen to me, Mr. Channel Islands, I want adventure, too. But look at what happens in this world when man takes charge." He looks down at his missing leg while hopping to get in position directly in front of Kai. His eyes are on fire.

"I was once young, like you. I loved to fish, like you. I fished every day, and I was very good. I never went a day without a full belly. This was long before fish contained excrement, drugs, and chemicals. Now those once yummy anchovies taste like a combination of cardboard and aluminum."

Kai is unfamiliar with cardboard and aluminum, but having tasted the local anchovies, he is sure that it cannot be good.

"I was once a proud fisherman. I worked the pier, fishing boats, bait balls, and fishing barges. I fished the area with great success. I was well known and respected and at the top of my game. In those days, there were plenty of fish to go around. So, we all existed together. It was very nice.

"One day, I noticed a bait ball just off the end of the pier. There were sparkles everywhere, indicating lots of fish close to the surface. I thought it was going to be a cinch. Because I was young, I wanted to show off for the people on the pier. Circling above, I made warrior-like sounds, hoping that I would be noticed. Then I dove from a greater than normal height right into the center of the sparkling fish." Colossus gets more and more agitated as he talks.

"How was I supposed to know that some fish on the surface were chum thrown out by fishermen on the pier? Among these were anchovies loaded on fishhooks. Just before I hit the water, my right wing bumped an invisible fishing line connected to a fisherman's pole.

"The fisherman, feeling the movement, thought he had a strike and yanked hard on the pole. His action sent hook, line and sinker ricocheting across the water. The whole mess swept around my leg with the hook embedding just below my tibia. There I was, hooked, wrapped in fishing line and burdened down by weights."

Silently, the gull takes three large gulps of air to help himself remain calm. Kai sees a deep sadness cloud the seagull's previously passionate eyes.

"Needless to say, I freaked out! I was captured and in great pain. Trying to escape, I did the only thing I knew. I started to fly. I stroked hard but got only about three feet into the air due to the weights. When the fisherman saw his line flying away, he was amused, and he began laughing loud enough for all to hear. He shouted to others on the pier and a crowd gathered. No one had ever seen a fisherman catch a bird.

"I heard the whining sound of the line escaping his reel, so I stroked harder. It seemed I was making progress until, in response to my success, the fisherman quickly set down on his drag. The resistance increased dramatically and the pain got worse. The line dug deep into my leg. For fifteen minutes, I struggled. It was horrific.

"In the meantime, a group of fishermen and tourists gathered to watch. They cheered the fisherman as he fought to bring me in. I struggled, unsuccessfully. I could fight no longer and had to give up. Steadying myself, I faced my enemy with wings in the air, and allowed him to reel me in. Exhausted, I landed with a thump on the hard, wooden planks of the pier, surrounded by dozens of people. No one offered to help me.

"The fisherman approached. He had dark eyes, a hairy face, and his breath smelled like rotting garbage. He quickly corralled me in hands that felt like rough coral, and with a flash of steel, he brought his knife down, separating me from my leg. In doing so, he was able to salvage his hooks and sinkers. He then lifted me up to the cheers of many and tossed me back into the air. I struggled to gain flight but plummeted downward toward the water. I pumped my wings desperately, trying to gain air and not hit the lower part of the pilings that were covered with sharp barnacles. I righted myself just in the nick of time and pulled out into a glide. As I flew to the shore, there were shouts and applause for the fisherman, as he held up my leg adorned with his hardware like a trophy.

"Instantly, I was no longer a sea creature in the true sense of the word. I had become land-bound, dependent forever on humans. People make, break, and bend rules any way they want. They are selfish. Nature is not important to most of them, so it is necessary for us to adjust, or perish. Man ruined my life with a mechanical rod and reel. I cannot fight that. Humans control us with their greed, inventions, and technology, making them the most dominating species on Earth."

"All that makes sense," Kai says compassionately. "But we must try to keep growing and learning. We must never give up. That is the key to success and happiness. Your bitterness only limits you," the young pelican states, like a motivational coach trying to relieve a troubled heart.

The gull, tired of the pelican's banter and inane philosophy, exhales a deep and depressing sigh. Looking at the youngster from behind saddened eyes, Colossus remains silent, remembering his life before and after that fateful day. The tough old bird knows the pelican is too young and inexperienced to understand the realities of life. Locked into a stare, neither of the birds know what to say. The seagull, set in his ways, lost his idealism a long time ago with the flick of a knife. He now lives the difficult life of a scavenger. His hardened exterior has been pierced by Kai's youthful idealism, but it cannot break down the cantankerous old bird's distrust of the world.

"What about the Magical Mountain that I seek?" Kai says interrupting the silence.

"It is there," Colossus says, pointing north as he pumps his wings and lifts off.

"Where? North? Is it still there?"

The gull ignores Kai's pleas and heads off to another food fight further down the seawall. Kai gazes back at the pier, the surfers, the battling birds, and the cars. Disappointed, but now hopeful, he now knows the way to the Magical Mountain.

As he watches Colossus join the fracas, Kai rises from the seawall and banks north.

ELEVEN

The least movement is of importance to all of nature.
The entire ocean is affected by a pebble.

– Blaise Pascal

Excited to be on his personal journey, Kai cruises easily above the breaking waves. He smiles, thinking about future adventures that lie ahead as an onshore wind massages his belly. The freedom of flight is one of Kai's greatest joys, floating alone in the sky, without the restrictions of being land bound.

Below him is an array of activities taking place up and down the beach. A meandering pod of porpoises acts like the children on the playground as they freely express an innocent love of life. Three of the young porpoises race a swell, surfing until it breaks. Like human surfers, the mammals catch waves as they form, ride them as long as possible, and breach into the air. They are superb gymnasts and the ultimate entertainers, loved by all. Humans point and cheer each time one of them goes airborne. Youngsters are infatuated by the mammals and want to get as close as possible. They run toward the receding waves and the surfing porpoises. In the instant the wave breaks, they turn tail and run to shore, screaming as the white water chases them. Once safe on the long sandy berm, they wait for the next wave, so they can do it over and over until they are exhausted.

Further offshore, a fleet of mid-sized sloops line up like pelicans in a train. The race begins with a cannon shot that sets the boats loose to zigzag out to sea. Skippers, trained to take advantage of every switch in the wind, fill billowing sails with as much air as possible.

On manicured beige sands, sun worshippers glisten while lying quietly on brightly colored towels. Musical sounds and the fragrance of sweet oil rise to meet Kai as he glides low over the beach.

Beachfront homes, perched precariously close to the breaking surf, have a permanent view of the sea. Many of them could easily be destroyed when tides, ocean warming, and huge swells combine to destroy beaches. In an attempt to protect these homes, rock fingers made of huge boulders protrude into the breaking waves. Too purposeful to be of natural design, Kai guesses they were placed by humans to prevent the loss of sand, in yet another fruitless attempt to restrict the powers of nature.

Small yellow shacks sitting on stilts are manned by red-dressed lifeguards. Their job is to search for unseaworthy swimmers. Scantily dressed beachgoers dot the beach and frolic in the sun. Close by, bicyclists and skateboarders dodge joggers and dogs along a wide boardwalk. There are sandy game players, surfers, walkers, and swimmers everywhere.

How can humans who seem to love the ocean so much treat it with so little respect? Kai ponders as he plays in the breeze.

Using an updraft created by the windowed face of a tall house, he shoots higher. Once skyward, he circles like a spy plane, taking in the many sights. The enormity of the human sprawl takes his breath away. As far as he can see are clusters of homes, businesses, and buildings. The houses are tucked together in tight rows, and taller structures are stamped with advertising and corporate logos. Kai stops dead, amazed by the vastness of human civilization. The roads, highways, and skies buzz with contraptions. Noise is everywhere. Everything is designed, decorated, and built exclusively for human use. Within canyons made of high buildings, many streets splay out like legs on a centipede. Distant colors are subdued by smog, and the horizon is dulled by what appears as a hazy film in the air. It is evident that man's domination over the landscape is absolute and shows little reverence for nature. The sprawling city has imprisoned all that is natural.

As he scans the distance, Kai sees a series of open spaces and enthusiastically rushes off in that direction.

Could it be that amongst all of this human development, there are natural fields? his inner voice asks hopefully.

"We will soon see," he answers.

Since his arrival yesterday, Kai has witnessed nothing but the indelible fingerprints of man. He rushes off to see if there might be a break somewhere in the Endless City.

Upon arrival, he glides slowly above a vast natural setting intersected by waterways instead of streets.

"Perfect," he says to himself. "This is much more my style."

There are scattered marshes, deep brush, small trees, plus three stately oaks. It feels as if they are welcoming Kai back to nature with an ambiance of country living. There are ravines and gullies weaving throughout the acreage and sandstone bluffs creating small cliffs.

Reflecting back to Master B's description of the mainland before humans arrived, Kai speculates, *This is but a tadpole example of what the Endless City was like before the arrival of modern man.*

Closing his eyes, he envisions what millions and millions of acres of open space would look like. He breathes a heavy sigh of relief knowing he is finally away from the intensity of the city and scouts for a place to land.

The fields, however, are not totally free from man's influences. Scattered willy-nilly throughout the acreage are large, metallic machines mimicking giant sandpipers bobbing for sand crabs. Rusted red with age, they speak a language of metallic grunts and groans.

"Can't humans leave anything alone?" Kai complains. "Must they infect everything they touch?"

Following a small dirt road, he lands on the hood of an abandoned truck. Parked nose to nose with another beat up and rusted car, they overlook a voluminous river. Its vastness is awash in cement. Stained with age, dirt, and graffiti, the riverbed is bone dry except for a slow-moving rivulet of green water. It is overgrown with moss and small plants and transports everything from paper, plastics, coolers, and clothes directly to the ocean.

"There are surely unseen dangers in that green water. Poisons and viruses for sure," Dread warns Kai. "Death lurks everywhere, just as your mother has warned."

As Kai drops his right wing and circles back toward the canals, he sees a grouping of gulls, a smattering of ducks, sparrows, terns, a pair of egrets, crows, and even two fellow pelicans.

"Lookie there!" he screams out loud, excited as an osprey floats into view. "What a beautiful bird," he yells with a youthful exaggeration. "With a body like that, I could be the greatest diver ever." The hawk's white underbody contrasts his dark wing feathers, striking eye-stripes, and rich colors. The raptor is stunning, looking like a Spartan warrior with an aerodynamic shape, giving him the appearance of speeding even when flying slowly. In pursuit of food, he uses his legendary vision to scan sparkling waters of the ocean or canals. Kai glides as close as possible to observe and learn from one of his heroes.

The osprey identifies his target, adjusts his wings and floats into position. This amazing predator is calm even as his muscles tighten. He is primed and ready for action. Thirty feet below, an unsuspecting silver mullet is betrayed by the reflection of sunlight ricocheting off his scales. He has no idea of the danger circling above.

In an instant, the raptor lifts his body and flaps continuously while calculating the needed speed and direction. Frozen in the sky, he suddenly flips downward, his angular wings swept back, twisting his body into a missile-like projectile. In a matter of feet, he doubles his speed and propels downward.

With perfect timing, he flattens his trajectory, lowers his legs, and drops razor-sharp talons into the water. The sharp claws grab the mullet's scaly back and clamp hard around the fish's spine assuring a strong grip. The hapless mullet squirms and flaps, trying to loosen the osprey's hold, to no avail. The fish is snatched from the safety of the canal and lifted high into the sky. As if boasting of his triumph, the osprey makes a wide sweep above the canals.

Once the fish is dead, the osprey returns to his nest atop a high pole donated by a group of admiring humans. There, he raises his wings in victory showing all that he is truly the king of the canals. It is yet another example of one species giving his life for the benefit of another. Death is not an arbitrary choice in nature but simply a way to perpetuate life and keeps the world in harmony.

"Nature does co-exist with mankind!" Kai celebrates.

What a refreshing break from those groveling birds at the pier, his inner voice says. *Unlike in the world of donuts and french fries, these wetlands still have a natural pecking order.*

Feeling really good about finding this place, Kai floats slowly to a dirt bench protruding from a sandstone bluff. There, he finds a cave that reminds him of his home on Anacapa. He glides softly to the embankment and lands.

This looks like the perfect place, his inner voice says optimistically.

Kai is cautious because the grotto's interior is cloaked in darkness.

This could be another's home, he thinks, remembering his encounter with the bratty pelican. But there is more to be concerned with here. *A hollow this size might be home to four-legged predators like foxes or coyotes. Either one would kill and eat me if they are inside.*

Kai stands silently outside the entrance. He listens and hears nothing. He looks for scat or pawprints but sees none. His conclusion is that the cave is empty. Looking into the darkness, he sees nothing. With no signs of occupants, he shuffles to the entrance. Silently, he asks Sorté for protection.

"Hello, is anyone home?" he asks, poised for a quick getaway. Getting no answer, he rounds the entrance to the cave and asks a second time. "Hello, anyone home?" Still no response. The back of the cave is totally black and a perfect place for somebody to hide. He strains his eyes to see through the murky darkness but still sees nothing.

"Hello," he repeats a third time inching into the cave. Preparing for the worst, he readies for a quick escape. "Anyone home?" he asks the darkness once again.

It is then that he hears a shuffling sound and senses movement in the back of the cave, just as a shadowy figure emerges. Anticipating danger, Kai back peddles out of the cave toward the bench's edge. Wings positioned for flight and eyes glued on the ghostly silhouette walking toward him, he feels his heart beating faster. Whatever it is, it is walking on two feet. Its body is shaped like an hourglass, and fortunately for Kai, it is not running, growling or snapping. It does not seem aggressive. In fact, it is walking with a kind of a waddle.

The stranger lets out a sigh as he emerges from the cave's umbra. It is an oddly shaped bird, smaller than a pelican, but too big for a gull. It is not a tern nor a sea hawk. It is a bird Kai has never seen. Based on its clumsy gait, he surmises it is some kind of seabird.

"Buenos días, señor," says the shadow bird in a soft and pleasant voice. "I did not mean to sleep in su casa. If you want, I will leave pronto," he offers humbly.

The bird's white chest is defined by a peppering of dark brown and black feathers. His neck is shorter than Kai's, but his head is similar, with a small straight beak. There is no pouch.

He must come from a place far out in the ocean, Kai speculates, cocking his head side to side as he studies the bird. He has a mid-sized body and a friendly smile. All in all, he seems pretty normal. But as Kai's eyes drop, he is shocked by what he sees.

"OH MY GOD!" Kai gasps. He shakes his head, and refocuses on the bird's feet. *His feet are BLUE,* he says to himself, *BLUE FEET, I have never seen such a thing!*

Gathering his wits, he looks to the strange bird and asks calmly, "Where are you from?" secretly hoping the answer is not outer space.

"I am from Baja, México, a small fishing village near Mulejé. It is beautiful and peaceful there, but I have been traveling mucho dias and slept here for only un día. I was muy cansado, very tired. Flying

from México was muy duro y peligroso—very hard on me and dangerous," the blue-footed bird answers.

Kai is concerned for the stranger's health and blurts out, "What is wrong with your feet? Are you sick or injured? Do you have bad circulation? Are your feet frozen? Why are they blue? I have never seen such feet anywhere."

Kai has seen colorful plumes and bright feathers among many species of birds. Plus, he has seen brilliantly colored fish, flowers, and reefs, but never feet the color of the Pacific.

"There is nothing wrong with my feet," the stranger responds with a heavy Hispanic accent. "Mis pies have always been this color. I'm a blue-footed booby," he pronounces proudly!

"I use my feet to dance and celebrate. Señoritas love blue feet and think them sexy. They are attracted by my dancing. Boobies dance together with great joy when mating. There are fellow boobies with red feet, yellow feet, and grey feet. Mine happen to be blue."

Kai senses an immediate bond with this unique new acquaintance.

"A blue-footed booby," he mutters under his breath. "How about that?"

"Boobies live in the warm waters of the tropics. We are of the same family as gannets and pelicans," he continues.

"We may be related—I am a pelican!" Kai interrupts.

"I can see this," the booby responds politely. "And quite a handsome pelican también. Boobies somos buena onda. We are very nice. We live near the sea, just like you. We dive for fish, just like you. We have a lot in common. Pero, Señor Pelican, you do not need to worry about me. I will leave if my looks offend you. I will return the cave to you. It is a very nice casa with una vista grande. You are a very lucky bird to live here." The booby lowers his head and glances down in a show of respect.

"Oh no! I am not offended by you!" Kai states adamantly. "I'm sorry if I came across that way. You just surprised me, I have never heard of a blue-footed booby. Plus, I was nervous about what other critters might have been in the cave. I want very much to be your friend. I am also new to the area. It is hard to make friends here. Besides, this cave is not my home. I am traveling like you, so we can stay here together."

The two birds stand opposite one another. They look eye-to-eye in search of the other bird's essence and soul. This is how birds of the sea evaluate others. Both birds are honest and decent and must decide if they can become true and trusting friends.

"Mr. Booby, I am on an adventure. You are welcome to join me," Kai proposes. "I am in search of the Magical Mountain, and I will fly until I find it."

"Sí, yo será muy contento ser tu amigo," says the booby, slipping back into his native Spanish. He says with delight, "Somos amigos, we can be friends! If you travel norte, through the great city, I would be honored to fly with you. Together, we will be safer and problemente have more fun. Pero, I know nada de nada—absolutely nothing—about the 'Montaña Magical.' But amigo, I want to go with you."

Kai's adventure suddenly changes for the better. Here is another sea bird to share in all the risks and excitement. Along the way, they will bond and build a strong friendship. Additionally, they can use this cave as their base of operations.

Everything is coming together, his inner voice says, making Kai smile. The two birds step close to each other, knock beaks, and touch wings. In the world of sea birds, this signifies a partnership being born.

Facing the open marshlands, Kai says, "I keep wondering about man's dominion over this land. Those I have asked can't explain why man is the way he is. I see very little that's still in a natural state. There are people, houses, and contraptions everywhere. All of this results in incredible waste. Humans have invented something for everything. It is so sad."

"Éstos son muy diferentes y malas aquí," says the booby. "I'm sorry. Me llamo Pancho. My name is Pancho."

"I'm Kai, very glad to meet you!"

"Hola, Kai, placer de conocerte—it's a pleasure to meet you," answers the booby, nodding his head.

"What is it like where you come from?"

"Mi familia lives near Mulejé on the enorme Sea of Cortez. Life is wonderful, and the weather is mild and beautiful. Hace mucho calor—it is very hot—and the sun is very powerful. It rains and floods when there are los huracanes—hurricanes. Our bay has mucho fish and our pueblo is chiquito, only one hundred personas. Life is peaceful, and we are contentos. We have no big cities nearby. I love mi casa. I love mi novia, Estrella. Desde que eramos pequeños, since we were quite young, Estrella and I have been dancing and in love. We are como dos medios de una naranja—two halves of the same orange. We met at the beach. It was a birthday party, una quinceañera. I saw her, smiled at her, and she smiled back. We danced all night and planned on being together forever. We will have many pajaritos—little ones."

"That's exactly like Feathertop and me. We have a friendship from childhood, and it is a well-known fact that we will mate someday. I'm happy with that," Kai says. "Why are you here if you are so in love with Estrella and your hometown?" he asks, hoping that Pancho's answer may clear up some of his own reasons for leaving home.

"Mi decisión was not simple. Mi corazón—my heart—told me, I have toda mi vida, all my life, en mi pueblo and con Estrella. I want to see the great ciudad del norte. California has many opportunities. I want to see them before I raise mi familia."

"Oh my gosh! That's just like me," Kai erupts. "We are truly meant to be amigos. There is only so much time, and I want to know everything about everything," the pelican adds with exuberance. "We can do this together. I am going to see the Magical Mountain where the Creator lives. Once I see all of what mankind has and visit the mountain, then I will go home to Feathertop and my colony."

"Estrella told me that she will wait five full moons. If I don't return," Pancho says very seriously, slipping in and out of Spanish, "she will forget me. Sería terrible—that would be terrible! Pero—but even so, I am curious. Many en México come here for a better life. ¿Por qué? What makes this ciudad del norte better than Baja? If it's better, I will return to Baja, get Estrella, and we will live in California. She already said yes, but tengo que volver, I have to return, in five full moons. So, entonces, I am here." Pancho continues, "Right or wrong, bueno o malo, I am now in the north! But very far from my sweetheart Estrella, mi amor."

Kai's mind fills with images of Feathertop and her soft, strong voice. Her patience is what he loves the most. She gives her love and support so easily.

Guilt interjects into Kai's thoughts.

"You should have talked to her. She may not want you back. You left so rudely. You disappeared without even saying goodbye. Ladies do not like that, Kai."

I probably should have discussed it with her, he thinks, realizing that for the first time in his life he is thinking about someone other than himself. Dismissing Guilt as an alarmist, he convinces himself that he will see her again, sooner rather than later.

"Mamá y Papa, as well as my uncles and aunties and Estrella, told me not to go," Pancho confesses as his mood darkens. "Boobies belong en los trópicos, no en la ciudad—in the tropics, not in the city. But still I am curious. If it's so bad, why do so many come here from México?"

"I can totally relate," Kai jumps in. "It is stupid. It doesn't make sense! The pelicans told me, 'Stay on Anacapa and enjoy the life the Creator has handed to you. Do not wander off to the unknown. It is dangerous, and you may get hurt or even killed. Do not go,' they warned me."

Kai and Pancho realize that they are driven by the same motivations. Despite what older birds are telling them, neither common sense nor blind trust will win over these two adolescents. Deep inside, they have a burning desire to explore the world. At their age, they believe this may be their only chance. Others want them to believe the rest of their life is predetermined, which is a ridiculous thought in the minds of a couple of teenagers.

Sitting down in front of the cave, the two discuss their lives. It turns out, Pancho's trip was full of struggle and danger. He had to pass over deserts that were dry and hot and go around large mountains that slowed his progress. Several times, the desert winds were so strong that he had to stop and wait for them to subside. Most of the trip, he was famished and thirsty. As he got closer to California, the Sea of Cortez became dirtier and had fewer fish to eat. Once out of México, things got even worse. The dryness, vast farmlands, and human sprawl seemed to go on forever. Pancho was exhausted after arriving at the cave last night. After a meal of tiny fish and lots of sleep, he feels like he is back to his normal self. He is ready for the proposed trip with his newfound friend.

Kai tells Pancho about his own observations and challenges. Pancho is inquisitive and eager to know about life on Anacapa. Kai shares his stories about his encounters with the shark, sea lions, cocky pelican, crazy dog, and the one-legged seagull. He tells Pancho of the surfers and his inspiration to ride waves. Pancho listens attentively and is certain they'll be close friends. It seems they agree on just about everything. They laugh for the first time since leaving their homes.

Like a globetrotting tern, Pancho has traveled over a thousand kilometers on his very long journey. This is remarkable for a bird used to living a peaceful lifestyle near his village. Kai's travels have been shorter, but the risks and the courage equal that of his compadre. They are perfect partners. No other booby, regardless of their foot color, has traveled this far north, and it has been over four generations since pelicans from Sorté have looked for the Magical Mountain. It is a collaboration of epic proportions; two excited partners-in-crime from totally different worlds, off on a challenge. Their laughter is loud and therapeutic as the bond of friendship grows. Both believe this will be a great partnership.

Kai remembers an old adage taught to him by the elders: *Relationships are like birds. If you hold tightly, they die. If you hold loosely, they fly. But if you hold with care, they remain with you forever.*

Hunger interrupts their conversation, sending them back to the canals for dinner. Amid joking and horseplay, they are compelled to do some hot-dogging as they fly. The booby is a strong flyer, and the pelican takes note. The pelican, on the other hand, is a powerful diver and never misses his intended target. Pancho rises and goes into a series of banks and circles, ending with a dive into the canal. He pops up with an anchovy. He challenges his new friend to compete. Kai accepts and follows suit. Both end up hollering and laughing hysterically as they thrash about in the water eating fish.

With full bellies and warm hearts, they fly to a nearby brick wall to primp and watch the sunset. They land next to an older house overlooking a canal, encircled by eighteen beautiful palm trees. There are three rusted beach bikes near the front door and a black surfer's suit hanging from an umbrella. A family of humans definitely lives here. It seems like a peaceful place to live.

As they primp and share experiences, they are silenced by an eerie sound.

"Meeeeeow, meeeeeow." It is a long and mournful plea for attention. "Meeeeow."

"El gato...cuidado," cautions Pancho. "Cats can be very mean when hungry."

The agonizing moan comes from a crowded planter box just beneath the two birds. Hidden behind a large philodendron leaf sits a scraggly black cat. Slowly, he steps out into the light. He is quite the sight, looking like he is dressed in a muddy tuxedo. His white chest hairs are brown with dirt, and his long charcoal coat is matted into Rastafarian-style dreadlocks. The cat appears either neglected or possibly injured. As he looks up at the birds, he blinks his yellow eyes as if trying to say something.

"Is this your home?" Kai asks softly, so as not to startle him.

The cat answers quickly, obviously anxious to talk.

"I have no home. I am homeless."

"How come a cat of your strength and beauty is without loved ones?" Kai asks, using a compliment to help soothe the feline.

"My family left, and I have nowhere to live. My name is Ted. I used to live right there for many years," he says pointing at the house. "It was a good life. I was named after some rude stuffed animal in a human movie. I never knew what I had in common with this character, but when my owners drank, they oftentimes made bad decisions. Naming me Ted was one of their mistakes, but their worst decision was leaving me homeless."

Ted steps forward, his sad face highlighted by outdoor lights. He is disheveled, with wild whiskers going off in all directions. His eyes are caked in dirt, and part of his left ear has been bitten or torn off. Ted is like a tragic portrait painted by an angry artist.

"For many years, I was the center of attention," he continues. "There were three kids and me. We used to play all the time. They picked me up and loved me every day, many times a day. Each time I awoke, I counted my blessings because I had a home, food, and a loving family. Later, two yappy Schnauzer dogs came to live with us, and they never liked me. But I remained the favorite of Rosalie, the youngest girl in the family. She was so full of happiness and joy. The two of us spent most of our days together." Tears roll down from his yellow eyes, and he needs to clear his throat in order to continue. His hurt is obviously very strong.

"Rosalie and I were true pals. She would pet me while she did her homework or played games on her computer. The two of us would lay in her sweet, pink bed for hours. When she was gone, I explored the canals and captured small rodents and bugs, but always came home when the school bus dropped her off. I was there every single day. Rosalie was everything to me.

"A year ago, there were problems with our parents. Discussions between Mom and Dad grew intense and at times, they were outright mean. I think they ran out of money. They could not agree on anything. I stayed upstairs with the kids and comforted them. The parents drank and argued downstairs. As the fighting intensified, the kids, both dogs, and I felt a big storm was approaching. And it didn't take long after that for everything to change."

Ted steps out from the protection of the plant and moves closer.

"A wave of despair overcame the family. The mother and the father were angry most of the time. Sometimes after drinking, they were mean to the children. As pets, we became a burden. One day I got so upset, I scratched Father's desk to let him know how unhappy everyone was. He responded in anger, and the next day took me to the vet to be declawed. He waited in a bar next door and became drunk once again. 'THAT WILL SHOW YOU, DAMN CAT!' he shouted when picking me up from the veterinarian.

"A short time ago, a group of men in white overalls came to the house with a big truck. The first day, they packed everything into boxes. On the second day, they placed all the furniture and boxes into the truck. There was so much noise and disruption, I went outside where it was quiet. I chased butterflies for fun and enjoyed my favorite flowers near the canal.

"Just before sunset of the second day, I heard the truck engine start and drive away. I ran back to the house, and the truck was gone. The family car was driving down the street, so I desperately chased after them. As it pulled away, Rosalie was staring at me from the rear window, sobbing. I heard father yell at her to sit down and turn around. It was too late. I sat in the middle of the street and watched as my home, my family, and my entire life turned left and disappeared. The house was sold and my family was gone."

Ted drops his head in silence remembering this fateful day.

The birds do not know what to say.

"They just up and left me! Do you believe that?" Ted continues. "I am reduced to begging for food. I have no claws, so I cannot fight for food or protect myself, and I have no home, so I am hoping for a miracle. I am a hobo. A homeless cat amongst many feral and homeless pets in the fields. The spoiled house pets in the neighborhood call all of us 'coyote chow!'"

"Ay! What will you do?" Pancho asks compassionately.

"Where is the justice in all of this?" Ted continues. "Regardless of who it may hurt, my humans were able to change their priorities on a whim. What happened to love and loyalty? What happened to commitment?" Ted paces uttering a low and mournful moan from deep within his gut. It is a horrific purr emanating from a dark soul.

"This is not fair," adds Kai. "I wish we could help."

Ted looks directly at Kai and says, "I want my old life back," and breaks into tears.

Off in the distance, a coyote howl rings out somewhere deep in the open space.

"The varmints are always on the prowl," Ted warns, having dodged this pack ever since his abandonment.

"Cuídate," Pancho calls out. "Ted, you be safe!" as Kai and Pancho fly back the short distance to the cave for the night. They decide to sleep outside the cave, just in case those coyotes know of this place.

TWELVE

The day is done, and the darkness
Falls from the wings of Night,
As a feather is wafted downward
From an eagle in his flight.

– Henry Wadsworth Longfellow

Kai settles in for the evening. He is weary and craves a long night of sleep. Staring into a milky sunset dulled by haze and an encroaching marine layer, the Endless City comes alive in a blaze of electricity. Suddenly, Pancho jumps up.

"Compadre, I have un buen idea!" he says excitedly. "Vamos juntos, let's go together on a trip to see the wonders of the city at night. Seguro encontraremos sorpresas. I'm sure we will find things we would never see during the day. It will be a night flight full of surprises."

Kai is startled and annoyed by this unexpected proposal. He straightens up and looks at his friend, somewhat mystified.

"Let's get some sleep. We need to rest," Dread counsels him.

Pancho stands tall, wings on hips, looking down at the pelican. He pushes harder, "Well, what do you think? A night flight? Let's call it 'la noche especial en la ciudad norteña.' Suena muy lindo, it has a nice ring to it, don't you think?"

Kai is quickly becoming accustomed to Pancho's manner of speech. Even words in Pancho's native language are becoming clearer. The booby's facial expressions, his eyes, movement of his wings, and his dancing blue feet help communicate his mood. Pancho is quite animated, making his point.

But Kai is conflicted. First and foremost, he wants a solid night's sleep. However, after thinking about it for a few minutes, he realizes Pancho's idea is beginning to make sense.

"Night flights over the ocean are one thing, but over a big city?" he asks Pancho, still unsure. "I am born with instincts, a built-in time clock, and the ability to land on the water in case of emergencies. These skills will be useless when flying above the Endless City. We would not only be without the ocean as our guide; we would be totally out of our element. I can only imagine the many disruptions that we will encounter. Noises, lights, tall buildings, flying machines, wires, and darkened mountains will be all around us. There may also be many other unknowns. It could be very dangerous!" Kai declares.

He takes two steps toward Pancho trying to emphasize the importance of his concerns.

"I have never encountered any of these things at night. I would prefer to wait until morning for our first exploration, especially if we plan to fly away from the ocean."

No sooner were the words out of his mouth than his inner voice reminds him of the purpose for this trip.

Adventure, pure and simple. Nighttime is totally different than daytime and, therefore, a more exciting opportunity, his inner voice drives home.

"But it could easily end in a disaster," Dread interrupts, sounding like the savants at home. "We are not here to die for some stupid stunt."

"Courage starts with decisions, and decisions lead to discoveries," Kai explains out loud, looking straight at Pancho. In him, Kai sees confidence, courage, and enthusiasm. Kai is weakening and almost ready to override his worry, because Pancho acts like a wise mentor with all the virtues that Kai admires most.

"Yes," Kai finally declares. "Let's go on a night flight! But remember, Pancho, we need to watch out for each other. There will be many obstacles. We are partners bonded by friendship, so we travel as one, not two. Whatever dangers we face, we conquer them together."

"¡Qué bueno!" Pancho states, overjoyed, dancing enthusiastically. He lifts his wings, executes a hop, a spin, a twirl, and yells out loud "¡Vámonos, let's go!"

Rising into the night sky, their new adventure begins. The eastern sky is glowing from a colossal sea of lights. They mentally prepare for whatever may happen as they stroke toward the golden glow. Within the boundaries of the canals, they are silent, like invisible phantoms shrouded in the night's darkness. Immediately upon crossing into the blaze of lights, they hoot and holler as if they are flying for the first time. Almost instantly, they are overcome by the toxic air. Their eyes burn, and they choke on noxious fumes. It is like flying above a volcano. Blinded by the boundless illumination of the city, they struggle to see where they are heading. Still another example of mankind's demented effort to turn nighttime into day.

A maze of asphalt and concrete roads spread out in all directions. Each has multiple lanes carrying an incalculable number of motor vehicles. From the main arteries, hundreds of smaller streets spiral off like branches on a tree. It is controlled chaos. An unbroken line of cars stretches as far as they can see. Inching along, each car is so close to the next it looks like they are pushing one another. Thousands upon thousands of vehicles slither along in opposite directions like two monstrous snakes. One travels north, clad in lights of ruby red, and the other moves south, sparkling in white lights. Wanting to follow this massive movement of people, they fly to the center of the biggest road they can find. Immediately, they are overwhelmed by a nasty and poisonous updraft. The sickening air shuts down their lungs. Their eyes burn so badly, they must close their eyes. Kai and Pancho are immediately unable to function and are flying blind.

"We must leave this terrible place. We must escape this air! Keep flying, no matter what," Kai hollers between coughing spasms. Both fear the fumes they are inhaling may kill them, reminding Kai again of his mother's warning: "The mainland is like a rattlesnake—full of poison."

"This has to be the origin of the brown line," Kai yells to Pancho, as they bank away from the monstrous serpent. Making a hard right, they fly desperately seeking cleaner air. They must get as far away from the freeway as possible.

Finally, with distance between them and the cars, the toxicity lessens, and their symptoms start to ease. But even this far from the freeway, the air is still much dirtier than the clean oxygen both birds are used to back home.

Everywhere they go, streets of the city are congested with human activity. What they are experiencing tonight is exponentially more aggressive, confusing, and scary than what Kai saw this morning. Lights are everywhere. Some flash off and on with great frequency; others are steady but very bright confusing the birds. Larger buildings are lit up with letters spelling out *Monsanto, Bank of America, General Motors, Amazon,* and *Google.* Flying through canyons created by the tallest buildings, the sound of sirens warp like echoes in a cave. Everyone is in a great hurry. The intensity of the people's hustle reminds them of a mega-sized colony of ants. However, the humans seem far less organized and more frenzied than the ants.

To lighten the mood, Kai proposes a game of follow the leader. He swoops down with Pancho right behind. Popping and buzzing electrical wires hidden in the night make them rethink this idea. Playing games is not a good idea when your life is in danger. It is simply too dark and too hazardous to fly for fun surrounded by blinding lights and disturbing noises. They must have full concentration.

Closer to the ground, they fly over blocks of dilapidated tents and shanties put together with a variety of throwaway items. Sadly, the humans living here give the appearance of injured animals, like the homeless cat, Ted. They live amongst foul odors that emanate from within the homeless city, contrasting the high-class downtown buildings.

As Kai and Pancho turn away from the business district, they see a black hole deep in the distance. Surrounded by a carpet of lights, this darkness appears as if a portion of the city has been ignored. Optimistically, they aim in this direction, hoping to get away from the dense urban jungle that they have just experienced. Realizing they are totally lost, they rise so Pancho can help navigate out of the city and toward the black hole. The birds hope the dead zone might be vacant land like the canals.

It turns out to be exactly what they hoped, an expansive area, void of electricity, structures, and roads. There are no people, only large lanes of grass, ponds of sand and small lakes. The entire area is surrounded by trees. Curiously, they find everything is arranged systematically like the rest of the city. Oddly, there are no rivers or water sources feeding the small lakes, and the beach sand looks totally out of place. It has to be another creation of man because there are small cement walkways crisscrossing the entire area with benches and outbuildings. Tonight, it lies in darkness, like a fallow field surrounded by the madness of the surrounding city.

"Let's take a break," Kai suggests. "This place is perfect. We can catch our breath and figure out how to get back to the ocean."

"Sí, perfecto."

They proceed down one of the tree lines, leading them to a small wooded area. Here they find a large ash tree wedged between two old silver oaks. Most of the ash's leaves have fallen due to the time of year, exposing lower branches, which are as big as some tree trunks. They agree this is a suitable spot for two clumsy sea birds to land. Pancho comes in slowly. He stops mid-air, rises, and then hovers just above, allowing him to set down gently upon the ash.

"Come on, Kai," he shouts happily. "Your turn."

His partner copies the approach and settles on the large branch without a problem. As the two travelers sit in peace, they look like two tiny infants resting in the strong arms of a loving father. After overcoming the challenges of the toxic updrafts and the confusion of man's world, it feels good to once again be alone in a natural setting.

"Wow, dude, that was a tough start. This place is much more insane than I expected," Kai confesses. "Humans have created an unbelievably complex lifestyle. Do you think there is always this much poison in the air?" he asks mystified. "Who could possibly want to live like this?"

"I think we are flying in the belly of your brown line," answers Pancho. "Dawn to dusk and into the evening there are many, many people. I saw lo mismo, the exact same, on my way here. City after city with cars and roads everywhere. But THIS is many times bigger y más loco que los otros, crazier than the others. The Endless City must go on forever.!"

They sit quietly listening to the surrounding sounds. The hubbub is non-stop. Like a stereophonic noise track, the hum comes at them from all directions and in varying decibels. They quickly agree that it is important to find the ocean as soon as possible.

Suddenly, Pancho senses an unknown presence in the darkness of the surrounding trees. An uneasy feeling crawls over him, causing him to shiver. Pancho motions to Kai to be quiet and stay still. The birds do not move or make a sound. As they peer into the labyrinth of dark tree branches, their delicate ears detect rustling noises. Kai suddenly sees movement on his left. Almost immediately, both hear numerous crackling twigs, and there is motion all around them. The trees are alive.

"There is something out there. Cuidado," cautions Pancho.

"What can it be?" Kai whispers. Dread also wants to know. "Be vigilant, Pancho. Something feels very wrong," Kai states quietly, straining his smog-irritated eyes in an attempt to identify the source of the sounds.

From out of the blackness, a gruff voice breaks into a chant:

> *Hey, what are you doin' in the 'hood?*
> *You have entered sacred space.*
> *Gettin' out of here, is what you should!*
> *Leave now or feel the sting of a million bees,*
> *these trees are not for travelers, and we ain't sayin' please!*

From an opposite tree, a different voice belches,

> *You freeloaders will bleed.*
> *This is our home, not a place to plant your seed!*

The two sea birds are in shock. These bullying voices are so full of contempt. They wonder how many there are. Cracking and popping sounds increase as branches move and an unseen enemy begins to surround them.

You do not belong here, this is our canopy.
We are tellin' you to leave.

This third warning comes from a deeper and even more menacing voice and is followed by a medley of threats. Each rhythmic sound is profane and used to scare the travelers.

"There are a lot of them," Kai whispers. "Be careful! If given a chance, they will hurt us. We must leave NOW, or we'll have to fight our way out."

"I've got your back, compadre," assures Pancho. "No problema."

The trees go silent for a few agonizing seconds. Pancho continues to peer into the shadows. As he plans the escape route, dark and shadowy figures can be seen bouncing from branch to branch in an effort to get closer. The voices are backed by a steady thumping sound. It is a hypnotic form of music that neither bird has ever heard. The lyrics are mean, threatening, and hostile. Despite all this, Pancho's blue feet instinctively move to the powerful beat. Kai fears that his friend's love of dance will give them away.

"This is not the right time or place," he scolds Pancho. "We are in great danger amidst this horde of night stalkers. They are heading toward us like flies to rotting meat."

Kai feels overwhelmed. His simple life on Anacapa has not prepared him for so much negativity and pure evil. He looks to Pancho for strength. Pancho, sensing all of this, is ready to take charge.

The first bird shows himself from the darkness. It is an enormous raven with long, matted black feathers. As he steps forward, the others chant, "Solomon Grundy, Solomon Grundy, Solomon Grundy," as if he is some kind of god.

Grundy limps closer, the moon illuminating him against the darkened tree. He is missing his right eye, and his facial feathers are in total disarray. To the naïve travelers, he looks beyond menacing. Grundy struts back and forth on his branch only yards away. His head bobs to the throbbing percussion as he paces. Oversized body feathers stick out, making his image appear devilish in front of the eerie and abstract shadows of tree branches. He glares at the two gatecrashers, motioning the others to come forth. The pounding from within the nearby oaks gets louder, and in seconds, the raven is surrounded by crows. Dozens of crows. The sea birds are face to face with an aggressive murder of crows pledged to protect their neighborhood from outsiders. The one-eyed raven is clearly their general.

Strangers, you have come where it is not your place,
you are not welcome, so do not stay!
Dressed like jungle panthers, we are brothers of darkness
and have no grace.
If you linger here, there will be a fray!
Even though you simply have lost your way,
we will make you pay.
For this is OUR home, bonded in brotherhood.
With our treasure, we live quite grand
but don't doubt, we will always make a stand.
Hear our words and
TAKE THIS CLUE:
You will die, you will die, YOU WILL DIE!
Like the bothersome fly!

More crows step forward, all bouncing on tree limbs. They continue to honor their leader as they screech, "Solomon Grundy, Solomon Grundy, Solomon Grundy!"

The shaken visitors watch as the big raven orchestrates the scene.
The crows work in perfect harmony as they chant their leader's name.

Feelin' extra low...maybe you should go!
Your lives are of no use to us, this you need to know.
Be ever so wise
it is time to dematerialize.

Make yourselves scarce, so your family won't cry.
What excites us most is that you will die.
If you stay, your lives will not last!
Trust us, because it's happened in the past
we stay strong.
Lookin' for birds like you,

Livin' the normal life,
with no worries or strife.
One day at a time,
havin' no problem fightin' or doin' crime.
Many deteriorating bones bleached below
are those who did not go!
We battle with fools who do not listen;
their gravestones in tonight's moonlight glisten.
Their families thinkin', they are simply missin'.
Many don't like us 'cause we're not compatible,
so we make them accountable.
For sures,
you will die, you will die, YOU WILL DIE!
Like a bothersome fly!

The crows chant this tune, pulsating like a beating heart. It is apparent that this demonstration of power has been rehearsed over and over. The crows rock back and forth as they sing.

They stare at the two frightened sea birds. The branches of the oaks shake violently as the song burns a hole into the souls of the unwelcomed visitors. It is as if Kai and Pancho wandered into a warzone between the crows and the rest of the world.

The friends are unnerved by the level of hostility. Never before has Kai heard anything like this. Never before has Kai felt so despised. Kai was taught that violence begets violence. He has never seen anger and hatred of this proportion. Once again, he looks to Pancho for guidance.

"Mala onda, amigo! Está bien gacha. The vibes are very bad aquí. Let's go quickly, compadre, we are in mucho danger."

The murder of crows advances even further as obscenities and exclamations get louder and louder.

"Órale! We must go!" Pancho yells to Kai, signaling they are running out of time.

They drop from the branch to catch air. Kai hits the ground, forgetting that the branch is so low. He ends up lying in a discombobulated jumble. Struggling to put his body parts back into the right places, he runs along the grass, frantically pumping his wings.

Seeing all of this, the crows scream like banshees and take to the air behind their leader. They rise and form an organized strike force. The raven flies point, with the crows in a formation shaped like an arrowhead. They are inflamed with a mob mentality and continue to scream at Kai and Pancho. In an attempt to buy time for his partner, Pancho rises to face the antagonists.

"Pinche crows, back off!" He fluffs his feathers to make his body appear as big as possible and distorts his face to look mean and ugly. "One against thirty, pero no tengo miedo—I am not afraid," he shouts as he readies for battle.

Pumping his wings hard, Kai finally makes air. Looking over his shoulder, he sees his wingman, Pancho, positioned behind him readying for a fight. The crows pursue the pelican. Pancho gets directly in their way. The crows yell insults about blue feet, giant pouches, and fat bellies.

"Uno por uno—one-on-one, not so bad," Pancho yells. "Let me have you cobardes one at a time, and things will be different. You are all cowards." A group of five crows are upon him, so Pancho pivots. "¿Quieren unos chingasos? I will fight you to the end," he bluffs with the bravado of an Ultimate Fighting Champion.

Individual crows position themselves to attack Kai from above. He is a perfect target. But each time a crow dives toward Kai, Pancho places himself between the attacking bird and his buddy like a shield. Pancho's superior size causes them to veer off. He scares off the first two easily. A third comes from a different angle, looming close enough to reach Kai. Pancho swings back around and dives hard. Using his blue feet like fists, he hits the crow broadside with all his strength, delivering a devastating punch to the thorax of the smaller bird. The crow falls to the ground gasping for breath, causing shock waves among the rest of the murder. The war is on!

"Solomon Grundy, Solomon Grundy, Solomon Grundy," the attack force chants as they pick up speed.

Kai pumps his wings and reaches full speed as he elevates. Wing to wing with Pancho, they outrun the attackers and the horde finally slows down. But as bullies often do, they break into humiliating taunts and laughter. Unable to hurt their opponents physically, they use derogatory words like sharp daggers.

Pancho and Kai blast out of the darkness and into a neighborhood lit by streetlights. Having made a successful retreat, they find themselves totally disoriented. Flying above the lights of the city, they have no sense of direction. Kai feels his heart frozen with frustration. Just as he feared, the risky night flight has taken its toll. They parallel another giant serpent of cars, hoping this freeway will take them back to the ocean. They are ready to get back to the safety of their cave.

Unfortunately, they go deeper into the Endless City. This snake-like line of vehicles bottlenecks into a colossal domed structure. The monstrous building is surrounded by a crush of cars along with thousands of pedestrians. Giant entrance doors are encircled by large bands of light emanating from huge spotlights. The scene is exciting, the commotion stimulating, and quells the lingering bad vibes of the crows. The seabirds have found yet another adventure.

Massive crowds encircle the property creating a wall of noise. The dome is extremely wide and voluminous although not as tall as other buildings they have seen. Shaped like a gigantic abalone, it is one of a kind. There are no windows, only doors. Stroking toward the entrance, they are fascinated by the sight of a huge electrical sign emblazoned with the words *Home of the Mighty Ducks*.

"Dude, check this out, this is the house of mighty ducks."

Though they have heard of many legendary birds, neither Kai nor Pancho have seen a mighty duck. Kai believes that if Sorté can be a demigod and there is a Magical Mountain, then certainly there is a place on Earth for mighty ducks.

"Mighty ducks would surely know about the Magical Mountain. We must find them!" yells Kai. "Let's go."

"Look Kai, there—a mighty duck," Pancho yells, pointing at a large statue of a stern looking duck sporting protective human clothing, a helmet and carrying a big stick. Groups of humans are standing in front of the god-like figure like worshipers. They have devices in their hands that emit quick bursts of light, eliciting large smiles. The human excitement is contagious, inspiring the two birds to find a place to observe these extraordinary ducks.

"Compadre, look, the sign has changed. It now says *THE MIGHTY DUCKS* versus *THE PENGUINS*. There's going to be a bird battle aquí. Órale, we must watch. Estará padrísimo—it's going to be awesome. I never would have thought so many humans would come to see a bird battle. Forget those pinche crows, we are about to see algo increíble, something incredible—ducks fighting with penguins."

Anxiously, they fly closer to the building and are immediately whisked up the wall by an updraft. This leads to a vast, rolling roof, with rows of giant skylights that open to the inside. There are no human spectators, only groups of birds scattered atop the windows.

"We can watch the battle from here," Kai announces. Most of the windows are already taken by pigeons, field birds, and even some sea gulls, but one window sits empty.

"Mira, ésta está libre, this one has an open space," Pancho says. "This will be our spot. Perfecto."

As they land, they feel and hear the uproar from the arena below. Powerful vibrations rise through the open windows like sea water from a blowhole. The energy and noise from within the building creates its own wind. The two amigos find a spot and settle in for the show. Next to them is a window occupied by a varied group of sparrows; crowned, black chin, sage, lark, fox, savannah, and song sparrows. The little birds sit in a large crooked circle looking down into the building, exchanging excited banter. They look like Mexican jumping beans as they hop around in anticipation of the event.

The street savvy Pancho recognizes this behavior.

"They are placing bets on the two teams. Their loyalties are divided, each one gambling for profit."

As the building erupts, Pancho steps away to avoid the deafening roar of the crowd.

"Kai, these are humans skating on a sheet of ice. No veo ni un pingüino ni un pato. I do not see a single penguin or duck. There are lots of people, lots of smoke and noise, but not a single bird. ¿Cómo puede ser? How can that be? A battle of the birds with no birds?" he asks. The question is lost amid the loud racket.

The combination of clamorous music and thunderous human voices saturate the arena. Row after row of people eat, drink, and cheer. They watch the center ice, where dozens of uniformed people skate with large sticks chasing a small black object. When the crowd yells, so do the sparrows. Kai is mesmerized by the fracas just as much as the sparrows, but he has no clue what is happening. He sees two different uniforms. Each time one group of skaters gets to the other side, pandemonium breaks loose. The crowd goes ballistic when the little black object ends up in a net.

Chants of "Wild Wing, Wild Wing, Wild Wing!" pulsate through the arena. A large human dressed like the statue answers the call, skating around the ice bringing the audience to its feet. The crowd is frenzied.

At the conclusion of the game, the energy subsides quickly. The crowd takes all the noise and excitement with them as they exit the building. Soon, there is an empty shell littered with debris and discarded food. On the roof, the sparrows bicker and taunt one another, eventually settling their debts. The big winner is the savannah sparrow, a smug, confident, and very happy bird. He dances his way to the edge of the rooftop, looks back at the sea birds and then drops into the city lights.

Thousands of people gush out of the arena and into their cars as if pulled by a strong rip current. Masses of vehicles return to the roads, creating two new auto serpents moving in opposite directions. Kai and Pancho drop from the roof's ledge and head toward what they think is the southwest. It is getting very, very late. They are tired to their bones.

Beneath them, the Endless City's montage of lights is still fully ablaze. It seems that mankind never sleeps.

THIRTEEN

We have become a nation of thoughtless rushers, intent on doing before thinking, and hoping what we do magically works out. If it doesn't, we rush to do something else, something also not well thought-out and then hope for more magic.

– Len Holman

As Pancho and Kai ride acidic thermals high above the mayhem of man, they hope they are heading west. Neighborhood after neighborhood goes by in a never-ending display of man's successful effort to pave over nature. House after house, building after building, road after road, all so wearisome in their monotony.

Flying in silence, they review in their minds the wild memories of this long evening. With an occasional inquiry of "¿Todo bien—is everything all right?" They work hard to find the peace and safety of the ocean.

Their tedious flight is suddenly blasted by a horrific clatter coming from above. In an instant, they are surrounded by repugnant decibels of sound, so invasive, it feels like they are drowning in noise. A helicopter of man-made metals whirls nearby. Obnoxious to the eye and abhorrent to the ear, this two-manned vehicle gyrates in mechanical madness. The rear end spins one way as the top twirls in another, disrupting the air like the winds of a tornado. From its underbelly, a column of bright light bounces over the ground in large circles exposing everything within it. The commotion brings the birds' attention to an incident playing out below.

The copter's torrent of light exposes a swarm of siren-screaming cars, pulsing blue and red. They race through darkened streets, awakening entire neighborhoods one after another. The vehicles are chasing a red car, darting in and out of traffic. Kai and Pancho quickly bank left and follow to see what is happening. In order to stay with the action, they are forced to cut across streets, go over buildings and dive under electrical wires at a torrid pace. It is frightening and exciting at the same time. Their bodies are running on a rush of adrenaline.

In a magnified mechanical voice, the copter shouts, "Stop! Pull over! Stop and get out of the car!"

The order is repeated several times as the chase continues. The red auto speeds down streets and around corners with tires screeching. Kai and Pancho fly recklessly above the fracas.

Dodging and weaving, dropping and rising, they try to keep up while avoiding any hazards. They are as much pursuers of the fleeing car as are those in the police cars. The exhilaration is excruciating. Kai peeks over at Pancho and sees an intensity that is counter to his usual laid-back style.

"¡Por aquí—this way!" Pancho yells.

He carefully dives between two neglected buildings, careful to avoid a dilapidated fire escape. More cars join the chase. Residents run out of their homes or lean from windows to watch the action. Some shout at the participants. No one notices the two black shadows speeding above.

Sirens from the pursuit push hard on the driver's psyche. He turns too sharply, causing his tires to shriek in protest. Suddenly, the right wheel breaks loose, and the car swerves out of control. It bounces over a curb and crashes into an electrical pole. Sparks fly, the pole leans, and then falls to the ground.

Pancho and Kai swoop down, landing on a nearby rooftop. Now voyeurs, like the human gawkers, they watch to see how this thriller will play out. Time slows to a crawl as the players position themselves for a grand finale.

Uniformed men, with weapons drawn, exit their vehicles. They move in like hyenas stalking an exhausted wildebeest. The helicopter drops down not far from the two birds, pounding them with turbulent winds. The birds hunker down so as not to be blown off the rooftop. They are fascinated by all the happenings. Suddenly, shouts break out as the driver of the red car jumps out and faces his hunters. In an act of desperation, he drops behind his car door. There are three quick flashes of light followed by popping sounds. Six officers answer with their own flashes and popping, too many to count. In just moments, the driver of the red car lies still in the street. The energy of the scene slowly ebbs as the hunters move closer, still tense and poised to react.

"He is dead," yells Kai. "I know it. It is just like what we learned in school. Man kills man for reasons other than food and basic survival. Sorté warned us that humans have wars, battles, and conflicts, killing each other indiscriminately."

Kai is saddened and disappointed by this realization because it confirms yet another truth about the mainland as predicted by those back on Anacapa. The Endless City seems wrought with tragedy, as well as waste and unhappiness.

By this time, officers have surrounded the red car and its motionless driver. The copter retreats to a higher altitude and shuts off its light. The birds look at each other, their hearts pumping wildly. Feeling as if they were participants in this grisly affair, they know that senseless killing is grieved deeply in nature, but apparently not so much in the world of man.

"This type of orchestrated death is not what we are used to. Esta muy malo," Pancho states coldly. "This is human nature. Mankind treasures his own life but is willing to take that of another cuando lo conviene—when it suits him."

"Senseless deaths are acceptable among humans, just as I was told," Kai responds, wishing he understood human behavior better. He is beginning to realize why nature's inhabitants cannot trust humans.

Dismayed by the intensity of this event, Kai and Pancho fly parallel to yet another large freeway. They hope this one will take them back to the cave. But all these roads look the same with their eight lanes, signs, and spin-off ramps. How are strangers supposed to know the difference between them?

Cars move more freely this late at night and, fortunately, it is much less toxic. Eventually, the air feels heavier, as if they are entering a marine layer. They know the ocean is getting closer, so they stroke harder.

After many miles, Kai concludes that they have picked the wrong road once again. None of the buildings look familiar to those near the cement river. He is sure the ocean is near because the temperature has dropped and moisture in the air has increased. Eventually, far in the distance, they see a huge black expanse.

"There it is, the Pacific! That is the ocean! Keep going!" Kai exclaims enthusiastically. They push forward despite exhaustion setting in. "Food will have to wait until morning. Sleep is overcoming me," Kai confesses, shaking his head to stay awake.

"De acuerdo," Pancho agrees.

With eyes half closed and intermittent yawns, the two finally find the ocean. It lies just beyond a harbor many times bigger than the one near the cave. Directly in front of them are three large black shadows sticking high into the sky. Small red lights outline their shapes. The huge tubes are dark and quiet. Kai, convinced the structures are safe from predators and mankind, glides down and drops softly onto the roof of the first tower. The two exhausted travelers huddle together and immediately slip into a deep sleep.

FOURTEEN

To me the sea is a continual miracle,
The fishes that swim—
the rocks—the motion of the waves—
the ships with men in them,
What stranger miracles are there?

– Walt Whitman

The two companions awaken from a fitful night's sleep after loud and repetitive sounds invaded their slumber. Their eyes open to an astounding tabletop of sights and noises. Unveiled beneath them are two immense harbors jammed with all types of equipment. The complexity of it overpowers the hungry and sleep-deprived travelers. Massive multi-colored machines line up like soldiers. From north to south, as far as the birds can see, is nothing but steel, cement, and huge structures. Next to these are endless rows of docks, cargo ships, and tankers. Hundreds of wharfs are stacked with different colored boxes and containers. The domination of mankind is so far-reaching that the ocean and its waters appear insignificant in contrast. From their perch, they have a perfect view of the mayhem around them. Outside the harbors, their beloved Pacific Ocean is littered with giant ships, similar to those lining the docks.

Unknowingly, they have slept atop a famous old cruise liner, *The Queen Mary*. Once a ship of dignity, it is now a fun zone and hotel for tourists. Surrounding the *Queen* is a complex industrialized landscape, whose activity is the beating heart for mankind's vast urban sprawl.

To the west, Santa Catalina Island sits on the horizon, punctuated with the large tankers waiting to unload. The power and immensity of Earth's largest ocean is reduced to a mere backdrop behind man's kaleidoscope of wharfs, piers, docks, roads, huge contraptions, and ships, all running along waterways controlled by man. The area is literally void of anything natural. Huge ships, rusted orange by the salty oceans, sit deep in the water. Stacked with orange, red, and black shipping containers, the monstrous vessels travel between faraway ports around the world. Containers are scattered about like children's toys waiting for places to go. Trains and trucks come to carry the cargo inland for distribution. Empty sister ships sit high in the water, ready to reload for return voyages to Asia, Africa, and South America.

The birds' ears are irritated by a wide range of harsh metallic noises. Running engines, grinding machines, and steel boxes crashing to the ground cause them great discomfort. Tugboats hustle about like referees, their horns responding to deep bellows of arriving and departing ships. Two horns here, several blasts there. Kai and Pancho know nothing of what is being said, but it is obvious these ships are communicating in some strange language. The conflict of sounds never ends.

"Is all this really necessary?" Kai questions as he watches groaning monster cranes loading cargo. "How can anything be this complicated? Does mankind really need this much stuff?" he asks in bewilderment.

"No sé cómo es existir como ser humano—I do not know what it's like to be human but obviously they think they need it all," answers his partner.

Changing the subject from these unsettling thoughts, Kai asks a timely question: "Hungry?"

"Órale, sí," responds Pancho, already in the air.

As they fly past four huge hammerhead cranes, Kai sees a peregrine falcon patrolling the skies. The raptor has just left his home atop one of the huge cranes where his family nests high above man's concrete arroyos. Just as his ancestors did thousands of years ago, he searches for food. Kai appreciates the ability of this bird to use man-made structures in place of non-existent cliffs, showing once again nature's ability to adapt when forced to live amongst man.

The falcon is eyeing an old warehouse strewn with graffiti. Kai hears the familiar coo-cuk-cuk-cuk-coo of its residents. The dilapidated old structure is home to hundreds of pigeons. These birds are scavengers, much like the seagulls at the pier. The falcon knows their routine, as pigeons are birds of habit. This particular flock leaves its warehouse each morning and returns late in the afternoon. The falcon floats high in the sky, waiting for them to emerge from the safety of the abandoned warehouse. Similar to a bait ball of fish, the pigeons live with the code of safety in numbers, sacrificing a few to protect the whole. The pigeons provide easy access to an abundance of food for the predator.

"Check this out, Pancho!" Kai says to his companion.

The flock rises, and the peregrine falcon swoops down. His speed is equal to one of Kai's fastest dives. With sophisticated vision, he picks one target among the hundreds of birds. The falcon's exceptional coordination and phenomenal flying skills make him a master hunter. He manipulates his wings, body, head, and rump, which results in quick and decisive turns.

Observing the falcon in perfect harmony with the environment makes Kai twitch midair. Kai feels like a child pretending to be an adult as he mimics some of the raptor's moves. Once over his prey, the falcon drops his legs and digs his talons deep into the pigeon's torso. In an explosion of feathers, the pigeon struggles to escape but is quickly overcome. The hunter makes a wide turn and flies back to his lair, ready to share this prize with his family.

Nature, once again, is in forced harmony with man. The entire process does not take long and will repeat itself each and every day as long as the dilapidated warehouse exists. This animal haven is scheduled to be torn down as man expands and improves the harbor. This will force both species of birds to adjust yet again.

"Pancho, did you see that?" Kai calls out bubbling with excitement. "That bird can really fly!"

"Si venga, compadre, á comer—it is time for us to eat, I am very hungry. We can watch later."

They exit the harbor and come upon a small fishing fleet. Four syndicated boats roll gently in the calm ocean as they work a large school of anchovies with a maze of nets. Once the fish are trapped, the boats' winches bring the net over the gunnels and dump the fish into the hold.

"There are plenty of fish to go around. Let's go," Kai says, not noticing an armed lookout on one of the boats. The scout's job is to scan the skies for large flocks of seagulls. The gulls steal fish, costing the fisherman money. Men, driven by money, are willing to do almost anything to protect profits.

Pancho and Kai, unaware of the complexity of the fishermen's system, see nothing but the sparkling confusion of thousands of struggling fish. As the nets shrink in size, fish stack up on top of each other. It is simply too tempting to pass up. Smiling, they dive into the fracas and are immediately immersed in anchovies. Kai fills his gular, while Pancho gobbles down all he can eat. Chomping and chewing, chomping and chewing, this is one of the highlights of their trip. They eat fast and furiously, loving every bite. As the nets shrink, the boats get closer, putting the hungry birds within shooting range of the man with the shot gun.

"Get out of here!" the sentry yells at the frolicking birds who are completely absorbed in their feeding frenzy. He aims and shoots his shotgun in an effort to spook them. The pellets splash the water only feet away from Pancho. The man reloads and continues his rant.

"¡No manches—you're kidding me! Vámonos. These people are mean," Pancho yells. "We do not want to get shot."

Neither of them realize that Kai's endangered species status protects them. The fisherman does not want to risk paying the hefty fine for killing a brown pelican. "Are you okay, Pancho?"

"No hay de que. It's okay, we are lucky. I don't think he was trying to kill us, but let's get out of here. Ahorita!" They fly quickly away from the trawlers, leaving the pellets behind.

"Sígueme, follow me if you can!" Pancho yells.

The challenge is on. It's time for fun now that their bellies are full. In a game of follow-the-leader, Kai mimics Pancho's every move. They head north, passing several beautiful coves. Forgetting the challenges and bad vibes they experienced in the city so far, Pancho skims the water, wings to the waves, rises suddenly, and finishes with a speedy dive into the water. Kai follows obediently. Laughter overcomes them as they pop in and out of the water on their way north. Gliding and diving among the incoming swells, all their tension and tiredness is erased. Pancho rises again until he is high in the air. He executes multiple barrel rolls and then dive bombs back into the ocean. Kai follows with his best imitation of a raptor scream. The sun is warm, the weather is nice and they are free and full.

"What could be any better than this?" Kai asks himself.

Nothing, his inner voice answers.

They arrive at a beautiful beach protected by a large rock reef with three to four-foot breaking waves. Kai drops down and glides across the top of the water. These waves are bigger than those at the pier, and Kai wants to ride them. He will have them all to himself because there are no surfers. An empty break is a surfer's paradise. Picking out a spot to take off, he glides low to the wave, turns right, and tucks into a curl. In front of him is a magical face of spiraling blue-green water. As the wave closes in on the beach, its energy hits the rocky bottom, making it grow in size. This causes the top to throw water over the bird's back. Kai tucks tighter, gains speed, and slides perfectly into a small green tunnel. Pancho, seconds behind the adept pelican, is too late and must straighten out. He watches intently as Kai hangs inside the wave. Right wing tucked, the pelican raises his left wing for lift, allowing him to float a few more seconds. He gently glides over the exposed shoulder of the wave and back into the sky. Behind him, the wave completes its barrel and breaks into millions of droplets, disintegrating as it rolls onto the beach.

Pancho yells, "¡Qué olas excellentes! Perfect wave, compadre!"

"Can you believe that?" Kai asks, incredulous. "I surfed my first real wave!" Kai is so excited, he whips around and returns to the exact spot where he caught this perfect wave.

Flying in slow patient circles, he scouts the ocean. Eventually, another swell shows itself. In the shallower water, Kai pumps his wings and strokes into a takeoff. This wave is bigger than the last. Cutting to the left this time, he digs his left wing into his body. He knows the wave will have additional power, so he works to increase his speed. His left eye is inches from the moving water as he looks down the line. Unfortunately, the wave is too fast and closes out. Kai is deep inside when it explodes. It grabs him and throws him downward into the swirling white water. He lands hard on his head, and his body gets pounded by the wave's energy. Nervous, but not afraid, he balls up and lays limp in the water, awaiting release. When free from the water's grasp, he pokes his head up, screams to Pancho, and then breaks into loud and satisfying laughter, slapping his wings onto the water.

"Qué onda? Are you okay, compa'?"

Dripping wet and heart pounding, Kai is all smiles when he returns to his friend.

"That was awesome. I've never felt anything like that before. The thrill of riding waves is fantastic, even when things don't go so well. There's nothing like it! So much happening and there is so little time to appreciate it. The wave I wiped out on was just as exciting as the one I made. I want more waves; I want bigger waves," he announces to the world.

Kai has been born into the life of surfing. It has grabbed his psyche and won't let go. He believes it has brought him closer to his Creator.

He flies to a tall boulder to dry out, rethinking the entire event and savoring the experience. Another of his dreams for this trip has come true. He thanks Sorté and vows that he will find more waves. Pancho joins him, and they chat with great enthusiasm.

Just on the other side of their rocky perch is a beach similar to the one he just surfed. The side-by-side coves are like identical twins, but there is one big difference. Multitudes of humans are gathered on the northernmost beach while the southern beach is empty.

"Pancho, look at all those people. What are they doing?"

Kai notices that they do not look like a typical beach crowd. Three surfers paddle in the water, but they are not paying attention to the waves. Lifeguards sit in two yellow jeeps and a large number of spectators, some in street clothes, are talking and pointing into the ocean. Many are walking about and taking photos of a huge cucumber shaped object lying in the breaking waves. The two birds lift up from the rocks and fly closer to get a better view. As they bank toward the object, they are immediately shocked by what they see. It has fins and a tail and lies limp in the water. It is a creature, but virtually unrecognizable to the young birds from this distance.

"It's a whale, a dead whale," Kai suddenly hollers as a great sadness wells up inside him.

The mood of the onlookers is also somber and downcast. These humans seem to have a deep admiration and love for the deceased mammal. Several onlookers are crying. The leviathan lies rotting in the sun, just like many millions before her have died.

Kai calls out, "It's a Pacific gray. A female. Something must have gone terribly wrong on her passage back from México. She is one of many on their migration."

"I worry about her chamaco—her little one," Pancho adds empathetically. "Surely, she had a calf. These creatures are fabulous and spend much time in México. Cuando vienen, temenos una fiesta, y cuando se vayan, les deseamos éxito y suerte—everyone celebrates when they come and wishes them well when they go. They are some of México's greatest amigos."

"Why do you think she had a child with her?"

"Por eso viene, that is why they come to México," Pancho answers. "Most females are carrying a calf and give birth in Ojo de Liebre Lagoon, across the Baja Peninsula from where I live. This one appears to be the right size and age to be a mother."

"Gray whales are wonderful and pass Anacapa in both directions," Kai adds. "I love watching their parade each year. They are so peaceful yet so strong. There are fewer whales left, and every death hurts their chances of survival. I really hope her calf was adopted by another. That way, it can live despite the mother's death. Once a powerful and graceful swimmer with a song in her heart, this mama gray lies dead and decaying in man's world. She has lost her essence."

Kai and Pancho are emotionally affected by this death. Whales are one of nature's mythological spirits, and this is indeed a sad day for all. Passing low over the carcass, they dip their wings out of respect. As the water sloshes around her bloated body, it is now easy to see why she died. She is wrapped in a series of heavy ropes and netting

similar to those used by the anchovy fishermen earlier. There are deep gashes in her tough skin wherever the ropes sit on her body.

"Pancho, look at the damage those nets have done. That is beyond cruel," says Kai, his voice rising with anger. "She must have dragged that net for a long time until she tired and eventually drowned. Surely, she fought hard to stay on the surface to protect her young one. This whale was killed by fishermen who neither knew nor cared about the consequences of their actions. Like the sentry with the gun, the killers were probably only concerned about making money."

"Sí, compadre, it is muy triste—extremely sad," Pancho agrees. "Seguro que ésta viene de México. I'm sure the whale is from Mexican waters because in Baja, I see many of these nets. They say fishing nets kill many mammals all over the world."

"Pancho, gray whales are very strong. For her to drag it this far is quite a feat. Oh, I do pray for the little one. Let the child make it safely north. Without the help of others, killer whales and sharks will be its biggest threat. The poor mother, unable to watch out for her loved one, is stripped of dignity and lies here decomposing amongst strangers."

There she lies, rotting like a stolen starfish left in the sun by a careless child. Close to the carcass are four scientific looking humans toting clipboards and taking notes. They crawl about the scene like vultures on roadkill. These humans are investigating the cause of death.

"Typical, they think they know everything. ¿Qué está pasando aquí? Look at them trying to figure out how the whale died," Pancho says with resentment. "Look at the net!" he screams at the people. "It is obvious that careless humans killed this whale with their trash. People are terrible at preventing disasters like this. I have seen enough. Vámonos."

An emotional Kai nods and banks away from the beach. The two of them continue their climb up the coast in silence. Thinking about the complexities of the harbor, the fishermen with guns and now the dead whale, Kai wonders if there is a solution to this never-ending conflict between man and nature.

"Does it need to be this way?" Kai asks Sorté.

I hope not, his inner voice answers back curtly.

Riding a consistent updraft banking off a long series of sandstone bluffs, they make a huge curve around another rock reef fronted by large estate-like homes. Impressed by their size, long driveways, and swimming pools, the birds follow a small coastal road that leads to yet another city. This one has a circular fishing pier, a small rock harbor and is packed with boats, buildings, people, and cars like they have seen elsewhere. At the foot of the pier is a smaller version of the building that housed the battle of the birds. Round like a scallop, it has images of the sea and its inhabitants painted on its three-story walls. Artists' renditions of whales breaching, pelicans flying, and colorful fish swimming are posted for all to see.

"We must look and see what those drawings are about, son muy especiales," says an excited Pancho. "Maybe, we can find some information about la Montaña Mágica aquí."

"Let's hope," Kai responds, feeling cynical as they approach the colorful building.

Landing in front of a large sign that says *Pacific Ocean Palace,* they are surrounded by drawings of seals, dolphins, whales, and schools of fish cruising among hammerhead sharks and jellyfish. The semicircular building is clean and attractive, giving the appearance of a shrine or museum.

"There must be some friendly creatures here. Let's talk with them and find out where we are," Kai proposes. "Maybe they will have directions to the mountain."

Kai pumps twice, gliding around the exterior of the building. Behind the rounded walls, the backside of the building is not covered. There are many different sized pools of crystal-clear water occupied with a variety of sea creatures. Two orcas swim lazily in the largest of the pools, which is surrounded by a seated arena. Many pinnipeds bask and sleep in another pool, dolphins and porpoises in a third and a plethora of other fish, sharks and sea life in still another. Further back, are empty pools hidden from the rest.

Kai settles near one of the roofless ponds surrounded by fake rocks painted partially white, representing either snow or bird poop. Kai is not sure which. Among the occupants are several walruses moaning in the very back of the pool plus a number of seals and sea lions. Nearby, he sees a smaller pool containing a bale of sea turtles, a smack of jellyfish, and a shiver of white-tipped sharks. The smallest of the pools is a sea otter environment complete with a slide.

"Pancho, this is cool. It looks like a place where humans are kind to sea life. Maybe it is a hospital or a sanctuary of some type."

When Pancho lands, he is face to face with four sea lions. The most curious of them pokes her head up very close to him. She is most attractive with stiff, strong whiskers.

"Hello," she says, brandishing bright, white teeth and a big smile. A dozen other seals swim in the tank or bask in afternoon sun.

"Hello," Kai and Pancho answer in unison.

"I am so happy for your visit," she says excitedly. "Can you stay a while? I have not had the opportunity to talk to an outsider for a long time, and I have so much to discuss. On occasion, a crazy sea gull flies in for a visit, but it is hard to believe anything he says. He is a bit contaminated in the head. Too much human food, I think. His stories keep getting wilder, and make absolutely no sense." She scuttles up closer to the two birds.

"How is it on the outside these days? Has much changed? Tell me all about the sea and tides. Are there still great migrations? I have heard so much about all of this, and I would love to know more. Is the ocean water clear and clean? Are the fish bountiful?" Her questions are coming like an endless set of waves breaking on the beach.

"I would love to catch my own fish someday. I would love to dive deep into the ocean far enough to see where blackness sets in. There are so many things I want to experience, but it is not possible. Here, the water is always full of sunlight, and we are spoon-fed by people. Can we hurry? I have so much to talk about!" she exclaims, repeating herself.

The booby wants to answer her many questions, but she doesn't stop talking.

"It is so confining here. An aquarium is not a bad place. We are safe, and the food is good, plus the medical benefits are the best. But who cares? The tradeoff is that we give up our freedom to roam the open oceans. I will never get to migrate and feel the change of seasons or the varying sea temperatures. I hear the ocean is vast and mysterious. I have never lived in the wild nor caught my own food. Our human keepers do everything for us. I have not experienced fear, pain, or worry. Life is simple. I am like a house pet. My human family comes daily with healthy food, and they make sure I am clean and illness free. All the humans ask is that I remain confined and entertain human folk. Thousands of people come here to wonder at us. We have little in common with the visitors, yet they seem to feel like we are one."

She wriggles up the rock to get closer to her newly discovered friends.

"How come humans come here to see what life in the ocean is like?" she asks with a bemused look on her face. "Think about it. People come to a cement palace full of treated water and captive animals to see what ocean life is like. This place is nothing like the real oceans, yet people get so excited when they see us. They cannot wait to be splashed by whales as if that makes them kindred souls to sea creatures."

She is now so close that Kai can smell fish on her breath.

"Our water is filtrated and a perfect temperature. This helps us live longer and look prettier. If only I could swim in real saltwater and follow true ocean currents. Instead, I sit here barking and smiling at people in the arena. The day will never come that a big bull fights over me, or I have to dodge sharks looking for their next meal."

Pancho looks around.

"So, this place is not as it seems? My friend and I thought it was to honor you and your way of life. Like a museum or something."

"This is another example of mankind doing something for himself at the expense of nature," she responds. "It appears as if they are trying to protect us and the natural world. But that is not the case. All of us at *Pacific Ocean Palace* live in enclosures, as if no other world exists. We eat, sleep, and swim on a schedule, all for the benefit of tourists. Day in and day out, our lives are very repetitive. I wish I could fly off with you. We have been robbed of our right to live in our god-given marine habitat."

Kai notices the reflection of the sun against the sea lion's gray brown skin. How beautiful she is, from her mustached face, down through her body, and all the way to her fins. She is free from scars and barnacles as if she were bred for beauty, not by natural selection. She looks very different from the sea lions on Anacapa.

As her discourse ebbs, Kai and Pancho have a chance to tell her about their travels and adventures. For most of the afternoon, they discuss a myriad of topics. At times, they are interrupted by other sea lions. They talk about the changing oceans, its inhabitants, and the many threats from man, as well as the life of these captives. Kai explains that natural inhabitants are in a fight against a changing environment. Mankind and the Endless City are usurping all that used to be natural; leaving so many without a habitat.

Other pinnipeds, many of them lifers, contribute further to the conversation. They agree that it is difficult to believe life on the outside is so hard. They are so used to this entitled lifestyle that they take it for granted. Many of them express dissatisfaction with the way they have been treated by humans, from their capture to their imprisonment. There is an underlying resentment among most of them. They all dream about being free.

The pretty sea lion relays the story of how she was captured.

"As a pup, I was taken from San Clemente Island. I will never forget the horrors of that day. The kidnappers came in a sleek and powerful boat with huge letters on it: *P.O.P. ENVIRONMENTAL SERVICES.* Disguised as ecologically sensitive fishermen, they captured whatever sea creatures they wanted. After they found me, I was placed aboard with many others. I was terrified. Separated from my folks, I was brought here to live out the rest of my life. Those fishermen were from *Pacific Ocean Palace,* one of the world's most recognized aquariums. When I arrived, I was told over and over that 'Visitors think we are happy at *P.O.P.*' But I, like so many others, resent the fact that my opportunity to experience the type of life that nature gave me was taken away.

"My new friends schooled me in how-to live-in captivity," she continues. "As I grew older, I realized that in an aquarium I must ignore many of my inborn instincts. Here, we are simply actors. We are told to be docile and friendly. We must never show any aggression. If one of us hurts or shocks a visitor, he or she is restricted, sold or just disappears. We must forget the outside world and never discuss family or independence. If I follow the rules, humans bring me plenty of food, take care of my health, and provide for all my needs."

Two of the front-line performers join in.

"We are trained to be clowns," one shares. "Each performance, we clap our flippers, swim about, jumping and splashing the humans to make them laugh. We are taught to target the kids because if the youngsters are laughing and happy, their parents are pleased and spend more money. This is good for *P.O.P.*, and we get rewarded with extra fish." It quickly became clear that *Pacific Ocean Palace* is as much a business as it is an ecologically oriented refuge.

An old and more cynical sea lion disagrees. He would rather be here than out at sea.

"There are no surprises here," he states without passion. "Just look at us with our glossy skin, healthy teeth, and peaceful ways. This is an easy life for a pinniped. We are spoiled, and we should appreciate all they do for us."

"All the other species are pampered, too," a third lion chimes in. "Whales and dolphins are the most popular, so they get the most attention. It seems like they talk to the humans. Even all those miscellaneous fish in the main fishbowl are performers. Sharks are taught how to swim in circles and look menacing. Schools of fish purposely dive in fear when approached by a hammerhead, creating drama. It is a well-kept secret that by the time the visitors are allowed in, all the species have already been well fed."

"Even the knifefish is a victim of this kind of fraud," the first lion interjects. "This electrified eel is kept in a glass enclosure where visiting children are allowed to pound on the window, creating tension and fear inside. An 'electrical shock assessment gauge,' attached to the window shows how much energy the eel is expelling. The more he is agitated, the higher the gauge goes. A kind of 'ring the bell' carnival game, but in this case using a living creature."

"The last thing the aquarium wants to show," says the second lion, "is what life is really like in the oceans. They avoid bloody feeding frenzies and prohibit hostility amongst the various species. Deaths, births, or any other event that may dirty our perfect water, mar the glass windows, or scare or offend the visitors takes place in the back pools."

"In aquariums, life in the ocean looks like what people want it to be," the first lion interjects. "It is not how it really is. All jellyfish must be long and elegant, sharks huge and mysterious, otters cute and fuzzy, whales docile and regal, and so forth and so on. The best of each species, according to their coloration, personalities, and demeanor are chosen for the center pools. Others become second stringers or are sold to other aquariums with lesser reputations. This aquarium must look perfect so that humans believe all is fine with regard to the real oceans. We all know this is not the case."

"Thankfully," the old sea lion adds, "those of us here have been given an opportunity to live the easy life. Our pool is for display and for us to put on a good show. We provide a glimpse of the wild, but in reality, all the landlocked yearn for is a taste of the sea. Visitors get a look at an ocean that does not exist. We are like lions and tigers in a zoo, living life behind a mask. Mankind imagines a relationship based on fantasy, then sells it to naïve people who do not understand the realities of the natural world."

Turning around awkwardly, the old sea lion dives back into his forever home. The younger sea lion jumps off the rock and returns to her foster family, and the two performers go back to practicing their tricks.

Kai and Pancho, who have not said much, are stunned. They did not realize the extent to which man makes nature work.

"Pancho, it seems very few of the inhabitants are happy. They are under great pressures and restrictions while living a false life."

Disillusioned, the two birds rise and fly westward, hollering loudly

"Thank you!...¡Gracias!" to the sea lions.

Kai is deep in thought, troubled by the lives of so many in the Endless City.

"I cannot wait to tell my father," he tells Pancho. "He always told me that living among mankind was hard. I did not expect the bad feelings to be so widespread. These animals are essentially captured into a life of labor that they did not choose. Their freedom was taken away. It sounds like the form of slavery that Master B talked about in history class. Let's head north," Kai declares.

Miles into this leg of their journey, they see a large city perched atop a sandstone cliff. There is a long pier jutting out from the shoreline topped with a carnival and fun zone. Many of the human visitors are gamers, who are oblivious to the beauty and complexities of the surrounding ocean. Tired from the long day, Kai and Pancho find a comfy spot below the pier and snuggle up. Under a blanket of moist marine air, they fall into a deep and healing sleep.

FIFTEEN

Life is life's greatest gift.
Guard the life of another creature as you would your own
because it is your own. On life's scale of values,
the smallest is no less precious to the creature
who owns it than the largest.

– Lloyd Biggle Jr.

Awakened by a loud beeping sound attached to a noisy trash truck, the birds begin stretching in preparation for the next leg of their trip.

"Let's make this a day to remember," Kai proposes, his words oozing with optimism. "We do not know how far the Magical Mountain is, but we must be getting close. We will keep moving north until we find it. Today will be the day that we land at the Magical Mountain and drink its holy water," he declares. "It is out there, and we will find it!"

"But amigo, the more I see of this city, me extrañan más mi puebla y mi Estrella, I miss my home more. It seems this place is very complicated. My life in Baja is simple. Estoy confundido, y no sé qué hacer—I am confused and don't know what to do. I really want to see the importance of this land and, por supuesto, of course, the Magical Mountain, but so far, all of this land is muy extraño and uninviting. Compa', I'm thinking about giving up this search and going home."

"Pancho, you can't," interrupts Kai. "Not yet, anyway. Let's find the mountain and then, I agree, we will both go. I am tiring of the humans' way of life, too, but once we breathe the fresh air and drink the healthy water of the Magical Mountain, it will be worth it. Today, we fly hard and far. The Endless City has taken too much of our time, and what we think is important is not here. What we are looking for is elsewhere. We started out to find the mountain, and that is what we are going to do. You must come with me." The pelican's voice is strong, and his eyes full of determination. "So, let's get to the mountain, and then we can return to our families and friends as soon as possible."

Both birds let their frustration and exhaustion speak. They have been pushing hard ever since they left home, and after what has recently happened, both are overwhelmed by all the negativity. Having flown so far in such a short period of time with little sleep, they are nearly beyond their limits. What weighs on them most is missing those they love. This is especially true after seeing the alternative here in the Endless City.

"We will find it today, I promise! The mountain is close. We must keep going!" Kai says sounding like a gambler telling the dice what to do. "Are you ready, amigo? Vámanos!"

"Bueno, this will be a great day," Pancho responds gathering up his partner's positive energy. "I feel good! The Magical Mountain is ours. Vámonos! Here we come!" Pancho does a booby quick-step jig as he talks, making Kai laugh.

"Let's go! Remember, we fly as one, not as two!"

"Compadres para la vida—friends for life," is the booby's response.

After a quick stop for breakfast near the pier, they continue their trek north. Their flight plan takes them toward a large mountain range north of the Endless City. They agree that this is the likely place for the Magical Mountain. They hug the coastline until late morning. The landscape beneath them begins to open up. There are fewer streets and less people out and about. Life along the coast is more rural and less congested. Only the homes along the oceanfront hug up next to each other. Most of the houses inland are separated by open space. Huge freeways have given way to smaller highways paralleling the beach with country roads going east into valleys and canyons.

"We need to pick one of these inland routes," Kai declares. "Hopefully, the one we choose will take us where we want to go."

"Not yet. Ésperate, compadre, it is too soon to go inland," Pancho counters confidently. "Let's stay near the ocean a little longer. I have a feeling."

Wing to wing, they continue up the coast. It is very beautiful. There are many triangular reefs and rocky beaches. Most of the coves are different from the sandy beaches to the south.

As they glide around an outcropping of rocks, they see a large bird off in the distance. It looks like a huge gull. They agree that he'll be able to give them directions. As they approach the bird, he looks less and less like a sea gull. He is much bigger with striking colors. His wingspan is expansive with knife-like wing-tips.

"This must be the legendary Ancient Mariner of sea birds," says an excited Kai.

Another one of his history lessons is about to come alive. It is an albatross. In the avian world, an albatross is renowned for its life at sea. Albatrosses are the oldest symbol of the sea. These hardy birds fly over vast oceans, returning to land only to mate. Going back to the beginning of time, the albatross was mythical in history. Not even Poseidon is more famous than the albatross. When mankind first sailed the seas claiming lands, gaining treasure and killing whales, the albatross was considered a spiritual guardian of the ocean. Sailors believed it was bad luck to kill one.

This albatross's dark body, black outer feathers and gray-brown back, contrasts with his white vest and rump. Black eye patches and lightly streaked inner wings give the appearance of a handsome film star in a tuxedo.

Kai remembers more of his lessons. Albatrosses are known to travel long distances, mate for life, and of the twenty-two species throughout the world, unfortunately *all* are endangered. Albatrosses have run head on into the encroachment of mankind, and because of their passive nature, they are also victims of man.

"It is sad that these birds are losing their battle to survive. Pancho, just think, if it is bad luck to kill one of these birds, then mankind has accumulated a lot of misfortune by killing millions over time. If they end up killing off the entire species, life on Earth for man will be at great risk. This wise bird will surely know about the mountain. Albatrosses are known to be smart and trusting."

They hurry toward the majestic bird.

"Hello," Kai calls out several times.

The albatross ignores him.

Perplexed by this snub, Kai circles. The albatross is flying at a very slow speed for a bird his size. The closer Kai gets, it becomes obvious that something is terribly wrong. He looks very old. His flying is hiccupping and erratic. He lacks the grace and beauty for which albatrosses are known. The bird rises and drops as if fighting winds of a fierce storm even though the air is calm. He mutters to himself and yells to nobody. To Kai and Pancho, the albatross appears feeble and sick.

"Fishy, fishy, where are you? Fishy, fishy. I am hungry. Fishy, fishy, where are you?" he sings like a small child repeating a nursery rhyme. He repeats this over and over as he flies.

His voice is high and squeaky, not befitting his handsome looks. The gray around his neck gives him an air of sophistication and a look of wisdom, despite his bizarre behavior.

Pancho gets closer and asks respectfully, "Señor, have you lost something?"

"Can we assist you? Are you okay?" adds Kai.

The albatross looks at the booby and asks, "Where are the fishes?" This seems an odd response for such a veteran sea bird. It confirms their suspicions that something is definitely wrong. Pancho moves in closer to see if the albatross might be hurt, but sees no indication of injury.

This behavior is not appropriate for such a smart and brave bird, Kai's inner voice thinks. He flies right up to the albatross, so they are looking eyeball to eyeball and exchange thoughts without speaking. The old bird's eyes are cloudy, dark, and distant; his face reflects a deep sadness. He is so skinny that his rib cage shows through his feathers. He may not have eaten for a long while, making it very clear to Kai that this old albatross needs help.

"Maybe he is blind," Kai whispers to Pancho. "That could explain his strange behavior." The bird's nonsensical mumbling continues. "We must try to help him."

It is obvious by his appearance that the albatross has not preened in a very long time. Some of his main feathers are out of place, and there is a bald spot on his neck. A crop of crooked primary feathers on his left wing is probably the cause for his erratic flight. The remainder of his body is worn and dusted with dirt and dried salt. This makes no sense for a bird that doesn't visit land very often. He looks more like a tramp than the greatest of all the sea birds. This neglect plus his anti-social behavior are indicators that he may be getting ready to die.

The albatross repeats, "Fishy, fishy, where, oh where are the fishies?"

Pancho looks to Kai in a silent plea for support. They want to help, but neither is sure what to do.

"Are you okay?" Kai asks again. "How can we help you?"

"We saw a small ball of fish one cove to the south if you are hungry," Pancho offers as he points to the location.

The albatross says nothing. Then as if coming out of a coma, he turns, looks directly at them and starts talking.

"I have lost Lanikai, and I have no one. It has been a long time since I have seen my family. I miss them so very much," he says in desperation.

"How can we help?" interjects Kai. "I will be happy to fish for you. Do you need help getting food?"

He ignores this offer of kindness.

"I cannot find my loved ones. Have you seen my family? My mate is missing, and I have lost all my children. When I was younger, I met Lanikai, the most beautiful of all the albatrosses. We made life-long vows of love. We traveled the oceans. She is so wonderful, so soft, yet so strong. She loves me, as much as I her. In the early spring, after our travels, we always return to our favorite nesting spot where we hatch our youngsters.

"Our home is deep in the Pacific on the island of Kaua'i. Our nest was on the front lawn near a large African tulip tree at the home of our friends Herb and Nancy. They were such wonderful people. They shared everything with us. Herb and Nancy talked to us, protected us, and treated us like part of their 'ohana. We were all one big happy family, and life was good. Wherever we went, they were always happy when we returned to their home. Their love and aloha always welcomed us back.

"Year after year, we came back to nest on the Garden Island. Lanikai and I were a great pair, and over the years, we had many fledglings together. I never imagined anything could ever change."

As he tells the story, he drops and rises in the air. It is impossible for him to relax, much like a soldier recovering from fierce combat. Kai and Pancho are baffled, never having seen this behavior.

"We had seven chicks, and each grew to adulthood. They have all found mates and moved on. One by one, they stopped coming back to Kaua'i. 'Too many people,' they said. I believe that they now mate on a small unoccupied island further to the west. I have not seen them for years, nor do I know their whereabouts. They have either been killed or continue to nest elsewhere. We have not been together as a family for many seasons. But it was okay because I always had Lanikai. We returned to Herb and Nancy's every year for ten years. Our love was as strong as the great blue whales that swam beneath us."

The albatross continued, sadly, "Three seasons ago, we arrived outside the house and started preparing a nest. Everything had changed. The house was no longer a pleasant green, but it had been painted bright yellow. Several of our favorite trees and bushes were cut down—the landscape was completely different. The smell of chemicals all over the grounds replaced the natural odors we were used to. Two of our favorite nesting holes were covered with decorative rocks. Worst of all, Herb and Nancy did not come out to greet us. Other birds told us they had simply gotten too old and were moved back to the Endless City by their family. The home had been sold, and the new owners were not friendly. They rearranged many things, making us feel unwelcome, so we found a new nesting ground nearer the golf course.

"Last season, I arrived early, built a fine nest and waited for Lanikai. I waited and I waited, but she didn't come. I became so worried that I could not sleep. That entire season came and went. Many times, I searched the island looking for her. I asked friends, but they knew nothing. I flew every day, hoping that she would turn up. In the end, I could not find my beloved. Lanikai had disappeared, and I nested alone. I was devastated."

As the birds continue chatting, it becomes obvious how sad and lonely the albatross is. Pancho and Kai look at each other, realizing that the despondent bird needs someone to talk to. So, they stay and listen attentively to their newest friend.

"This year, I arrived early once again. It has been over a year since I last saw my beloved. I was full of expectations that this year would be different. Lanikai will show, and all will be fine. Life will be like it used to be, I told myself. I found a perfect location under the cover of an expansive koa tree. Our nest was next to a cliff with a fabulous view of the ocean. I asked all the other birds to look out for Lanikai. I settled down to wait for her, but she was late once again. After a moon cycle passed, I flew about looking for her. For the second straight season, she did not show. Other albatrosses gave birth to handsome young chicks. I was forced to nest alone, yet again. Sadly, I accepted the fact that my wonderful Lanikai is gone forever. She must be lost and is probably dead. So many others had gone through the pain of losing a loved one, but I never thought it would happen to me. I left that place and started flying, and I have been flying ever since. I am old, broken, and now alone. I have lost touch with my children and grandchildren, but most painfully, I have lost the love of my life. There is no reason to live without her."

Tears cloud his eyes, showing a depth of sorrow Pancho has never seen before.

"I want my Lanikai back," he shouts to the sky. "I want to see my children once again." He drops his head and begins to sob. Kai and Pancho feel his pain and are not sure what to do.

"I am so broken-hearted, I can no longer be the great navigator I once was. Nor can I fish anymore or fly long distances. LOOK AT ME! I am alone and lost somewhere near the Endless City. I HATE the Endless City. Since leaving Hawai'i, I have wandered, lost in a cursed depression with no hope for the future. I am running out of strength. Without a loving family, there is no reason for living."

"There must be some way we can help?" Kai asks again.

Before Pancho or Kai can finish their attempt to help, the big bird disengages and quickly strokes off, despite the crutch of his tattered wing. Dumbfounded, they watch him head toward the cove mumbling, "fishy, fishy." It is evident to both Kai and Pancho that he will never be the same dynamic bird he once was. He has given up hope and is preparing for death.

Neither bird has experienced the death of someone they love, nor do they understand the depth of the loss the old bird is feeling. Reflecting on their own families and their girlfriends, they feel empathy for this poor bird.

This encounter, more than any other so far, changes their perspective about what is important in life. Loved ones fill your soul and make life meaningful, more so than adventures and selfish personal accomplishments. The old albatross appears smaller and smaller as he flies in erratic circles and passes right over the bait ball without stopping. He is truly a lost soul.

Kai shakes his head, returning to the reality of their situation. He hollers to Pancho, "Let's get going. We still have a long way and we must find someone to give us directions to the Magical Mountain. We must keep moving."

Using only logic as their guide, they turn eastward and into the hillsides. The valley beneath them is full of manzanita trees and canyons that are lined with pines. Believing the Magical Mountain is nowhere near the sea, they aim east toward a set of gray-blue mountains far off in the distance. Even in the daylight, they are once again navigating blind. Flying wing to wing, they ready for a challenging flight. Everything will once again be unfamiliar, and there will be no ocean.

Immediately, the temperature rises, and the air becomes drier. A small dust devil dances down a dry creek bed below, welcoming them inland. All signs of the Endless City have vanished. Beneath them is wide open terrain, virtually uninhabited by humans. Some of the steep hillsides are covered with only brush but are quite pretty in their starkness. Even the sparse human dwellings have a rural feel. The occasional home is surrounded by open space and blends with the woodlands. Playing the rolling hills like giant swells, the two of them surf up the hillsides and down into the valleys.

Unlike the ocean, these monster waves are stationary and do not move. There is not much of a thrill because the tall trees prevent them from gaining much speed. Kai, however, figures out a way to slalom among the trees, which adds to the difficulty and increases the fun. They must use quick turns to dodge the many branches they come upon.

They surf the mountains for much of the afternoon, eventually cresting a tall mountain peak. Just on the other side, their positive attitudes evaporate in an instant. The scene in front of them is hellish.

It is a world literally devoid of anything living. All plant life and vegetation has been burned, leaving everything bleak and blackened. Landscape from the valley to the mountaintop has been destroyed or permanently scarred by what must have been a huge fire. Dead or dying trees with grotesquely burned limbs stand like guardians to the underworld. Ashen black rules the day. Ground cover has morphed from pine needles and brush to a lighter-than-air dust. Soot paints the ground. Rocks and skeletons of dead trees are colored a gruesome black. Poison air has replaced oxygen and hangs over the valley like the devil's breath. Homes appear as if they were beaten down by huge hammers, then lit with matches. Lonely chimneys and plumbing pipes stand like wounded warriors on a battlefield. The entire scene is heartbreaking, as if they have just entered a horrible nightmare.

As he tries to talk, Pancho chokes from a severe dryness in his throat.

"¿Qué pasó aquí? This is very bad, there must have been a huge fire," he wheezes.

"Great harm has come to all who lived here, both human and

natural. This is an unbelievable tragedy," Kai agrees. "I have never seen such annihilation."

Neither one of them come from an area prone to this type of wildfire, so the scene and the reality of its destruction are hard to grasp. Rising high into the air to escape a toxic dust swirl, they are met by eight turkey vultures circling above a corpse of a burnt deer. Having nothing in common with these scavengers, Pancho motions Kai to keep a safe distance. Looking off into the distance, there is nothing but destruction covering hillside after hillside with no signs of people, animals, or birds. Only an eerie silence exists.

"Let's look for survivors. I want to find out how this happened. We surely can be of help to someone," Kai suggests.

Floating high above, like the vultures, they are searching for anything that may still be alive.

"Pancho, I see nothing but ash and cinders. Where has everything gone?" he asks, interrupted by a chesty cough. Ash drifts around them like a light snow on a windless day.

"The fire was recent," he calls to Pancho. "Keep looking. Someone is nearby and in trouble. I know it."

They take respite upon a large blackened boulder. As they land, small puffs of ash rise from their feet. Pancho lets out a moan.

"¡Ay! Compadre, look at my feet. They are not blue anymore. They are covered with this death powder. No me gusta este lugar— está de la fregada. I don't like this place, Kai. Me siento muy mal aquí—I feel really bad. Let's get out of here."

"Wait a minute, Pancho," Kai stalls, his mind working overtime. "The amount of destruction here looks like what I learned about in school. The savants described the aftermath of war where huge bombs were used. These bombs are made to lay waste to everything. When evil fights evil, nature loses, and lives are lost. I hope this is not part of a war. If so, we could be in even greater danger."

The loneliness and despair of the situation is broken by a swarm of buzzing insects. They startle Kai, making him jump from his perch.

He lands leg deep in the black and grey residue. As he hops away, a rooster-tail of ash follows.

"¿Á dónde vas?" asks Pancho nervously.

"I'm going to look for anybody who has survived this disaster. Maybe, we can be of some help," Kai repeats.

"It has been too long. No podemos hacer nada. We can't do anything. Let's leave now," Pancho pleads, fearing that they are surrounded by death and evil spirits. He tries to convince his partner that searching for others is madness. "We will only get sick from all this waste. What about the Magical Mountain?"

Kai hops down onto an asphalt street where there are the remains of human homes. The structures are now ghostly piles of pipes and other metal objects. On the corner is a burnt and dusted street sign that says *Buena Vista*.

"Buena Vista...not so much anymore," Pancho murmurs, muffling a cough.

Kai's instincts tell him there is someone nearby.

"Hello," he yells. "Anyone out there? Hello?"

Kai flaps his wings, glides a few yards, and lands at the base of a fallen tree next to one of the smoldering homesites. The bottom third of the tree did not burn. Kai is optimistic that someone might be hiding there.

"Who is there?" demands Pancho.

From a dirty hole in the tree trunk, a small round-faced bird with yellow eyes emerges. Like a kid in a Halloween costume, her brown and white features are covered with a coat of charcoal dust, making her appear old. She stands and swivels her head to see who is calling.

"Hello, are you okay?" asks Kai. "The two of us are traveling, and we came upon this wasteland. Are you hurt? Is there anything we can do to help?"

"Hello, back at you," she says with as much cheer as she can muster. "You are odd looking birds, and I do not recognize you. There's nothing left. Why are you here?" she asks emerging from the

tree, facing the two sea birds. "My name is Fancy, I am a spotted owl."

"Oh, I love owls!" Kai exclaims.

"I used to live over there," she points toward a ravaged and blackened ridge. "That is where my nest was. It was twenty feet up an old coastal chaparral."

From where they stand, the ridge line looks like a line of dark, mutant trees standing on volcanic rock.

"I've been staying here until I move to the new growth area. Living this close to the ground mimics my cousin, the burrowing owl. I must look for family and friends. But I have found no one. They are probably all dead. It's time I admit the truth and abandon this futile search. I need to fly north and start my new life. The number of spotted owls is very low, so it will be hard to find a new mate."

"Where did this fire come from?" asks a curious Kai. "There is so much destruction. Was this a war? I cannot imagine fires come here that often."

"No, it was not a war. But fires come much more often these days now that there is the Endless City. My ancestors dealt with lightning strike fires, but the open spaces around them were more plentiful, allowing birds and animals to move about easily and re-establish their lives. Besides, fires came as nature's way to cleanse the forests. All of that has changed since the coming of man. These days, there is very little open land left for relocation, and forests have become part of the human settlements."

The owl shakes her body, ejecting a cloud of dust and ash from her feathers, exposing her true colors.

"Today, the Endless City surrounds us in almost every direction. There are simply fewer places to settle after a fire. If that is not bad enough, these large cities create more houses, and with more houses come more people, and with more people come more fires," she says with a tinge of resentment in her voice.

"More people demand more wood, so more trees are cut down, and the forests shrink. This leaves more space for more buildings and homes for humans. But the worst part of all of this massive growth is that it brings more careless people to start fires. Human-caused fires are more common than lightning fires. Electrical poles can start fires, and some really sick people wait for strong desert winds and purposely start fires. They like to watch fires burn. Can you imagine that?"

"¿Mande? ¡No manches! No way! Fires hurt people as well as nature," an angry Pancho responds. "Did people start this fire?"

"Yes, a group of young humans were playing and partying in the woods. They built a warming fire and lost control of it. The rest is history. Open fires are forbidden in this forest, but these people did not care. They were cold, so selfishly they built a fire. The flames raged on for three days and have smoldered for another two. It finally died with the help of an offseason rainstorm. My home was destroyed, and my family has probably been killed."

The look on the owl's face quickly shifts from victim to advocate.

"I have lived here all my life. When I was young, my family lived in a tree just one hill over. Before these houses were built, this was a quiet area. People did not live nearby. One day when I was a teenager, men came to mark trees. Later, others came in trucks and in two seasons changed the face of our grove forever. First, they cut a road all the way to our stand of trees. Then, they used noisy chainsaws to clear out trees that were in their way. They were followed by large bulldozers. When the men with their machines came over that ridge," she pointed to a rise in the hillside, "we knew we were in danger. Like prehistoric monsters, these machines took enormous bites out of the Earth. Insects, worms, rodents, snails, frogs, birds, squirrels, foxes, skunks, snakes, possums, raccoons, bear, deer, trees, scrub brush, and bushes were all displaced with each truckload of soil that was removed. Bite by bite, the old inhabitants disappeared, and a vibrant natural community was ended. My father moved three times during his life due to the encroachment of man.

"Needless to say, I was livid. These men and machines showed up and took away everything important to me. This is where I grew up, and this is where I belong. But in the world of man, nature is not important. Man's own special needs and comforts come first. I will always remember my daddy's words, 'Sweetie, one day, you will learn.' And today is that day.

"When humans came to tear down our neighborhood, I was so angry. I left our tree and went straight to the man driving the big machine. I buzzed his head and dropped dirt on him. Then, I screeched, but nothing worked. In fact, the men were amused and mocked me. On the second day, a man in the huge yellow tractor was pushing dirt straight for our home. I flew to the machine, back-peddled in front of the driver and made my dissatisfaction known. The driver, seeing me just feet in front of him, stopped the machine and called his friends over. I had their attention, so I dropped to the ground in front of the monstrous machine. I defiantly held my wings high in the air."

The owl stops, raises her wings, and stands perfectly still as if the machine was still there.

"Workmen sucked on small burning sticks as they watched my tirade. I believe they were impressed by my pluck. Watching me for a few minutes as I stood brave and strong, I believed I had stopped them. In my heart, I sang a song of victory.

"*Rad da tat, rad da tat, rad da tat, rad da tat,*" the huge Deere tractor answered back. The diesel engine revved up, sending rounded puffs of black smoke skyward. I stood firm. The driver ground the huge machine in gear, and it slowly moved forward. It moved closer and closer but I stood firm. We were in a game of chicken; the monster tractor and me. Nature versus the machine. Me versus mankind.

"This went on for several minutes until my father came to my side and forced me to leave. He knew my life was in danger. The tractor operator, seeing his opportunity, quickly accelerated and pushed a large wave of dirt toward our home. With a loud thump, the machine's blade hit our beloved tree. It shook violently in protest.

"We left home that night and moved to the top of the next ridge. Within a very short period of time, our original tree, nest, and home had completely disappeared. It angers me to this day. All I wanted was to enjoy my life in a natural forest like the ones my ancestors enjoyed. As an owlet, I can still remember how the old life was lived." A smile breaks through on her angelic face.

"We are sorry for your loss," offers Kai. "It seems so sad that you are not allowed to live the life that you want. Is there anything we can do for you? It seems everywhere we go, there are stories like yours, and it saddens us greatly. Please accept our support and wishes for a better future."

Pancho is uncomfortable with this line of discussion and wants to move on to the important question. He knows the sooner they accomplish their goal, the sooner he will be able to go back to México. Tired of the constant disappointment in the Endless City, he has had enough.

"Let me ask you a question," says Pancho, "Owls are very wise, and hopefully you can explain something to us."

"Of course," Fancy answers.

"We are in search of the Magical Mountain? They say it is the spiritual home for all animals and birds, a place of harmony. Are you aware of such a place?"

Fancy's expression quickly changes.

"The Magical Mountain, of course. We all have heard stories about it. My grandfather told me that young birds from far, far away flew to the Magical Mountain. It was the rite of passage to adulthood. It was the greatest of all destinations for young birds across the mainland."

"That is where we are going!" interrupts Kai. "That is why we are here! Please tell us where it is."

"Granddad said that his generation was the last to fly there because the mountain had lost its magic. He spoke about it being overpowered by man and his technology. That is when the spirits left."

"Have you been there?" Kai asks. "Do you know that for a fact?"

"Oh no. No one goes there but scavengers. It is home to only vultures, pigeons, and crows."

"Do you know where it is?"

"Not exactly, but my father said that it was a half day's flight to the north. Like my grandfather, my father told me not to go there."

"That way?" Kai asks pointing to some distant mountains.

"Yes."

"Do you think we could get there by nightfall?"

"I don't know. I need to fly in a different direction, otherwise I would show you the way. There have been no recent fires where I am heading, but it is time to move on and start my new life. My days here are over."

Fancy, looking past the sea birds in the direction of her next home, gives them a masked smile and says, "Goodbye."

"Goodbye, Fancy," they answer in unison. "Thank you."

"Que le vaya bien," adds Pancho, wishing her well on her journey.

"Go with safety," she says in return, rising from the fallen tree trunk and banking to the northeast with dreams of green woodlands in her mind.

Kai and Pancho turn to each other with anticipation and then fly due north.

SIXTEEN

Regard not your past failures nor successes.
All the past is equally a failure and a success;
it is a success in as much as it offers you the present opportunity.

– Henry David Thoreau

Kai and Pancho hope this will be the final day of their search for the Magical Mountain as they pass over the coastal range heading north. The intensity of the Endless City is now far behind them. The terrain beneath them gets prettier as they fly.

"Keep going, we will find it," insists a determined Kai. "I feel it in my heart. Can you imagine what it will be like to taste perfect water and see its heavenly beauty? Oh, I hope it will be like the stories we were told."

"The mystery will soon unfold, compadre. No te preocupas. Don't worry; just keep flying."

Below them, an explosion of golden poppies blankets a large elevation of the mountains. Thanks to the recent rain, a boulevard of small bouquets shows them the way north. These unspoiled mountains and their wildflowers are untouched by the millions of wilderness-starved people trapped in the Endless City. For a short time, mankind is absent.

"This is what it must have looked like long before the Endless City was built. It is as beautiful as I had thought," Kai shares. "Our Mother of Nature does not forget anything, right down to the bugs and the blossoms."

A distant mountain range looms over a vast valley, giving them hope.

"That is the Magical Mountain," Kai speculates with increasing exhilaration.

"I'm getting hungry. What do we do for food?" a more practical Pancho says, changing the subject. "No ocean, no agua—no fish. Could be a problem for us. What will we eat?"

"One day's hunger is worth getting to the mountain," Kai responds. "We have sacrificed so much to get this far. We can't get sidetracked by an empty stomach. Pancho, we are going to the greatest place on Earth. It will provide whatever we need. Just be patient and think about the pure food, healthy water, and the soothing rest that awaits us."

"Y si no existe, if it does not exist like they say, ¿qué hacemos? What will we do?" asks Pancho earnestly.

"If there is no food, we become scavengers like all those others we have met. We will eat enough human food to get us back to the ocean. All will be fine," Kai says, trying to convince himself as well as Pancho. "Look over there!" Kai shouts excitedly.

In the distance is a small house fronting a huge expanse of open land. Standing next to a gate are two humans dressed in brown uniforms with big round hats.

"Pancho, those are the people who watch over us on Anacapa. They are park rangers, and it's their job to protect nature. Maybe they are doing the same here. This is good. This place will be safe. Let's find someone who lives here to show us the way to the mountain."

They drop low to the ground and glide toward the gate. One of the guards spots them right away. She immediately puts black viewers to her eyes and watches as the birds pass. She talks excitedly to the other. Sea birds this far from the ocean surprise the rangers. She yells for others to come look. Soon, four officials come together to speculate about these two ocean dwellers and why they are such a great distance from the sea; one all the way from México. They have never seen this before. Just beyond the rangers is a wooden sign that reads *Sespe Condor Sanctuary*. Kai is familiar with the word sanctuary because Anacapa is also a sanctuary.

"We are very lucky to have found this place. Let's look around. We can rest up for the final leg of our trip," he says to Pancho.

"Rest? ¡Compadre, no descansamos, no resting! ¡Seguimos! We'll keep going! This is not the Magical Mountain that we seek. We must find it today, so we can be back at the ocean by tomorrow and start our trip home. I don't want to delay any longer."

"Pancho, we are not sure how far the mountain is. Seeing how we're this close, let's make sure that we know what we are doing and don't get lost."

"Confianza, compadre. Trust me, I will not let us get lost," Pancho answers without hesitation.

Once they pass beyond the gatehouse, a wide area lined with hills, arroyos, and grain-colored grass opens up. Recently blossomed wildflowers are sprinkled among clusters of oak trees and old chaparrals. Huge granite boulders are scattered about haphazardly as if placed by children. The scene reflects the natural perfection of early California as captured by many master artists. The two friends perch on a high ridge to scout the area. In the distance, large mountains loom prominently. Both birds are growing anxious. They believe these peaks will surely be home to their Magical Mountain.

"That is our destination!" Kai shouts.

They are suddenly engulfed by a large shadow coming from something passing overhead, momentarily blocking the sunlight. Looking skyward, they see a large outline of some type of airplane. But it is silent, like a glider. From its motions, it becomes obvious that it is an extremely large bird.

"Look at how big he is. ¡Mira sus alas! Look at those wings! So much bigger than yours or mine. The tips of his wings are shaped like human fingers."

Squinting into the lowering sun, they look for more details about its identity, but the size of the bird is overwhelming.

"Have you ever witnessed anything like that? asks Kai, with a combination of awe and trepidation.

After a close examination, Pancho responds.

"This is not like our golden eagles in México. Son grandes, pero—how do you say?—más aerodinamizados—they are more streamlined. This one has the look of a vulture but is much bigger than vultures I've seen. And see how easily he flies!"

Impressed by the bird's long glide, they watch him casually work the various drafts of wind, then float across the valley and land on an opposing ridge in only a few flaps. He settles on a large rock, stretches into a standing position, and then turns his large head to stare at the two sea birds.

"Kai, let's talk to this hombre. He will surely know of the Magical

Mountain," suggests Pancho. "From his appearance, he's been here mucho tiempo, a long time. The montaña cannot be that far away. ¡Órale!" says Pancho, his enthusiasm now running high.

"Whoa, Pancho, are you sure that's a good idea?" interrupts Kai. "Check out how he's staring at us. What if he is a large raptor and wants to kill us to feed his family? He's big enough that both of us could be fed to his little ones or simply eaten by him. I think it is dangerous to trust such a large bird. I do not want to satisfy his hunger instead of my own."

"I disagree, Kai. Look at his body and remember how he flew. He's a scavenger, a very big buzzard. Mira esa cabeza. Check out that head. He definitely is not a hunter. He eats dead things. Confianza," says Pancho. "Todo va a estar bien. Trust me, we will be okay," he says, trying to convince his cautious friend. "Seguro, nos va a ayudar. Surely, he will help us find what we are looking for."

Kai agrees reluctantly, trusting his partner once again. They drop off the ridge together and fly cautiously toward the big bird. Kai flies several body lengths behind Pancho in case they run into any trouble. The closer they get, the bigger and scarier the buzzard looks. There are no feathers from his neck up. His large head is a reddish-orange with what looks like reptilian skin. He has beady eyes, fat jowls, and a sharp can opener-shaped beak. A ring of white feathers encircles his neck like a tight-fitting lei. His body is bigger than a turkey and covered with black plumage that looks like an oversized trench coat. Two very large, elongated feet extend from beneath the dark plumage. On each foot is an oversized middle claw to tear apart dead bodies.

"Señor vulture, we are not from here and need your help," Pancho says, landing several yards from the bird. Kai stays back a few feet, ready for a quick getaway in case this conversation does not go well.

"I am a condor, if you must know," the bird says sternly, turning his large body to face his unexpected guests. His dark eyes, set deep in his scarlet head, examine the two misplaced aviators. The initial silence is powerful and lasts for what seems like forever. This bird is definitely a mystery. Being birds of the sea, they know nothing about this unique creature. Neither sea bird can recall hearing any stories about condors.

"I am a condor," he repeats. "You are sea birds, are you not?" he asks politely, in a deep voice. "I recognize the pelican, but who are you with the oddly-colored feet? I have no idea who you might be.

"What brings you to the condor sanctuary? We get very few natural visitors. Condors are dangerously close to extinction and we have learned not to trust anybody. Our tourists are mostly human. They come in cars and walk about with black viewing devices. People come to see us because there are so few of us left. They want to be able to say they were one of the last to see a condor. We condors are losing our fight to survive," he says with both sorrow and scorn.

"Condors are left alone for the most part. Other birds do not want to chat with us and do not come to the sanctuary because of the cloud of melancholy we live under. We are dying off. Most think we are ugly and scary and do not trust us," he continues without taking a breath. "Maybe two hundred of us are left, and this sanctuary is one of the few places we are safe. We need a large area to live, and there is very little open land left anymore. So, we are forced to stay in our sanctuary. It is best not to wander off the reservation because, with all the people and buildings, there is a good chance of getting hunted or attacked. I have no offspring and no spouse, so upon my death, it will be the end of my family line that dates back to long before modern man. All my descendants are dead. I am the last of a royal line."

"We are honored to meet you, Mr. Condor," says Kai. "We are not here to disturb you. We simply need directions."

The big bird is disappointed by this response. He hoped they might want to be friends and talk for a while. With each day, the condor grows older and lonelier. The only thing he has left is to die and join the many before him.

Unfortunately, these travelers do not want to talk. They are on a timeline, and the sun will be setting soon. But the condor has much to say about the outside world. Once considered a mystical and spiritual bird by early man, he is now restricted to the sanctuary. This does not give him the opportunity to talk to outsiders. *Sespe Condor Sanctuary* is quite small compared to the days when his ancestors roamed the entire southern mainland all the way to México. In those days, they were able to fly free. Even though there are no walls confining him, his fear of what may happen off the reservation is as powerful as steel bars. He hides from modern life at *Sespe*.

"My friend and I are on a long journey to find a very special place," Kai says to the condor. "Our forefathers used to come to a mountain nearby that was known as the Magical Mountain. We are here to find it. Can you help us?" Kai's feathers puff when he says the words Magical Mountain, as if it was an award being pinned to his chest. "We've been told that it is nearby."

"We want to get there by sunset, so we can be closer to god," interrupts Pancho. "We need to keep moving."

The condor is baffled by his young visitors' request.

"Let me get this straight," he says, wanting to make sure he understands. "You two have flown an incredibly long distance to find a Magical Mountain?"

"Sí," responds Pancho enthusiastically.

The condor leans back in silence and momentarily goes into deep thought. Slowly, he breaks into a low chortle that grows into a deep chuckle, and ends up as a booming laugh from deep within his belly. The condor laughs so loud that he begins to wobble. He wraps his huge wings around his jiggling belly, causing him to suddenly sit down.

"Magical Mountain is closer to god," he repeats and goes off again, this time in a wild guffaw.

Kai is confused and feels belittled by the bird's reaction.

"What's so funny?" he asks the condor, glancing over at Pancho.

"Un momento, Señor Condor," Pancho interjects. "Why are you laughing at us?"

The hysterical condor takes a minute to wind down like a toy top losing momentum. Looking back at the two of them, he explains.

"I am sorry to have to tell you this, but I think you may want to turn around and go home."

"Turn around? NO WAY!" shouts Kai angrily.

"Okay, then I will do as you ask. I will tell you how to get to the Magical Mountain. Or at least, what's left of it."

"Bueno," says Pancho. "We have come a long way, and sí, we are very serious."

The condor settles down, clears his throat, and tells them the story of the Magical Mountain.

"I'm not going to tell you the long version because it is a waste of time. Birds have come to the Magical Mountain for centuries. It was very near here. For eons, my ancestors were the gatekeepers for the mountain. Condors thrived by feeding off all the magic that existed. Visitors came from all parts of the world just so they could experience the wonders of the mountain. Local birds, regional birds, and migrating birds from as far away as South America, Russia, and Alaska came to be 'one with god,' just as you have said. They came for the medicinal water and spiritual healing. It was a coming-of-age journey for many young birds like yourselves."

The condor stands, then paces back and forth on the boulder. His mind is exploding with personal memories that he has not visited in many years. He seldom speaks about the mountain anymore because the new generation shows no interest in its story.

"I was told that it was an exciting place, but I never got a chance to experience it. By the time I was old enough, it was in decay and condors were in grave danger. Many stories of the mountain have been passed down, but they are slowly dying just like the mountain. Mankind killed the magic long ago. Didn't anyone else tell you this?" he asks incredulously.

Kai thinks about his father, his savants, and Auntie Aphrodite. He recalls, plain as day, the look of frustration on his father's face each time he brought up the subject.

"Please, believe me son," his father had pleaded, "the Magical Mountain is no more."

Now this condor, who lives close to the mountain, is confirming all that his father said. The condor leans closer to the two of them. Beak to beak, eye to eye, his fearsome face begins to show some tenderness. He continues his story.

"Grizzly bears were in charge of security. Eagles taught courage to young birds, and all residents of the mountain worked together to perpetuate the ways of the Mother of Nature. Creatures of all kinds came for the mountain's positive power. Birds and butterflies staged long migrations to experience its magic. Every year, four distinctive seasons came and went, setting into motion the perfect sequence of events that nature wanted to provide for its children. All creatures flourished and grew to great numbers. Legends say the Mother of Nature came to live within the mountain because she was so proud of her family.

"Today, the bears are gone as are almost all of the other animals," continues the condor dejectedly. "In recent years, man built structures around the base of the mountain and created roads all the way to its peak. Today, noisy vehicles transport humans to fancy resorts near the top. This activity has changed life on the mountain forever. This former magical place is now for the exclusive use of humans. Most of the animal life is gone. In a nearby valley, man built a shrine dedicated to the magic of man and his successes. Now, humans, not critters or birds, come from all over the world to worship a different god. You will see all this when you arrive there. It is but a short distance from here. As the crow flies, it's just on the other side of that third ridge line." The condor unwraps one large wing and points to a large snow-covered mountain sitting high above the final ridge.

"Have you been there recently?" asks Kai.

"No, I don't leave my sanctuary. It is unsafe to leave. Last time I left the reservation, I was shot," He holds up his right wing, unveiling a nasty scar on his upper wing. "I was lucky the bullet went clean through. I will never again visit humans. They must come here if they wish to see what's left of our species. It is not a natural world out there anymore. Why do you think they call this a sanctuary? A sanctuary from what? From humans. I remain safe as long as I avoid the outside world. Be very careful," he says, his face lined with a deep trench of sorrow. He turns and stares at the snow-covered mountain in silence as vivid memories flood through his thoughts.

"If we go now, can we get there before dark?" asks Kai. "Should we leave now?"

"You are not my responsibility—you do whatever you want. Aim at the snowy peak, count the ridges and just after the third one you will come upon a valley and a large asphalt road. Fly over that valley, and you will see what you are looking for. You cannot miss it!"

"If the mountain is truly there, then why laugh at our questions?" Kai asks.

"You are looking for a mystical place, are you not?" he says, his red face looking ghoulish once again.

"Sí," answers Pancho.

"I laughed because the god you are looking for left this area a long time ago. Today, a different one runs our lives, one created by people."

"But, but..." Kai stutters. "But there must be some magic left. God does not leave behind empty temples," he says, looking to the condor for support and gets none.

"You go. See for yourselves. You decide whether it is the place you are seeking." The condor's demeanor immediately shifts at this point. He has tried to reason with these youngsters for quite a while. Now, it's time for a nap.

"Let me apologize for my previous rudeness. I am getting on in years, and you two are both so naïve. It has been a very long time since I have laughed. There is no humor in living with extinction. I apologize, but I could not control myself. Laughter feels so good," he says, his red face softening once again. "I greatly appreciate it. Plus, it is nice to hear your perspective. That, too, I need. You remind me that in youth there is optimism. With youthful optimism comes hope, and with hope comes a purpose. For that, I salute you. Have a safe trip to your Magical Mountain. You should easily reach there by sunset."

The condor turns his head into the breeze, raises his enormous wings, gathers up wind like an Aztecan god-bird, and rises slowly upon a thermal. He drops his head and glides gracefully across the canyon toward his lair. They watch him land softly. Without looking back, he slips back into a darkened cave and disappears.

Pancho, ignoring his growling stomach, yells out, "Órale...we must get there before night comes!" He does not want to waste any more time.

Kai mimics the condor and rises up on the same updraft. Pancho follows. They turn east, flying low to avoid an opposing wind. While hunger is a growing concern, they have no conventional food available this far from the sea. Never having been a scavenger, Kai is concerned that human food may not be good for them. As they close in on their destination, anticipation overrides their empty bellies.

"That is exactly like the condor described. We are at the third ridge," exclaims Kai, "we are almost there!"

"No lo entiendo. I don't get it," says Pancho. "There is no mountain close by. Is it just a large valley?"

"Let's find out," Kai cries out with encouragement. He pumps hard, ready to solve this lifelong mystery.

Digging their heads into the breeze, they set their wings into glide position, which helps them pick up speed. Kai thinks of Anacapa, his family, and his speed dives. It seems like a lifetime ago.

Pancho, yells, "¡Sale, vamos! Let's have some fun."

Like two air show performers, they sweep down the hill performing huge crazy eights.

As they get closer to an odd arrangement of structures, they hear unfamiliar noises. It is a confusing mix of screams, screeches, ringing bells, blowing horns, shrieking sirens, and grinding metal. It is everything that they have heard in the Endless City, but now it is all in one place at the same time. This wall of racket and its invisible energy feels like flying into a thick wind. Waves of sound rise and fall like ocean swells, making the birds' flight confusing. The harshness of the noise starts inside the human encampment and spreads out far beyond its walls. As they approach, they are flying not only against the wind, but are also confronted with the thrusting power and thunderous sounds emanating from the area. It's as if they are swimming through turbulent surf with the sea pushing them in the opposite direction.

The young birds are overwhelmed by the sight of flashing lights and throbbing colors encircled by a vast sea of cars. The intensity of the scene reminds them of the Battle of the Birds, only bigger, noisier, and out in the open.

"The condor must have been wrong. This cannot be the Magical Mountain!" screams Kai above the clatter. "It must be further."

Pancho makes a hard right to gain altitude as Kai follows. Flying over hundreds of parked cars, they come face-to-face with a gigantic sign with pulsating letters. They hover in the air as they watch the letters spell out *M-A-G-I-C M-O-U-N-T-A-I-N* over and over again.

"This is it, this is *Magic Mountain*," Kai screams, trying to be heard over the many layers of mechanical din. Disappointment does not have time to register. The young pelican goes straight to anger.

"This is wrong—so, so wrong, and in so many ways," he yells to Pancho, who strains to hear him.

Guilt, who has been absent for most of this journey, appears and says, "I told you so!"

The mass of writhing humanity beneath them is beyond comprehension. It looks to be the invention of a madman. People by the thousands are riding and twirling around on mechanical devices, swinging in the air and diving down man-made waterfalls. Large crowds of humans line up at the front gates. Throngs of people are everywhere. There is no mountain, no natural streams or trees, and no wildlife. Everything of nature has been removed and has been replaced with plastic, cement, and steel, all created from the minds of man. It is a tribute to human ingenuity and their progress, innovation and greed.

The many machines of *Magic Mountain* crank, rise, fall, spin, drive, twist, and whirl. Giant wheels turn at incredible velocities, and despite his love for speed, it all makes Kai very uncomfortable. The overall scene is one of organized pandemonium as screeching customers ride *Tsunami*, dodging great walls of water, *Galactic Starfighter*, the black belt of roller coasters, *Shrieks and Terrors*, a free-falling machine that must be stomach-sickening, and *Gargantua*, a twisting and turning speed monster among many others designed to thrill and scare the people.

Trying to separate themselves from all of the negative energy rising into the air, Kai dives under it, and Pancho follows. They alight upon the roof of one of the food wagons. Sitting there speechless, they observe the chaos surrounding them. Hordes of tourists wait in long lines to get burgers, hot dogs, potatoes, and sodas. There are even longer lines waiting to ride the wailing machines. A beautiful young child notices the birds. She is the only one observing nature within this insane asylum. Her parents do not pay any attention to her efforts to get them to look. She eventually smiles and waves as her parents grab her hand and walk her off toward the rides.

"This cannot be our Magical Mountain," mumbles Kai with a deep sense of dismay.

"The condor said it was a mountain of a different god. ¿Recuerdo?" Pancho reminds his friend. "This is very different, ¿no?"

"Yes, but this is not even a mountain," Kai objects, his ire obvious. "It is a valley surrounded by mountains! It is not magical, it is mechanical! It is not holy, it is ungodly! There is nothing here even close to the legend. How could this be allowed to happen?"

Noise from the park continues to roll over them with the energy of a twelve-foot shore break. The closer they get to the rides, the louder the mechanical noise and the human screams. And the louder the screams, the longer the lines. None of this makes sense to either of them.

"Amazing..." Kai mutters. Despite all the warnings, he is simply not ready for this radical of a departure from the natural world. His dream has been shattered into thousands of little shards of glass. And worse yet, it feels as if he is walking on them.

Behind them are three large green trash receptacles. Four overweight pigeons are rummaging through and eating the human leftovers. Pancho bumps Kai.

"Aquí, hay comida. There's food here. Por lo menos, at least, let's eat."

Together, they hop off the trailer and land with the pigeons.

"Pardon me, can we eat with you? We are very hungry," Pancho questions politely.

The pigeons ignore him. They are fighting each other over discarded bags of fried potatoes and have no time for manners. Kai sees another such bag and reaches over with his cumbersome beak. Finally, he will taste human food. Whatever these things are, they look like dead caterpillars. Once he manages to snap one, he tosses it in the air and lands it in his gular. Up against the inner skin of his pouch, it feels slimy and foreign. He swallows the fry, but there is no discernible taste.

"These are horrible," he complains. "How can anybody eat this?"

Pancho is having less trouble because the shape of his beak is better suited for human food. He has found some frijoles and rice, two of his favorite human foods in Mulejé. He chows down.

"This is not so bad. I will pretend I'm back in México."

They sit atop a heap of trash and discarded food. It smells terrible, and it is demeaning for them to eat what humans do not want. Kai chokes down a few more bites of food, but nothing about it is desirable.

"Hey pigeon, what do you know about the Magical Mountain?"

"You mean *Magic Mountain*?" answers the male.

"No, I mean the Magical Mountain, the mountain for birds and animals."

"Hey, Rosa, do you know what he's talking about," he shouts to his friend with a mouthful of food and ketchup in the crease of her mouth.

"He is probably referring to the old legend of la Montaña Magical."

"¿Hablas español?" Pancho asks, excited that she might know Spanish.

"I pick up some here and there. There is a lot of Spanish spoken aquí," Rosa answers.

"Cuéntenos de la Montaña Magical. Tell us about the Magical Mountain," says the booby.

"I must tell you in English. Mi español no es muy buena. I only speak bits and pieces. The story of la Montaña Magical is that before mankind invaded this area, the montaña was nature's shrine to itself. It was a supreme example of how the natural world ruled in a logical and fair fashion. Nature was not arbitrary nor did life favor one species over any other. The mountain existed when the number of people on Earth was like a single grain of sand on a vast beach. Humans did not affect life; they were simply another member of the natural world. But the montaña disappeared many generations ago as nature lost out to mankind's overpopulation."

"If that's true, then what is this place?" Kai asks, sweeping his wing toward the madness in front of them.

"Much later, this was built, and man's technological magic was put on display. It has grown in size and spread around the world," she says. "For us, this is the best place to scavenge for food. We do not need to hunt anymore; we just eat leftovers. We come when we're hungry and leave full. Day in and day out. It makes life quite easy."

Looking back over the park, Kai asks for the last time, "So, god does not live here anymore?"

A short distance from the trash bin, *Superman, Escape from Krypton* launches a carload of screaming humans. With their hands raised, they speed along at a rate faster than Kai's last speed dive. The clamor from the screamers plus the grinding sounds of the metallic wheels drown out the question. This intervention acts as a divine message for Kai. Certainly, all of god's magic has left, and he clearly does not live in *Magic Mountain.*

Kai spits out the two fries he is eating and, without another word, takes off. The noise from the park feels like a strong wind on his back. Pancho bids farewell to the pigeons and quickly follows. Both fly in silence back toward the ridge. They are alone in their thoughts as they head into darkness. It is a very long way to the ocean.

SEVENTEEN

Life is a series of waves to be embraced and overcome.

– Danny Meyer

Kai and Pancho are anxious to put distance between themselves and the overwhelming disappointment of *Magic Mountain*. They have no idea how far they are from the ocean, but they are determined not to give up. All they think about is getting back to their beloved Pacific Ocean.

A powerful depression has shrouded Kai's once optimistic thoughts. He struggles with the memory of the mechanical mountain and how insulting it is to the ways of nature. The extent of disrespect that man has shown feels like the ultimate betrayal. To make matters worse, both birds are experiencing upset stomachs. The human scraps and junk food did not agree with them. Extreme hunger and the failure to find the Magical Mountain of their dreams adds to their mental misery. The best medicine is to get back to the healing sea.

They fly hard throughout the night. The coastal mountain range is dark and undulating with much of the terrain uninhabited. The small moon does not help in this difficult journey. Trees, electrical wires, and ridge tops are all potential hazards that may pop out of the darkness if the birds do not concentrate one hundred percent. All of this is taxing on their exhausted minds.

As the night wears on, the need for sleep attacks them unmercifully. They discuss strategies, direction, and precautions for the flight, and when those fail, it is only meaningless babble that keeps them awake. During lulls in conversation, they imagine what they will do when they get home.

With the coming dawn, the sun spreads light from beneath the eastern horizon. Inspired by a lightening sky, the birds sense that they will be out of the mountains soon. Kai smells the moist, thick air that signals the approaching ocean. He fantasizes about feeling the cool, clean ocean water and eating lots of fresh fish.

"Let's have breakfast first thing. I want to savor every single anchovy," Kai says with a big grin on his face.

"Agree. My belly hurts from those pinche frijoles. I would not make a good scavenger. Fresh fish is definitely my thing."

The sun's corona peeks over a low spot in the eastern mountains as they summit the last ridge before the ocean. Floating toward the deep blue sea, a band of wispy clouds stretching over the ocean give the flyers a last needed hit of adrenaline. Looking at each other, they break into wild and therapeutic laughter.

This joy sparks a special memory from deep in Kai's mind. It is of a celebration chant from the heart of Anacapa culture. Overflowing with thanksgiving, he sings the ballad about coming home after a long flight.

Going home, going home, my wonderful home,
we no longer need to be alone.
As we follow our beloved sea,
Anacapa's irresistible beauty pulls at me.
Flying with ancestors keeps our families alive,
sharing our love and building our pride.
Exuberant children born full of life
alongside elders ever weakening yet wise,
parents view us through excited eyes.
Anacapa sings and Anacapa cries,
birds are wed to the sea without choice,
frolicking in spiritual waters and unified in voice.
They're flying high above the sea,
accompanied by a song and a soft breeze.
Anacapa loves and Anacapa cares,
providing us a home with the purest of air.
Pacific waves crash upon rugged shores
talking in both whispers and roars.
We fly the oceans with nature's guiding hand,
no longer needing just the land.
Anacapa, home to me.
It is all I ever want to see.

Kai recalls gatherings where the entire colony sings songs. This one he remembers fondly because it talks about coming home. His whole life, he envisioned a day when he would be returning from some great adventure. Looking to the expansive blue horizon, Kai and Pancho are the happiest they have been since the day they met. Reunited with a salty sea, serene beaches, and clean ocean air, they skim the surface. Wing to wing, they drag their feet across the water. Their jokes and banter bounce across the sea surface like skipping stones. In a matter of minutes, they spot a bait ball. Landing smack in the center of the fish, they start eating. The fish, sent by Sorté, welcome her two children back.

"Tomamos una siesta, compadre, estoy muy cansado—I'm very tired. Let's rest before we go south. The flight will be long and hard. After everything we've been through, we deserve a rest."

Kai agrees. Floating on the surface, they relax into the consistent movement of the sea. The ocean sounds comfort them like a lullaby, and within minutes, they are both sound asleep.

Kai is the first to awake. Loud and repeating snapping sounds chase the comfort from his groggy mind. The source of the noise comes from large waves pounding on a nearby beach. They have drifted precariously close to shore. The swells have grown considerably in size and strength, showing up as a wicked shore break.

"Wake up, Pancho!" he hollers, "the waves are getting really big. We must be careful." He pumps quickly and gains air. "Let's head south. We need to get back to the cave."

Pancho nods and rises from the water, readying for the long flight.

They fly low, only inches from the crashing swells. Kai is pumped by the sounds of the breaking surf.

"Let's find some surfers, so I can surf alongside them," he declares like a teenage grom, who rides his bike to the beach with surfboard in hand. Side by side, they cruise the coastline. The surf varies from beach to beach and cove to cove. What is apparent is that the further south they go, the wave action increases.

Pancho is familiar with this type of energy and has seen it many times in México.

"Vienen desde muy lejos. These waves have come far. They must be part of a really big storm, un huracán to the south."

"This is the kind of swell surfers dream about," Kai yells over the roar of the exploding surf. The sheer strength of the waves gets Kai's blood flowing. He is jacked up with a combination of fear and excitement, similar to his feelings just before a dive.

"Today will be the day to answer the ultimate question. Am I ready for this kind of challenge? Can I accept the ocean's call and her dangers? I must keep a cool head," he says.

And remember to treat the ocean with the respect it deserves. Surely, human surfers are celebrating this day up and down the coast, Kai's inner voice reminds him. *Let's join them. Somewhere, we will find the perfect wave.*

As Pancho scans the west for signs of the storm, he sees a line of distant clouds sitting atop an expanse of watery billows. The pre-storm scene is calm but doesn't disguise the tremendous amount of energy moving in their direction.

"This storm must be from Baja and moving norte," Pancho states with authority. "Huracanes normally don't make it this far," he explains just before a massive wave hits the rocks and showers him in white water.

Banking left, they settle on the soft sand of a nearby cove. Watching nature's show, it becomes obvious that this beach has a deep-water footprint. Waves rise really fast and then slam onto the sand with tremendous power. Each one sounds like a cannon shot and sends seismic vibrations racing up the beach.

A family of humans share the shoreline with the birds. Their three young children are more fascinated by Pancho and Kai than they are with the ocean's display of power. This pleases both the birds and their father who knows the dangers of waves like this. Keeping his youngsters safe, the father herds them away from the dangerous water.

They run up the beach to join another group after taking pictures of the birds.

"Let's go," Kai demands. "We need to find a different kind of wave. One that stands up longer and does not have the guillotine-like lips of these monsters. These waves are not surfable."

Kai studies the waves at each subsequent cove as they trek on. There is tremendous energy everywhere they go. He is looking for a break similar to the one near the pier. They have yet to see any surfers because of the rocky shoreline and steep waves. Several swimmers with artificial fins catch some extremely dangerous looking waves. They freefall out of the face, travel a short distance, then disappear into rolling white water and get spit out the back side. One bodysurfer is clobbered by the force of the wave, leaving him in knee-high water to be struck by a second powerful wave.

"These are way too fast. I will get hurt," Kai tells himself after gliding just feet above the impact zone. "The strength of these waves is incredible, and there is no way these will work. Vámonos, it is time!" Kai says with a strong gringo accent.

"¿Mande? Time for what?" asks Pancho, stretching his neck, so he can hear above the crashing waves.

"This swell is rising. Your Mexican hurricane is sending me a wave to ride today. It is out there somewhere. My golden opportunity is rolling toward us and I need to find it. Keep flying!"

Pancho turns to the crashing waves and watches as yet another explodes on the sand.

"¡No manches, güey! Are you kidding me, dude? You cannot be talking about surfing today. Son como un toro loco—these waves are strong, like an angry bull!"

"I know, I know," the pelican answers. "We will keep going until we find the right place. I have asked Sorté to send me the perfect wave and she will do so. This is something I have been dreaming about the entire trip."

"But, compa', think about it—this is storm surf. Está gacho—

really nasty—tiene mucho poder."

"Well, my friend, there are three things I must do to be ready to ride these waves," Kai explains.

"¿Neta?"

"Number one, I must overcome any fear I have of the ocean, the wave, or its power. I must attack the wave with the same energy that it is delivering to me. I must be one with the wave."

"Compadre, I do not doubt your bravery—tienes coraje," responds Pancho. "Pero, you have never surfed waves this big. ¿Por qué intentarlo ahora? Why try it now?"

"Dude, I have swell-surfed miles of the ocean. I have studied and observed humans whenever possible. I surfed small waves near the pier. I studied these waves, their curls, and their motions. The only difference is that the waves today are many times more powerful. As a wave increases in size exponentially, my inner spirit must grow with it. A surfer's skills and bravery must increase at the same rate the wave increases in size and strength. I am equal to the wave and I will have my day in the water!"

Pancho is not sure if he believes all of this, but Kai is his best buddy, so he will be at his side no matter what.

"Pancho, remember the day I got pitched and landed in the white water. I felt the potential strength of the ocean that day. The ocean always wins, no matter what. Today, I just need to be smarter, stronger and braver."

"Órale. ¿Cuál es numero dos?"

"Number two, I must use my experience and style. Drawing upon my speed dives, and the danger involved with them, will give me the experience I need. I've also developed a style and determination that will get me through this tough day of surfing. My last dive was as fast as hurricane winds. Mi amigo, these are hurricane level waves. I will trade one for the other."

"¿Y tres?"

"Number three, is the most important. Timing is everything. Right place, right time equals success. Wrong place, wrong time equals disaster. Surfers who are too early or too late get into trouble. The ones who enter at the precise place and time make waves. These surfers are always stoked and exhilarated; they are the happiest people in the world! I am confident that I can confront this seaside beast and outrun it."

"¿Enfrentarte a la bestia? Confront the beast—that's all?" asks Pancho sarcastically. There is a moment of silence. But he relents, and with an excited, "Sí, güey. ¡A huevo!" Pancho agrees to go.

Kai's mind is made up. He will go deep when he finds his wave and that will be TODAY! Rising from the sand, they head south in search of Kai's perfect wave. The coastline is bursting with energy. They fly next to a barrage of waves hitting rocks, creating a loud noise and blowing cascading fountains of water high into the sky. The onslaught of big waves, as consistent and powerful as these is a rare event.

Pancho flies close to his friend for support.

"Compadre, estoy contigo. I'm your wing man. No te pasa nada— I'll help you if needed."

"Muchas gracias," Kai answers.

After almost an hour, they come to a large bay with many surfers. Kai surveys it from above. He scrutinizes the breaking waves and their riders. As the rolling swells approach, they hit a large bending reef that creates long, perfectly shaped waves. The surf stands up and becomes double-overhead faces pushing all the way to shore. Surfers excitedly race across the bay. Some go all the way to the distant fishing pier in hopes of catching the ultimate ride.

On the beach, Kai notices a small creek, a rocky bluff, and a parking lot full of cars. This is the staging area for the surfers. Large boulders are painted with graffiti. One rock exclaims in blue paint, *Bu is Ours! Go Home!* Another says, *Locals Only!* On the base of the pier is a sign with letters *M-A-L-I-B-U*. "Malibu," a Chumash Indian word meaning "surf sounds loudly," is one of the best-known surf spots in the world. Rarely does it get this big, but when it does, it is a sacred spot, and today's surf is larger and louder than ever.

Surfers bunch up at an outside break which seems to be the best spot to get the longest rides. Each ride starts with one surfer, but others often poach one another. There are as many as five people on some of the smaller waves.

Kai flies below the height of the waves. He sees a spot where he wants to take off.

Right place, right time, he thinks. *Because these waves are so big, they will be very fast. I need to fly fast and glide hard in order to stay ahead of the lip. I must attack these waves just as if I were diving.*

Dread shows up but says nothing, so it looks like he is onboard.

Above the action, Pancho flies in circles, watching and learning. The intensity of the scene is intimidating. He is fascinated by the power, uproar, and energy these waves and surfers create. The waves look as if they were crafted by an invisible artist. Anticipating long rides, the surfers get more intense as they wait. They paddle about fiercely and yell among each other in an effort to establish a priority.

Pancho yells support to his partner, "No te preocupas. Don't worry, I'm watching. Yo te cubro las espaldas. I got your back, güey!"

The booby stays high to keep out of the way but is only several yards from the pack. Pancho will be Kai's jet ski in case something goes wrong.

Kai nods. His eyes darken due to the adrenaline pumping through his body. He flips around, flies back shoulder high to the surfers, and glides into the prime spot. Kai is now one of them and can feel the competition. Watching the horizon, Kai meditates and gets into synch with the sea.

"These waves are coming from a hurricane blowing in the south," he tells himself. "My wave is out there and will come very soon."

Several swells hit the reef and heighten into big beautiful waves. As they pass under him, each one has at least one surfer locked onto it. Kai's heartrate quickens as his thoughts race in his head. But internally, he is purposely maintaining a calm demeanor. This is not the time to lose composure. Utilizing a one-two pump while circling, he positions himself just inside the takeoff spot. Each surfer looks to be half the size of the wave's face. As each one drops into the wave, they instantly pick up speed and cut toward a perfect line. The crowd seems to work with each other. Occasionally, an uninvited surfer jumps on the wave which does not go over peacefully with the other surfers. But the ocean is providing wave after wave after wave. There are plenty for everyone.

The surfers ignore Kai, not realizing he is in the line-up. A young boy paddles in circles, trying to get to the right place at the right time. The boy, with encouragement from others, catches a ten-footer and screams as he drops into place. The sight of so many scrambling for these waves is emblazoned into Kai's mind. He realizes that this is a once-in-a-lifetime opportunity. He must take advantage of it.

This is it. It is time, his inner voice instructs him. Dread remains silent. Kai inches closer to the face of a very large wave. It is so symmetrical, it looks almost unnatural. Malibu waves are said to be sculpted by a special god.

Surfer after surfer takes off and disappears, hidden behind the backside of the wave. After four consecutive waves, Kai has worked himself into the perfect spot. He has gained a special bond with the ocean, and he loves the feeling. It is intimate and loving, yet challenging and daunting. Anxiously, he watches two more surfers take off. His eyes clear, his mind keen, and his muscles taut, Kai glances up at Pancho and gives him the nod. Pancho acknowledges by dropping down to get into a watchdog position. Pancho will be outside the breaking wave, so he will be able to follow his buddy all the way.

Kai fails on his first attempt. Two surfers are right on top of him as he starts his entry.

"Remember, right time, right place," he chants.

Swinging back around, he gets into position for the next wave. This time he chooses a spot a few feet deeper. Surfers are starting to notice this brash bird and wonder what he is doing. This is the distraction that Kai needs.

"Here you go, Pops! This one is for you!" he screams to his father on Anacapa.

The wave jacks up to fourteen feet, larger than any before. Kai's eyes widen, his heart races as he drops down the wall, tucks his wing, and turns right. A couple of hard flaps puts him in a primo position. One of the most experienced surfers of the group drops into the wave with him. They are staggered perfectly. The surfer speeds down the huge face and cuts right, just like the pelican. Kai leans into the wave and draws his right wing tighter. Moving his tail feathers, he is able to position himself just above the accelerating surfer. The pelican's secondary feathers keep him in line, his primary feathers maintain speed, and his tail feathers move him up and down, just as he has been practicing. He tucks his head like in a speed dive to avoid wind resistance.

The sensation is incredible. Surrounded by nature at its finest, the pressure and power of the wave's rotating water is remarkable. The curl forms and crashes around him. It feels like he is gliding in heaven. Only feet in front of the swirling and rotating barrel, he strains to maintain speed. As the face collapses, the wave growls and pushes air out like a sideways thermal. This blast of wind pushes him forward.

His fellow surfer, only a few feet in front of him, is on a clear-colored board with red rails. His surfing style is smooth and graceful, even on such a large wave. As the wave engulfs the two of them, the human squats mid-board with knees bent and arms out. Kai stays just behind him, wings tucked and tail feathers hard at work. The surfer and the bird blast across the wave, totally coordinated. Spectators and other surfers are astonished by this tandem ride. Kai grins a gritty smile as he watches the human.

Pancho is ecstatic! From his position above, he has an awesome bird's-eye view. Both surfer and bird are hurtling across the wave at exactly the same speed. They are in total control and in sync with one another. Pancho hollers an indiscernible screech, as Kai and the surfer rip the wave.

Surfers down the line stare in stunned silence. It's the biggest wave of the day. Both bird and human are positioned perfectly.

Right time, right place, Kai's inner voice keeps saying.

Other surfers back off, giving them the wave out of respect. People in the water and on the beach watch this famous elder surfer ride a perfect Malibu wave with a pelican. Both Kai and the old surfer feel something epic is taking place. The surfer drags his hand, keeping the bird close. They fall back into the barrel. Kai is almost on top of

the surfer. In a quick glance, the human looks back and their eyes meet.

A deep feeling of respect is shared in that instant. Two species covered in a curl is something that has never happened before. The wave's barrel is a glorious cyan color and large enough to allow Kai to flap his wings. He keeps up with the surfer and stays ahead of the grinding barrel behind him.

Time magically slows down, and Kai is aware of every second. He feels humbled, knowing he is merely a guest of the ocean. The wave is in charge. In an instant, nature could push him violently into the white water to drown. But, at this moment, the swell, the surfer, and Kai are one. They are equals and a common bond is born. The Mother of Nature has gifted Kai with a wonderful trifecta, showing how nature and mankind can work together.

Kai feels deep reverence for nature, accepting all the millions of happenstances leading up to this moment. Inching through the misty barrel at a high rate of speed, he closes in on the watery edge. Holding position, the surfer rises up next to him. They almost collide. The surfer adjusts, making a large sweeping turn and heads back toward the curl. Kai moves up near the lip to give the surfer space. Water from his surfboard slaps the bird in the face. The board with its red rails glides perfectly up the face one more time and then off into space. The surfer jettisons his surfboard as he and his board dance in the air. Both disappear and fall back into the ocean behind the white water.

Kai is now alone. He makes two hard pumps to catch up to the sweet spot, totally in tune with the wave; he is nearing the pier and shoreline. The speed of the wave picks up as the water gets shallower. Unsure as to why the surfer bailed, Kai wants to ride forever but knows he has only a few moments left. It is as if he is flying behind a waterfall, totally covered by water. His wings are fully extended and a smile is pasted on his face. He enters the envied green room for a second time on the same wave. It is hypnotic, soothing and fulfilling.

Kai completely disappears as the crashing sea water surrounds him. Other surfers paddling out yell and whistle at him in acknowledgement of a great ride. He must decide to get out, just like in his diving. He outlasted the surfer, and now the final beach break is closing in on him. This has to be the end.

Kai flaps harder and harder as the wave picks up speed. He goes fast enough to exit the tube just as it explodes into a million droplets of water as a shore break. He pumps and flies over the top of the wave, then ejects himself over the lip much like the surfer. He, too, celebrates by dancing in the air and then falls ungracefully to the surface of the sea. The phrase "one with the ocean" immediately comes into his mind.

There is no time for self-congratulations. There is another wave right behind this one. The longer he lies in the water, the greater the chance of being crushed as it breaks. Mimicking other surfers, he gathers himself and turns to face the oncoming wall of water. The next wave is just as big, arching a ton of water. From his angle, it looks gigantic, angry, and mean. It breaks in a circular explosion, sending a wall of turbulent white water toward him. Caught inside, he dives like a duck, going as deep as he can. Using his feet like swim fins, he paddles underwater in the direction of the horizon. The rumbling mass of water passes overhead like a landslide on its way to the beach.

Keep moving, keep moving! his inner voice screams.

Clashing energy comes at him from all directions. Suddenly, as if grabbed by a giant, he gets pulled into a mammoth chamber of horrors, with water throwing him about as if he were nothing but a feather in a wind storm. Totally helpless, he is pulled and pushed, losing all sense of direction. He is thrown about until finally his back smashes into something hard; a painful sign that he has hit bottom. Tucking into an oblong ball, he rides it out until the wave's grip weakens.

"Okay, get your head on right and aim toward the surface before you drown," he instructs himself calmly.

He pushes off with all his might and heads toward the light. Finally, he breaks through to the sunshine and air, gasping for beloved oxygen. Starved for air, he mistakenly sucks down the sudsy foam created by the water's intense agitation. The irritating brine causes him to choke and cough.

Dread finally speaks up and scolds him, "Get out of the impact zone! Waves are still coming. You will get hurt."

Loosening his wings from the water, he flaps desperately as he runs across the surface. He chants "harder, harder, higher, higher."

Looking over, he sees Pancho low in the air, swooping down, repeating instructions like a frantic swim coach near the finish line, "Get up, hurry, hurry, go, go!"

A third wave is preparing to clobber Kai. At the last possible second, the ocean releases him, and he pops up into the sky, flying wing to wing with Pancho. The wave's powerful lip crashes beneath him, missing him by inches. The booby, a few feet in front, watches the final wave of the set crash. It is an eight-footer, steep and very powerful. Pancho yells encouragement while Kai closes his eyes and pumps hard. He is using nothing but spent adrenaline. Both exhausted and exhilarated, he experiences a high he has never felt before. He glances left to see his pal Pancho who is right there with him, just as he had promised.

"¡Cabrón!" Pancho yells at the top of his lungs. "You were inside the barrel longer than the surfer. You are amazing!" Pancho sits up in the air with his wings held up in the shape of a "V" for victory, unknowingly imitating the old surfer "hi sign."

"Awesome! That was epic!" Kai yells back, borrowing old surfer lingo. "That wave was a giant. The surfer and I bonded like the best of friends. Even the pounding felt good once it was over. I was in control the entire time. I knew what to do, and I didn't panic," he pronounces with pride. "I rode one of the biggest waves of today."

Pancho flies tight little circles around the pelican. Both of them are overjoyed.

"Wait until I tell my dad. He will not believe it. No pelican has ever gotten locked into the curl of a giant wave, and with a great surfer. That is a first!

"Wait Pancho. Come with me, quickly—I must find my surf buddy. Do you know if he paddled back out?"

"Sí, I saw him."

They hustle back to the takeoff spot. The waves are not as big, but still strong and consistent. A larger crowd of surfers has formed, and Kai can hear some yelling back and forth. Some of it is positive but there are also warnings and threats. That big set has made tensions rise. As waves come in, surfers hustle for the next one trying to find the ideal wave.

"There. There he is!" exclaims Kai.

About twenty yards up coast from the scrambling crowd is his buddy sitting calmly on his surfboard. Kai flies straight to him. Pancho follows.

The pelican and the surfer lock eyes once again. The bird circles him twice as the surfer rotates his board to follow. Out of respect, the smiling surfer makes a two fingered sign on his right hand, which looks a little bit like a bird with wings. "Aloha, friends forever," is the simple message he sends. Kai lands close. The surfer has a kind and weathered face, apparently an elder. He takes two paddles toward Kai who jumps on the nose of the board. In an instant, they find the other's essence and soul. In silence, they exchange respect; a bird and a human bond like never before. Kai has entered the world of pelican lore, and it feels really, really good.

In the midst of this sentimental moment, they are distracted by a whining noise overhead. It is a small white plastic copter, acting like the larger copter of the Endless City. The bird and surfer look at the drone. Unbeknownst to both, this unique friendship has been filmed for posterity. A filmmaker and his camera drone shot the entire ride from takeoff through the tube, concluding with this touching reunion. Kai and the surfer will be forever remembered in an upcoming surf movie. The opening scene will feature one of the best surfers in history sharing the perfect wave with an adventuresome pelican. Its title will be *Birds of a Feather Surf Together*.

EIGHTEEN

Since it is not granted us to live long, let us transmit to posterity
some memorial that we have at least lived.

– Pliny the Younger

The birds want to get back to the cave before dark, so they break from the spell of Malibu and start a strong stroke home. The overnight travel and the surfing have left Pancho tired and Kai spent. This next leg of the trip will be grueling. Kai's mind is in overdrive. It is time to start processing the many lessons he has learned since leaving Anacapa. Glancing over his shoulder, he sees Pancho working hard alongside him. Despite the brevity of their relationship, Kai feels a deep sense of security with the booby's presence. The booby has become one of the rarest kind of friends; someone who is trustworthy to the end.

Below them, the open lands have completely disappeared as the two birds fly over the expansive megalopolis with its overwhelming density. The Endless City is jammed with people, all vying for a home near the sea. The birds follow a course just offshore from the long sandy beaches.

As they pass the dual harbors, they begin to recognize some of the piers and cities. Outside the breaking waves, the wind shifts to a perfect angle, pushing them along like two sailboats traveling on a broad reach. It is an effortless flight badly needed by the exhausted travelers. After several hours, they see a high-rise near the cement river indicating they are almost home.

"Just imagine what a tern or albatross must go through. They fly thousands of miles between breeding grounds. We have gone a fraction of that distance, and I am beat," confesses Kai. "How about you?"

"Sí, también estoy cansado. It was very tiring to fly from Baja, pero valió la pena. It was worth it. We have seen so much. It has been a treasure. But I'm done. People make it so hard for us to live with them."

They push on, wings in perfect harmony, as they slip into a deep meditation. Unaware of a massive storm forming on the horizon, they work to get home.

Dark and ominous clouds march steadily toward the Endless City. It represents the front line of Hurricane Linda, which originated in México and is the same storm responsible for the large waves pounding the beaches. Due to *El Niño* conditions and ocean warming, Linda has travelled farther north than is usual for a southern storm. This hurricane follows a river of warm water and makes a rare right-hand turn. It is now heading straight for the mainland in full force.

Kai is the first to notice.

"Pancho, look! What is that? It does not look good."

"Sí, ya viene encima de nosotros—that storm will be on top of us soon."

"We better get back to the cave where it will be safe. We do not want to get stuck in a squall."

Pancho knows and understands large storms.

"Seguro es un huracán. See the color and size of the front? Es grandota—huge, with clouds higher than a mountain range. Keep flying, compadre! We do not want to be in the air when this thing hits."

They pick up their pace, passing an odd-looking platform sitting high above rainbow-colored sea water. The structure consists of small-sized buildings alongside noisy machines, giant hoses, long pipes, cranes, ladders, fences, and generators. Everything is tightly bunched together. Its purpose is to draw crude oil from beneath the ocean floor, so mankind can satisfy his addiction for fuels and transportation. The oil will be transformed into high-powered fuels to feed the many contraptions needed to keep the Endless City running.

The sea birds notice a small oil spill, resulting in a series of loud buzzers and clashing metal. Aboard the derrick, there is a skunk-like odor and toxic rain. Men, running about frantically, work feverishly to recapture the escaping liquid. With the storm approaching, these workers must fix the leak before Linda arrives, or there will truly be a disaster. It is a race against time.

Hit by small, oily droplets, Pancho yells, "¡Sal de aquí, luego luego—get out of here right now! ¡Aguas, güey—watch out! This is no good. It's another pinche human mistake."

They keep moving as blasts of whirling wind announce Linda's arrival. "Linda" means pretty, cute, or lovely in Spanish. She is dressed to impress, wearing a black cloud ensemble with earrings of flashy lightning as she struts confidently across the water. But Linda's attitude is less than beautiful. She is ready to decimate the mainland.

Pancho announces, "Son muy peligrosos—las olas sí vienen de México. These winds come from one of our Mexican storms. They will become ever more dangerous y pegan fuerte—they will pack a punch. We must find the cave pronto, compadre!"

"Roger, Pancho! There, over there. That is our cement river! And there, behind it are the bluffs! The cave is nearby. The wave maker is not far offshore, so hurry!"

The gusts increase in strength with each stroke. Their flight, though short at this point, has become a battle with the wind. Struggling to fly past the canals, they land on the dirt bench and waste no time determining if the cave is still unoccupied. Finding no signs of any inhabitants, Kai and Pancho are confident they are not in any danger either from the storm or four legged predators. They scamper inside to rest in safety,

Taking one last look over the canals, they see Linda looking like a black tidal wave rolling toward them. Lightning strikes are becoming louder and more frequent as the grumbling thunder arrives. The front wall of the storm extends from deep in the south to as far north as Kai can see. There is obvious chaos everywhere it touches. Linda will soon enter a totally unprepared city.

Kai worries about his family and friends on Anacapa Island.

"I hope they are far enough north not to be affected by this storm. Please, Sorté, watch out for all those I love. Keep them safe and tell them not to worry," he whispers in the form of a prayer.

Exhausted and sore from their arduous day of flying, the two birds huddle in the back of the cave and immediately drop into a much-needed sleep.

Kai begins to dream.

The flora is dense. Kai cannot see where he is or where he is going. Vines, trees, bushes, and brush restrict not only his sight but his movement as well. Several of his feathers are stripped from his body, snagged by sharp branches. Imprisoned by the green and shadowed forest, Kai tries to spread his wings and fly away. But the branches and mossy tree trunks smother him. He cannot move. Claustrophobia overtakes his body as he suppresses a strong desire to panic. Kai does not comprehend how anything could survive in such confinement.

Rustling sounds come from deep within the brush. This crackling is followed by a low grumble. It is like an announcement that someone or something out there wants to make its presence known. Seconds later, Kai hears a menacing growl. Whatever it is, it sounds evil. Fear crawls over him as the snapping branches and brush get louder and closer. The growls increase and soon encircle him. They are no longer warning sounds, but promises of harm.

"Trapped, lost, and unable to fly. What are you to do?" Dread screams impatiently.

Pairs of bright red eyes appear from deep within the shadows.

"You, in the jungle. Tell me how to leave, and I will be gone," Kai shouts. "Tell me what to do. I will obey. Where am I, and how did I get here?"

The night spirits ignore this offer of reconciliation. The invisible beings are moving closer, and their hostility is palpable. Panic knocks at the gates of his mounting fear. Kai is afraid that today may be his doomsday—the last day of his life.

Unexpectedly, an all too familiar voice penetrates this fear.

"Kai, do not be afraid. You can make this all go away. I will help you to safety! You are in control of your future," the voice guides him. The words are strong and comforting.

"Be patient, my son. I want you to know that you will be fine."

Piercing through Kai's thoughts of doom, it is the voice of his father reassuring him. His terror recedes as the voice continues, "Kai, I told you that someday in the future you will have to lead the family. It is that time, time to return home. Your mother needs you. Do not let fear stop you. These demons are of your own making. They do not exist. Cast them aside and remain strong. Come home to the family. You are needed.

"Look upon these red eyes as obstacles and mistakes you have made in your life. Your fears make them scarier than they are. They are not monsters. In reality, they are simply stepping-stones to a new and better life. Show the kind of courage and strength you show in your diving and surfing, and you will have no barriers. Seek only opportunities. Your young life is full of open doors. Stop wasting time trying to break down the doors that are closed."

Kai wonders how his father could be with him and know about his surfing adventures.

"Pops, why am I needed? Is there something wrong?"

"Growl back at these demons," his father instructs ignoring his son's question. "Growl back without fear, and they will go away. Now!"

Kai turns to face his red-eyed demons.

"Who are you, and what do you want?" he hollers, looking at the ring of evil spirits encircling him. He picks out the closest pair of glowing eyes. "Grrrrrrrrrr!"

"Louder," his father's voice orders. "Much, much louder."

"GRRRRRRR, GRRRRRRRRRR!" He takes a deep breath and repeats his challenge to the scarlet eyes. "GRRRRRRRR! GRRRRRRRRRRR!"

The eyes begin to vanish and the jungle fades a little.

Kai continues to follow his father's commands, and one by one, the demon eyes disappear, and the forest recedes further. By repeating this over and over and over again, it is not long before all the demons have vanished and he is standing alone, wings spread ready to fly away. He is ready to move forward in his life.

Kai awakens from his slumber just as a spirit light races from the cave. This rare vision comes only in times of great importance. The elders talk of them as messengers from Sorté. The manifestation of this spirit alongside his father's request to return reinforces his decision to go home.

My family needs me. I must get back to Anacapa, his inner voice insists.

Now wide awake, he walks to the entrance of the cave. Outside, the howling winds tell him he cannot leave because Linda has landed in full force. The violent winds now surround the cave. He is stuck for the duration of the storm. The spirit light and his return home will have to wait. He lies back down in the darkness, and Dread dominates his thoughts for the remainder of the night.

In his dream, his father told him, "*Growl at the demons, and they will go away.*" Kai realizes that it is time to take charge of his life. This means understanding his fears. He may not be afraid of speed or big waves, but there are other things that do scare him. What will it be like to grow up and live the life of an adult, caring for others instead of only himself? What happens when he loses those he loves? What about starting a family? All these are deep thoughts for the young pelican trapped in the Endless City.

"Thanks, Pop," he says out loud. "I look forward to seeing you soon. I must tell you everything. I have learned so much, and I love you a lot. We will talk about everything," he promises.

By morning, Linda's beauty is costumed in fury and destruction. She moves over the land slowly, unleashing her wrath with total disregard for the consequences. One hundred mile per hour winds and nonstop torrential rains are pummeling the city. Like a wicked witch in a fairytale, Linda parks over the mainland and stays long enough to destroy as much as she can.

NINETEEN

*A wailing, rushing sound, which shook the walls
as though a giant's hands were on them;
then a hoarse roar, as if the sea had risen;
then such a whirl and tumult that the air seemed mad;
and then, with lengthened howl, the waves of wind swept on.*

– Charles Dickens

By sunrise, the menacing winds batter the coastline like a tsunami breaking on the back of a finless shark. Kai feels a deep and ominous danger.

He shakes his partner.

"Pancho, wake up! Wake up! The storm is here, and it's very strong. We need to be vigilant. Others are in trouble out there. There must be some way we can help."

Pancho rolls over, stands up, and moves toward the entrance of the cave. Rubbing sleep from his eyes, he squints into the morning light and hears an eerie wail wafting through the air. Pancho's sleepy brain is jarred awake when a beach chair flies past at an incredible rate of speed. It is followed by branches, plants, small projectiles, and a plastic trashcan; all now lethal weapons. The rain comes down in sheets. The tide and storm surge have pushed the shoreline all the way to the bluff, crushing small structures and flooding homes.

"Es muy feo, this is very, very bad," Pancho gasps. "The storm is very strong and dangerous. Muy fuerte! Dude, you are right—many will get hurt, or even killed. Quedámosnos aquí. We must stay here, safe in our cave."

Yesterday, Hurricane Linda, spinning counterclockwise, turned on a dime somewhere in the Pacific Ocean. This new course put her strongest winds directly in front of the cave. She is now aiming at the Endless City with her huge eye staring straight at the two birds. Winds, air pressure and water team up to create a monstrous squall, punishing all in its path. The Mother of Nature is angry. She is reminding all of us on Earth that she is the strongest force on the planet. At times like this, mankind's weapons are useless, and he is forced to run, hide, and wait.

Pancho sticks his head out of the cave and receives a hard slap of wind and water.

"¡Híjole! We are near the center," he surmises due the strength of the winds and the odd color of the sky. "With luck, these winds will go down when the eye covers us."

Kai nods and cups his wings over his ears trying to block out the noise.

"Pancho, we must help others," he hollers. "There are fellows out there in the storm without the safety of our earthen walls. This is only going to get worse. If we can, we must let them know they can come here."

"Sí, this is only the beginning," Pancho agrees. "The other half of the storm is still coming."

Throughout the Endless City, humans usually live an entitled lifestyle. But not today. Linda will teach them the realities of life. Kai and Pancho take a deep breath, tuck their wings tight against their bodies, and venture out to the lip of the cave. The eye of the storm has arrived and everything settles down quickly. The sky is ringed with huge clouds and a halo of blue. Winds drop to a near calm. The surrounding eyewalls rise up like monstrous moving cliffs.

The two good Samaritans yell and wave to any fowl who may have survived the first onslaught of the storm. Their voices carry well in the eerie silence.

"Sanctuary, sanctuary. Come! Sanctuary, sanctuary. Come!" they scream, hoping to reach those in trouble.

A fair number respond by hurrying to the bluff. By the time the window of calm closes, there is a menagerie of weary and bedraggled birds in the cave. The group includes a turkey vulture, a pair of red-tailed hawks, a great blue heron, six mallard ducks, two pair of saturated sandpipers, a muddied egret, plus an assortment of sparrows, pigeons, and crows. They all huddle in the center of the cave to warm themselves. All of them are wet, dirty, and wind-blown. Several are injured. But thanks to the efforts of Kai and Pancho, they are now safe.

When the winds return, the group goes through a meet and greet. This is the first time many of them have been this friendly with birds of another species. Most birds stick to their own kind in day-to-day life, but these are extraordinary times. Chatter is brisk and friendly.

Only the red-tailed hawks act aloof. They are predators and feel uncomfortable making friends because the pigeons and sparrows in the cave would be food for the carnivores in any other circumstance. The sparrows are the first to approach the hawks with introductions. Soon, all are talking, thankful for their sanctuary. For the length of their stay, these natural enemies have become friends.

All talk stops when a pitiful "meeooow" rolls in from the cave opening. Backlit by diffused sunlight, the latest visitor asks for admittance. The bevy of birds tense up. Kai and Pancho immediately recognize the newcomer. It is Ted, the old cat, still looking like a sad hobo. He stands quietly at the edge of the cave's entrance. He is a disheveled mess. His coat is soaking wet, matted, and caked in mud. He looks thin and sickly.

"Can I join you? I almost drowned and don't have anywhere to go. The overturned canoe I hid under was blown away. It is scary out there, plus I hate water." He takes a tentative step forward, trying to give the birds a clear message of non-aggression.

"I promise I will not hurt any of you. I have no claws," offering his clawless feet as evidence. "I will not be a nuisance or a liability. I will put no one in any danger. I am alone and frightened. A dry place and your companionship is all I want."

Collectively, the birds glance at each other and then back at the cat. There is no love lost between cats and birds of nature. Feral and house cats are notorious for stealing eggs and killing chicks.

"I vouch for this cat," Kai inserts, stepping forward. "He has proven himself to be non-aggressive. We can trust him. He was abandoned by his humans and is now living meal to meal on bugs, mice, and human scraps. During these urgent times, we must help others. Today, he is like the rest of us and needs our assistance."

"Es la neta, compadres—it's the truth, guys. I also vote to let him stay," adds Pancho.

After considerable discussion, the group decides to allow the cat into their cave.

For the rest of the day, the winds increase in power and destruction. There are occasional lulls, and with each drop in wind speed, the group anticipates the storm's end. They are disappointed over and over when the fierce winds resume. The wind-driven rain is relentless, coming down at a high speed in acorn-sized drops. The mismatched, waterlogged group clusters together in the safety of the cave. Some birds pray, while others simply worry. Many of their family and friends are outside fighting, hiding, or dying. The storm's attack continues for the rest of the day.

At the dawn of the storm's third day, Kai walks onto the ledge and looks into the sky. The firmament has broken loose from the hurricane's grasp. Slowly, one by one, the birds stagger out, captivated by the beauty of orange-dusted clouds in a glorious sky. To the east, a bright, yet tentative sun peeks through the many ribbons of storm clouds. The heavens are so peaceful that the past two days seem like a hallucination.

Beneath this calm, lies a catastrophe of epic proportions. What was once an organized and well-functioning city is now a total disaster with man-made noises rising from the rubble. The roar of machines replaces the howls of wind. In ravaged neighborhoods, rumbling trucks and twirling tractors are already at work. The sky is full of the sounds of sirens, grumbling diesels, and whining saws. Convoys of relief vehicles, rescue boats, and helicopters crisscross the landscape, looking for the trapped and injured. The canals are gone, replaced by a littered and brackish lake. Flooded streets are distinguishable only by rows of partially submerged houses and car roofs.

Anxious to find friends and family, some birds take to the air. The snowy egret is the first to leave. She rises, her dirty brown back contrasts with the vibrant white cumulus clouds that are as fluffy as a newborn chick. All of nature's colors are distinct and clear, as if washed and put out to dry. As Linda thunders eastward toward the mountains, coastal nature celebrates the storm's exit.

Flooded homes are visited by people in row boats, on surfboards or anything else that floats. Broken and damaged items are everywhere. Boxes, bags, clothes, towels, umbrellas, surfboards, bicycles, and other human possessions spread out in the dirty brown water already full of plastic debris, snapped branches, and clutter.

From the instant Linda left, humans rush to repair the damage. People act impulsively, envisioning a quick and haphazard rebuild. Anxious to fix or replace their structures, they work as fast as possible without regard for long-term consequences. Humans have a distorted sense of time due to their short stay on Earth.

The Mother of Nature is subtler in her healing ways. She rebuilds, but it takes much longer. She knows time is on her side. Pride and patience are an important element of nature, so it may take years or even centuries to recover. The Mother of Nature wants her repairs to be true and everlasting.

Pancho, Kai, both red-tailed hawks, and the heron drop off the bluff to explore the beaches. The hawks rise rapidly into the newly washed sky, followed by the heavier birds. The rest of the gaggle leave the cave and scatter like shotgun pellets. Ted is left behind and alone once again.

Pancho and Kai stroke hard, following the hawks high into the air. At this altitude, it gives the squadron a panoramic view of the devastation below. The world of man lies in ruin, bleeding and gasping for life. The cement river is a raging torrent of brown water. The water carries mattresses, cars, wooden crates, trees, oil, fruit, and feces, all on a fast track to the ocean. The effects of this toxic soup on the ocean are immediate. Everything living near the shoreline is affected by the poisons. Fish and birds are first to die, their bodies are strewn across beaches and float in the waves. Pancho swoops to the surface looking for food, only inches above the ugly brown water. It has an acidic odor, making him gag.

"¡Ay, qué asqueroso! That is ripe," Pancho hollers, spitting out a few droplets.

Kai and Pancho hope food will be available nearby. However, everything is so polluted, it is not the time to eat.

"We are not going to find anything in this mess," Kai agrees. "The entire shoreline is contaminated. If we are lucky, we may find some healthy fish further out."

Kai takes in deep breaths to clear his lungs. Away from shore, the air is clear, the bitterness of the brown line they observed for weeks is gone; blown to bits by Linda's strong winds. They see the egret ahead and join her. All of them appear as small black dots against the beauty of the newly hatched sky. All are thankful they are alive and not land-bound like so many others.

Crowds of people and their machines move about like insects under attack. They dig, destroy, haul, and secure structures. Workmen in yellow trucks gather up the massive amounts of contaminated sea life dying along beaches. Skull and cross bone signs are placed on the sand, warning humans to stay away.

"Do you see what is happening?" interrupts the egret, boiling over with anger. "Look around. Do you see how powerful nature is? Mankind already thinks he's back in charge, not realizing that they are mere guests on this Earth, just like the rest of us."

The egret does a three hundred sixty degree aerial as she talks.

"Man makes his own rules and claims to be the most important species on Earth. Does this devastation look like he is in control?" The egret laughs at the irony of such a thought.

"Our Creator is in charge," she continues. "Humans did not make, nor do they understand natural cycles. A world in balance is best for all, and that is up to the Mother of Nature. Remember friends, endangered species do not exist when nature is in charge. We all live together." The egret rises seemingly effortlessly and the others follow suit.

"But look over there," she says, pointing to a huge yellow tractor taking monstrous loads of dirt and sand near the mouth of the cement river. The smoky machine is under attack by ten least terns. Endangered and losing hope for survival, the terns are battling back as man's machine runs over their nesting area. They jump, flutter, scream and squawk in the face of the driver. The birds' eggs are buried just below the surface of the sand and have miraculously survived the onslaught of the rampaging river. Now, the unborn terns are being killed by the machines.

"You see," the egret hollers in disgust, "humans are responsible for the terns being endangered in the first place. They pretend to protect them by putting a fence around a tiny nesting area. Now, they kill the same birds in order to save beachfront homes. It is nonsensical and crazy. Once again, nature pays the price."

Egrets used to be birds of the fields but had to move to the sea when the expansive meadows were developed by man. Cement overran the farms, and the egrets, like so many other species, were forced to become scavengers. Now they compete with seagulls, crows, and pigeons.

Her tirade continues, "Mankind lives alongside nature, but each time his inventions get more sophisticated, it makes it easier to kill nature. Humans believe it taboo to eat other humans but think nothing of killing creatures of nature for food. In fact, they kill us not just for food, but for clothing, decorations, and fun. Humans think they are the top species and can do no wrong. Well, believe me, mankind's comeuppance is near. This storm is only a taste of nature's anger. A sea slug has as many rights to be on this Earth as these humans. In fact, at times like this, I wish the sea slugs were in control."

The egret's words are full of contempt. She whips around and catches a wind slide that drops her down to the flooded canals.

Kai is dazed. After a short silence, Pancho states the obvious.

"Oye, güey, no los quiero comer—I do not want to eat these fish. They have the poison. Just the water itself will make us sick. Let's go back to the cave and wait for things to get better."

"That may take a while," answers a hungry Kai. Remembering the DDT stories and his mother's comment about the rattlesnake, he concedes. "You are right, we should wait."

"We need to be patient after this big storm. La naturaleza se re-cuperará, siempre amanece el sol—nature will heal itself, the sun always rises, and healthy fish will regroup."

"True. Let's get back to the cave for some rest. We can deal with our hunger later."

They turn to the shoreline, cross over the russet-colored river, pass two blocks of semi-submerged houses, and land softly on their muddy bluff. They remain outside the cave in the healing sun, listening to the sounds of mankind cleaning.

TWENTY

When the blood in your veins returns to the sea,
and the earth in your bones returns to the ground,
perhaps then you will remember that this land
does not belong to you,
it is you who belong to the land.

– Native American saying

One more day in the cave is about all Pancho and Kai can stand. They are anxious to end their time in the Endless City with its clamorous efforts at reconstruction after the storm. Human activity is frantic and relentless. The tidal surge, ocean waves, and river runoff have ebbed, and the streets are accessible once again. Structures within a quarter mile of the shoreline are ringed with brown dirt, indicating the high-water mark.

Kai and Pancho lack any definite plans and are frustrated by their own indecisiveness. Both are feeling very down, but neither wants to face the truth. *Magic Mountain* turned out to be a bold statement of man's contamination of the Earth and its mockery of nature. What other possible purpose could there be to stay here? Out of respect for one another, neither wants to admit the trip is over. Their loved ones are on their minds, and both are very tired of this hobo lifestyle. Home is calling. They need to leave.

Their thoughts are interrupted by a high-pitched howl coming from an adjoining bluff.

"¡Coyotes!" Pancho announces, his muscles tightening and body straightening. "They are not far away."

Known predators to all in the wild, their howl is followed by multiple yaps and shrieks announcing the successful hunt by the group. They are feeding on some unfortunate critter. Perhaps they couldn't find enough human scraps to eat in the devastated neighborhoods.

Pancho notes a prolonged silence after the kill. The jackals are on the move once again.

Familiar with these dangerous creatures, he warns, "Cuidado, compadre, stay alert, they may be coming back. Like sharks in the ocean, these skinny, dog-like creatures are always looking for a meal."

The birds watch carefully for movement in the brush. Suddenly, at the foot of the trail, just one bluff over, a family of coyotes emerges.

"¡Compa', ahora vienen! There they are!"

The pack turns and walks up the small path leading to the cave. Four skinny creatures, two old and two young, skulk straight toward the birds.

"Vámonos, they have spotted us. Rápido amigo, be quick, compa' or we will be their next meal."

Pancho and Kai take two steps, pump their wings, and scramble off the bluff and into the air. The young coyotes clamber across the dirt shelf, hoping to catch the birds. They are too late and end up sliding to a stop at the bluff's edge. The mom and dad join their anxious offspring who are now yelping at the retreating birds. The parents turn to reclaim the cave. Kai glances back just in time to see Ted dive over a bush just below the bluff. This movement attracts the attention of the two young coyotes. Simultaneously, both jump and scamper after the cat.

"¡Ay! El gato. Run, Ted!" The coyotes chase him. "Vaya con dios, mi amigo," says Pancho, as he prays for the cat.

The young coyotes are on top of Ted quickly. They pounce and immediately start ripping and biting at the old cat. In seconds, it is over. The young coyotes sing their victory to the delight of proud parents.

"Pancho, keep moving. How lucky we are..." Kai continues as they fly south. "Had the coyotes come back earlier, we might have been their meal instead of Ted."

In a moment of silence, they honor the old cat's circle of life.

"¿Á dónde vamos—where are we going?"

"Follow me to the old oak. We can rest and decide what to do next."

"Órale, compadre."

The old oak sits solemnly on a bluff on the western edge of a park. It is leafless due to the time of year. This century-old member of the beech family has just survived its second hurricane. It poises proudly above the canals facing the vast ocean, Catalina Island, and the curving coastline. The view is spectacular. Like the bluff supporting it, this stately oak is one of the last remaining vestiges of the past. Seeded long before the massive urban sprawl, it is the oldest tree in the area. The oak's lowest branch makes for an easy landing.

In an open knot above the birds, honeybees work busily on a hive to honor their queen. The birds listen as two drones talk about their lives and the old oak.

"They say they're going to cut it down," says a large drone, hovering stationary in the air.

"Lots of politics with this one," answers his partner.

"Yeah, but no one knows what we know. Most are too young to remember what has happened in the past."

"Should we tell them?"

"About the developers?"

"Yeah, the developers. Remember what they did to the huge grove of trees down the hill?"

"I remember it well. It is now the parking lot for many condominiums. Our home used to be in the trees where the tennis courts are now. Those were good days. Lots of room, lots of flowers and lots of freedom. There were many bee colonies back in the day."

"Great times. I loved it. Plenty of honey for all."

"Previous generations had it even better. Oh, what a glorious land."

"Plus, we lived with a view of the ocean."

"This is the last place left. Look at all those buildings."

"Remember how some people fought the bulldozers?"

"Yes, but their numbers were not large, so the machines easily won."

"The bees left because big tractors and men with chain saws came and transformed the natural hills into flatlands, so they could build many units. We were forced to look for new land to live on."

"Is that why your family left?"

"The many flowers with nectar disappeared as did the trees that we relied upon for our hives. We lost our homes and became homeless. Then we found this tree. This is the last bastion of nature in this part of the Endless City."

"This oak is the best tree of all the trees. It is the oldest and the wisest. Do you really think they will cut it down?"

"Yes, eventually" says the drone in disgust.

"What will happen to us if they cut it down?"

"We will be forced to move yet again."

"Maybe the group *Save the Oak Folks* will come back to fight and save the tree?"

"We will have to wait and see. Now that this storm is over, the protesters will return and the arguments will start up once again."

Suddenly, the bees are summoned to the queen. They belong to the oldest and most trusted of the hives, so they must hurry off to their leader.

Pancho and Kai are not aware of any fight to save the old oak nor any political battles to cut it down. It is yet another lesson in the ways of humans. The birds remain in the oak for the rest of the day, amid the hum of the hive. They re-visit key experiences of their adventure. Eventually, their talk turns to the future.

Both birds agree that their escapades have been the best education they could receive about the real world. They are wiser, braver, and much more knowledgeable. The Magical Mountain was not as they had envisioned, and they learned firsthand that the natural world is not valued by much of mankind. Technology has replaced nature, and this has resulted in toxic rivers, immense roads, and permanent brown lines in the sky. Mankind's addiction to contraptions, plus his need to consume, spells trouble for nature.

"Is it time to decide what is next?" queries Kai, asking the question that has been lingering in both of their minds.

"Compadre, te voy a decir algo, I'm going to tell you something. I am sure of one thing. I do not want to continue these travels anymore, even though te extrañeré mucho—I will miss you a lot. I have had enough of this city. I want to go home and be with mi familia. But most importantly, I want to marry Estrella. She is waiting for me, and I want to be with her always. We can live peacefully in Baja, away from all this madness."

"That is good news," Kai says excitedly. "If you are ready to leave, I am ready to leave," he declares.

Kai wants to be with his family and find out why his dream father has called him home. He yearns to see Feathertop. Even more importantly, he wants to learn how to love her forever.

"I will go back and share what I have learned," he says, promising as much to Pancho as to himself. "I pledge to teach other pelicans to keep Anacapa strong. My father is my hero, and I am ready to tell him everything. He will be proud of my accomplishments once I show him that I am ready to face my demons. I wish you could meet him," he states loudly. "Pancho, I, too, am ready to go home."

The booby dances joyfully and sings out, "Vámonos a casa—I want to go home and start the next part of my life."

Once the agreement is reached, a great burden is lifted from both their shoulders. The two pals thump chests and sit on the gnarled arms of the old oak. Their eyes lock. They thank each other in silence, pledging a lifetime of friendship. Simultaneously, they burst into laughter for the first time in many days, and it feels really good. But beneath this levity, there is an inner sadness. This is the last time they will be together. Kai jumps up and hops over to Pancho. They hug.

Their tears of joy drip down upon the oak's dry bark, immediately seeping deep into the tree and its inner soul. Wanting to help, the old oak responds by sharing the courage it has gathered over its lifetime. The oak will eventually be cut down, ending up in a pile of sawdust or as pieces of furniture and its wisdom and lifetime of knowledge lost forever.

Today is not the day for the oak to be crying, because he is still alive and looking out over another gorgeous sunset—number thirty-two thousand six hundred sixty-two—of his long life. The tree has learned not to worry about its future; it lives one day at a time, as is necessary in the Endless City. Sensing a deep bond with the birds, it canopies them with positive spirits and blessings from deep within its roots. The oak wishes them love, encouragement, and protection.

The two friends feel the oak's positive energy surrounding them, like an invisible cape with magical powers.

TWENTY-ONE

If I should go tomorrow, it would never be goodbye
for I have left my heart with you, so don't you ever cry.
The love that's deep within me, shall reach you from the stars.
You'll feel it from the heavens, and it will heal the scars.

– Anonymous

The sun slips beneath the western horizon as their last day together melts into dusk. As the sun vanishes, it leaves a rare green flash; an atmospheric marvel symbolizing the importance of their adventures together. There is total silence between the two.

Kai feels a darkening sensation inside him. His inner voice is jabbering about going home and being with the family. Guilt is arguing that his demon dream represented circumstances that need immediate attention.

"There is no more time for conversation. It is time for action. We must leave this spot and go home," his combined voices agree.

This interlude is rudely interrupted by the high-frequency noises of a low flying airplane, multiple chain saws, and a beeping truck in reverse. With thoughts of brotherly love in their hearts, both birds struggle to find a way to express their fondness for each other. Both fail. Instead, they turn, look into each other's eyes and tear up. Pancho nods and smiles that all too familiar smile, stretches his wings twice and drops from the oak. Kai watches as his friend banks south and succumbs to distance and darkness.

"Pancho is gone," he mumbles forlornly.

The pelican, fighting back tears, turns to face the northwest. It is time to start the second most important flight of his young life. He left home without telling anyone and will begin his return flight to his beloved Anacapa in the dark of night. Mimicking Sorté's legendary departure, Kai opens his wings, gathers wind, and rises easily. He has never before felt so light. It is as if he is being magically lifted from the oak. When he is above the tree, he stalls and, without a second thought, turns and flies toward his home and family.

His route retraces the same path he followed when he left Anacapa. With the new experiences now an integral part of his being, this flight feels very different. Once he is west of the two harbors, he heads to the open sea, utilizing a hypnotic four-count rhythm. The retreating hurricane has left a crystal-clear night sky, light winds, and a half moon to guide his journey.

As he searches for inner peace, his feelings crash into each other like battling robots. One at a time, he envisions images of his loved ones. He smiles each time he sees one of their faces. Kai is anxious to have grown-up conversations with his favorite savants and family members.

"Pops will be the first," he declares with conviction. "I am sure he will be satisfied. Dad, I'm coming home."

Visualizing beautiful Feathertop, he wants to talk to her right away, too. He can hardly wait to see her cute face and hear her voice when he proposes. He wants to start the courting ritual immediately. This will please his folks.

"Maybe I can dance like Pancho when I see her," he chuckles to himself.

These thoughts suddenly feel more unsettling than the nerves he gets when he is speed diving or surfing.

That is so strange, he reflects. *I am more scared about growing up than I am about risking my life. Becoming an adult is a brand-new adventure with many unknown challenges.*

But deep inside, Kai knows it will be the best adventure yet. The truth is that this new stage of life is not about danger or risk, but is about giving himself to others. It is about living for more than just himself. The challenges of creating a family seem much more daunting than any of his daredevil stunts.

"I will become a leader and serve our colony well," he declares boldly. "I will teach lessons about the Endless City, just as my elders tried to teach me."

By this time, he has put many miles between himself and the mainland. Skimming across the dark waters, watching reflections of moonlight, he adjusts his stroke down to relax and conserve energy. His internal compass is set and his mind is quiet, so he settles into a meditative state. From here on out, he is on automatic pilot.

Eventually, Anacapa Island looms as a dark shadow in the distance. Moonlit silhouettes of cliffs and Pinniped Point are his references. Nirvana wind whispers "welcome home" to one of her favorite sons. It is too early for the colony to be awake, so he drops into the familiar, cool Pacific waters of the Channel Islands. He will wait here until sunrise, anticipating a great and joyous reunion. He quickly falls into a deep sleep.

Like a proud rooster, a sea lion bellows the coming of a new day. Kai awakens refreshed, but anxious to get home. His mind is on fire with positive thoughts; he's ready to see his family.

Kai declares, "This is a great day!"

The sunlight gently lightens the windless sky. The ocean is like green glass, the air he breathes is pure and the water pristine. He rubs sea moisture into his feathers. No more brown lines or toxic fish, just the beautiful environment of Anacapa. Looking at the entrance to the Goldfish Bowl, he wings toward it. Rising into the morning sky, his head perched high and proud, he cuts above the rocks. Clans are forming in front of their homes in preparation for the morning feed. Many recognize him and wave. He smiles and waves back. He does one wide glide above the cove, taking in the sights, smells, and sounds. It is like seeing a trusted old friend. His heart flutters.

I am home, I am home. Oh, I am home, his internal voice chants gleefully. *This is where I belong. Thank you, Sorté, for watching over me.*

Leaning left, he adjusts his tail feathers and heads straight to the family cave. He is surprised to see no one out front.

Pops is usually up by now. The family should be out on the bluff getting ready for the feed like all the other clans, he thinks.

In his excitement, Kai does not think about this odd circumstance. He throws his wings back, catches air, and brakes. Dropping onto the bluff, his body stands straight like a soldier. Still, there are no signs of anyone. This is not the reception that he anticipated.

I want to hug my siblings and my mom and dad and dance with joy, he thinks.

"The mouth of the cave sits dark and quiet," Dread points out ominously.

Kai looks around, trying to figure out why his family is not on the bluff. He is shocked by what he sees. On the left side of the cave hangs a necklace of seashells and bird feathers laced together with seaweed. There are two large brown pelican feathers, two yellow feathers, and two smaller white feathers in this lei. The sight triggers a sinister foreboding in Kai.

This type of necklace is not a decoration. It celebrates nothing. Just the opposite, it is called the "wreath of death." It is a traditional garland made from the feathers of a deceased pelican. If the body is not available, off-spring donate feathers to make the wreath. This long-standing ceremony among pelicans is taken very seriously. Someone has died.

But my family is young and healthy. This is terribly out of place, his inner voice cries.

"What possibly could be the reason for the wreath? Do they think I am dead?" he asks, and it suddenly occurs to him what his absence may have meant.

He looks around confirming he is standing at the right cave.

It must be me that they are mourning, he speculates. *They will be so relieved when they see me. I can hardly wait to see the looks on their faces.*

"Pops, Pops! Mom, Pops where are you?" he calls out. "It's time to ready for the day. I am home, I am alive! It's Kai! I am here to celebrate. Where is everyone? Mom, what is wrong? Why is that necklace here? Please come out. Someone, please come out! It is Kai. I am home," he yells desperately at the dark cave, extremely concerned by the lack of response.

His thoughts turn ugly and panic begins to set in.

"Maybe an auntie or uncle has died? Maybe, oh my god, one of your brothers," Dread says. "I tried to warn you that your demon dream was serious, but you would not listen."

"What could I have done?" Kai answers back. "I was in the middle of a huge storm!"

Just then, his mother emerges from the cave. She shuffles slowly, her body slumped over as if she is carrying a huge weight on her shoulders. She puts her wings around her son and hugs him tightly. Kai feels his mother's heart beating hard, like a conga drum. He senses tremendous sorrow undermining her happiness in seeing him. She does not let go. She starts to cry. Intensified by the still morning air, this sad reunion has alerted neighboring families of Kai's return. Feathertop quickly joins them. With tears in her eyes, she watches mother and son embrace each other.

"You are scaring me, what has happened? Where is the rest of the family? What is it? Who has died? Where is my dad?"

His mother's body shakes with sobs as she clings even more tightly to her son. By this time, Kai is frantic! His mother finally speaks, sputtering her words, interrupted by moans of grief. It takes her several attempts to complete a sentence.

"Your...your fa...father is dead," she says, struggling to put together the thought. The words pierce Kai's heart like a spear. He staggers backward, carrying his mother with him.

"Dead? Oh no, dead."

Darkness wraps over him like a blanket. This news is too terrible to comprehend.

"What? That cannot be! I want to see him. I need to see him! I have so much to tell him. I want to see my dad," he begs, tears exploding from his eyes. "Dead, no, no, oh no!"

Behind him, Feathertop gently places a wing upon Kai's shoulder. Her angelic image is blurred and matted by tears. She too is weeping.

"I am so sorry I was gone. It is my fault! I will never leave again. It is all my fault—but what happened?" Kai struggles to ask.

He sees his siblings peering out from the cave. They too are crying, their faces distorted with sadness.

The cliffs rimming the Goldfish Bowl are packed with birds. By now, the news has spread that Kai has returned and learned of the tragedy. In unison, all birds in the colony raise both wings to show respect for the family in this time of grief.

"What happened? I want to know what happened," Kai demands, as Grief and Guilt overwhelm him.

His brother Churchill steps forward and sits in the dirt next to his mother and Kai. It is the exact spot where his father last lectured Kai about the dangers of going to the mainland.

"Kai, it was an accident. Dad was killed by the sea. The same sea that he loved as much as he loved his family," explains his brother, taking charge of the situation.

"Please, tell me what happened," Kai pleads.

"A destructive hurricane hit the mainland. Its outer winds and powerful waves were strong enough to reach Anacapa."

"And Pops, what happened to Pops?"

"High winds and large waves lasted for two days. During that time, none of us ate. It was too dangerous to fish. Dad told us to stay in the cave and not venture out. We stayed, but we got really hungry."

His mother intervenes, "Your younger brother Rikki was really frightened by the storm. He complained about the howling wind and had terrible nightmares. He was hungry, so your father decided that food might help him."

Churchill picks up the story.

"On the last day of the heavy winds, Dad decided to get fish for Rikki and the rest of us. It was not necessary, but Dad was concerned about our young brother, so he flew off into the storm. He knew that the ocean surface was too rough for fishing, so he flew through Fox Canyon, away from the direct winds. I trailed him in case there were any problems. When we got to the rocks at Landing Cove, he had me sit down on a large boulder, protected from the winds and the waves. Gusts were very strong, and Dad told me not to leave the boulder. He went to the water's edge and brought back a few crabs and gave them to me to store for the trip home."

Rikki and his sister MT join their brothers and mother on the bluff. Rikki is crying harder than anyone due to the tremendous amount of guilt he holds. The family and Feathertop surround Kai like a protective wall.

"Dad went down to the rocks three times," Churchill continues. "He told me the crabs were scarce, but he wanted to find enough for each of us to have a small meal.

"On the fourth flight, there was a strong gust of wind that bounced him against a boulder. This exposed him to the sea. I saw a rogue wave twice as big as the others come out of nowhere. He did not have time to fly or swim because there was nowhere to go and no time to react. The wave exploded with tremendous force right on top of him. Water was thrown high into the air, and when the white water disappeared, Dad was gone. I desperately tried to find him. I flew over the rocks for as long as I was able. Increasing winds and giant waves made my search too dangerous. He had simply vanished."

"He is gone," Rikki whimpers, between breaths. He then lowers his head in shame and starts to bawl. "It is my fault. I should not have complained about the food."

Churchill's eyes brim with tears as Kai chokes back tears of his own.

In this moment of clarity, Kai knows he must console his family.

"No, Churchill," he says. "You did what you could. Rikki, it is not your fault either. I should have been here to help. Pops warned me that life is fragile. It was as if he knew that something was going to happen. I am responsible for his death because I was not here when the family needed me. Now, both of you, hear me out. Our father was a brave and loving man. He did what he did because of his love for all of us. We must never forget that. It does not matter who did what or who went with him or who said what. It was Pops' time to die, so we must carry on. Pops was thinking of his family. We can only be proud of him."

Kai turns and takes two steps toward his mother.

"Mother, I am back and will help you. Churchill and I can watch over our family. You will be proud of us, just like you were proud of Pops."

His mother looks at her oldest child who carries his father's strength. It is this virtue that she fell in love with when she first met her mate. Now she sees the same quality in her oldest son.

Feathertop edges close to Kai and places her wing upon him.

"I like having you home. I will be here for you," she says in a comforting whisper.

Her words ease his feelings of loss and guilt. He hopes Feathertop will be at his side from now on. Kai lowers his bill and plucks the biggest brown feather from his wing. He then raises it in honor of Sorté and his father, walks over to the cave, and places it into the wreath of death.

TWENTY-TWO

*A human being is part of a whole, called by us the 'Universe,'–
a part limited in time and space.
He experiences himself, his thoughts and feelings
as something separated from the rest–
a kind of optical delusion of his consciousness.
This delusion is a kind of prison for us, restricting us to our
personal desires and to affection for a few persons nearest to us.
Our task must be to free ourselves from this prison
by widening our circles of compassion to embrace
all living creatures and the whole of nature in its beauty.*

– Albert Einstein

On this classic spring day, soft westerly winds and mild temperatures enhance the serenity and calmness of the ocean surrounding Anacapa. It is an example of the Channel Islands at their best. Surrounded by the pristine blue sea, Kai leads the family train to the morning feed. It has been two years since his trip to the mainland. Gazing down at his beloved Pacific Ocean, he feels confident, content, and thankful for all that life has provided.

As predicted by so many during his younger years, Kai's opinions and leadership skills have allowed him to become influential within the colony. As the youngest savant in Sorté's long history, Kai teaches birds of all ages. His favorite subjects are pelican history, pelican lore, and the world of mankind. Regardless of what he teaches, he feels it is important that students think for themselves about how to get the most out of their lives. His firsthand experiences with mankind and their ways, combined with his ability to weave fascinating stories about history, make his classes the most popular among the students. His style of teaching is similar to that of Master B, but much more upbeat and interactive.

Trips to the mainland are still banned. In fact, great pandemics, devastating fires, and increasing crime ravage the Endless City to this very day. It has gotten worse.

Kai advocates that young birds stay away from the mainland because it teaches the wrong lessons. He tells his students all about man's potential for good, but human shortcomings and their disregard for the *Laws of Nature* put the future at risk. Each and every class ends with examples of what makes life on Anacapa so special.

He and Feathertop pledged their mutual devotion to each other shortly after his return from the Endless City. They courted for a short period and are now parenting two young fledglings of their own. Completing their childhood dreams, their once strong infatuation has been replaced by a deeper feeling of love and respect. They vowed to stay together for the rest of their lives.

Kai talks openly about his own early struggles in order to help youngsters work through the many entanglements involved when growing into adulthood. He does this with constant reminders to each bird to be the best they can.

"Never lose sight of the gifts that nature has given us," he reminds them.

He believes strongly in the philosophy of "face your demons and growl back." This reverberates throughout his lessons, as does "always be true to yourself" and "remember that change is the gateway to a better life."

When reflecting upon his own life, some of his most treasured memories revolve around the conflicts he faced while growing up. Those with his father stand out. He tried to establish himself outside the influences of others, while at the same time, parents, savants, and grownups were telling him to conform. He sees this in youngsters every day.

Pops did not live long enough to see what I was able to accomplish nor did he get to meet his grandbirds, Kai's inner voice says with regret. *Pops would have relished his granddad role and have been so very proud of his two grandbirds.*

Fancy, named after the strong-souled owl on the mainland, was the first born and has grown into quite the leader. Following family traditions, she is outspoken, reliable, a strong fisher, and an excellent student. She is beginning to show the same sense of independence that her father possesses. Her younger brother, Titus, has yet to show his true passions. Still quite young, he brings great joy to all those around him. Titus is old enough to try most things but does not do them well. His learning curve is steep, and he is constantly testing others. He is still very dependent upon family members for support and is especially fond of Uncle Rikki. The two siblings are daily treasures for their parents.

Kai's train includes both his family and Feathertop's. It consists of numerous fledglings, six aunties and uncles, grandparents, eight cousins, a number of close family friends, plus three of Kai's students. His train is the largest of all in the colony. Kai choreographs a new flight plan each and every day. Today, he has them spread out like a boomerang. Kai leads alongside his mother with an unoccupied slot next to her in honor of Pops. Known as the "missing bird" formation, it allows designated family members to fly in the void representing a fulfillment of life's transition into the afterlife. Each trip is intended to be unique. Navigating various routes and in different configurations, Kai's trains are designed so that fishing does not become routine.

"It is not just a fishing trip; it is a real-life experience to be re-membered," Kai reminds his flyers.

Each trip is meant to be a learning experience in a safe environment. Flying behind him on his right are Rikki, Churchill, Feathertop, and MT. On his left are his mother and Feathertop's grandma, Grace. All others fall randomly into place behind the family; Thirty-three birds skimming gracefully near the surface of a gentle and loving sea. Travelling north around Pinniped Point is one of Kai's favorite trips. It lets him tap into the overflowing spirituality of Nirvana. She is always happy to see her old friend.

The group executes a series of lazy "s-turns," reminding Kai of the games he played with his traveling buddy, Pancho. From the ground, Kai's trains look like dancers in the sky. After making the turn at Pin-niped Point, the mainland comes into view. Its broad shoreline is dusted with the usual ominous brown line.

Man is up to his typical business, Kai's inner voice tells him.

As memories of the Endless City flash in front of him, Kai declares to himself. "The sanctity of Anacapa must not be squandered and the *Laws of Nature* must be followed. All species must learn to live together or all living things could eventually die."

Looking somberly at the Endless City, he thanks Sorté, his father, Pancho, and the brown line for the profound influence they all have had on him.

If it wasn't for the trip two years ago, his life would have turned out totally different. Had Kai never left Sorté, he would not have experienced the complexities of mankind nor had the opportunity to teach future generations about nature and the importance of a wholesome environment. Beneath the edge of a small line of stratus clouds, Kai turns and observes the formation strung out behind him.

Suddenly, a bright aura lights up the group. Disguised as a ray of sunlight tunneling though the clouds, Kai sees an image of Sorté, the greatest of all pelicans, standing in the center of the beam. The bird of legend has come to pass on an important tradition to the young savant. She wants Kai to know that by taking up his quest to save nature, he will receive powers far greater than himself. The spirits of all the birds of legend will accompany him in his journey to protect the planet.

Sorté spreads her wings and pumps out an orchid-scented breeze that engulfs the train. All the pelicans know something special is happening and look about to catch a glimpse of Sorté. Kai is stunned and humbled by the realization that he is now truly part of pelican lore. He turns to the god-bird, expressing his gratitude with a smile and a nod.

From that day forward, Kai takes his place in a long list of great pelicans and the name "Flyin' Kai" will be passed on for generations. Kai turns and gives a loving smile to his mother, who is now occupying his missing father's position. A silent thought rises up in the minds of all those in the train.

"Remember, life is good on Anacapa."

Thousands of miles to the south...deep in Baja México, a similar story plays out above the emerald blue waters of Mulejé.

THE END

ABOUT THE AUTHOR

Duncan P. Forgey is a photographer, teacher, writer and author who has been published in numerous newspapers, magazines and on-line medias. *Flyin' Kai: A Pelican's Tale* is his first novel.

He holds a Master's Degree in Education and has worked as a high school educator and private counselor. Duncan's heart lies with adolescents as they struggle to become adults in a constantly changing world. He is also a successful businessman and motivational speaker.

A thalassophile (lover of the sea), Duncan has lived with the ocean since birth. He honors the seas through his writings, travels, photography, surfing and sailing and now lives on the island of Kaua'i, after a lifetime of watching California's vast open spaces and much of its magical wildlife disappear.

DuncanForgey.com